Mary Cowper

Diary of Mary Countess Cowper,

Lady of the Bedchamber to the Princess of Wales, 1714-1720

Mary Cowper

Diary of Mary Countess Cowper,
Lady of the Bedchamber to the Princess of Wales, 1714-1720

ISBN/EAN: 9783337012250

Printed in Europe, USA, Canada, Australia, Japan

Cover: Foto ©Raphael Reischuk / pixelio.de

More available books at **www.hansebooks.com**

Diary of

MARY

Countess COWPER,

Lady of the Bedchamber

TO

THE PRINCESS OF WALES.

1714—1720.

LONDON:

Printed for John Murray, *Albemarle Street.*

MDCCCLXIV.

Introduction.

 HE Volume to which thefe Obferva-
tions are a Preface contains the Diary,
or rather certain Portions of a Diary,
which was kept by Lady *Cowper*, the
Wife of Lord Chancellor *Cowper*, while acting as
Lady of the Bedchamber to the Princefs of *Wales*,
Caroline of *Anfpach*, before her Acceffion to the
Throne as Queen of *George II.* The greater Part
of the earlier Portion of this Diary, in the Form
of Extracts, copied out by Lady *Cowper's* eldeft
Daughter, Lady *Sarah*, about the Year 1730, was
lent to Lord *Campbell* while he was engaged in
writing the *Lives of the Chancellors*, and was ufed
by him freely in his Biography of Lord *Cowper*.
So interefted was Lord *Campbell* by thefe Ex-
tracts, that he obferves, in Page 343 of his fourth
Volume, that ‘ a charming Diary of the fecond
Lady *Cowper*, beginning at this Time (1714), is

preferved. It remains in MS., but it well deferves to be printed, for it gives a more lively
Picture of the Court of *England* at the Commencement of the *Brunfwick* Dynasty than I
have ever met with.' It may be added to Lord
Campbell's Remark, that we are singularly de-
ficient in Materials of the same Class for the
Illustration of this particular Period. A Sort of
Hiatus in our political Memoirs occurs about
this Point, which renders almost any Contribu-
tion to the Void more than usually acceptable.

The Extracts which were taken by Lady *Sarah*,
and which were seen by Lord *Campbell*, were far,
however, from being so full as the present Publi-
cation, for this is taken directly from the original
Diary in the Handwriting of Lady *Cowper*,
wherein many Paffages omitted by Lady *Sarah*
appear in their original Form. Moreover, a Portion of the Diary, from *April* to *July*, 1720,
was not tranfcribed by Lady *Sarah* at all, and
therefore not seen by Lord *Campbell*, and indeed
it was only difcovered at *Panfhanger* so late as
laft Year. Thus the Diary as here published is
as nearly as poffible a Tranfcript of Everything
which Lady *Cowper* has left in this Shape. The
Names which were in Cypher are here given in
full, and the Spelling is fomewhat modernifed,
but that is all the Change it has undergone. As

the Writer ftates at the Commencement of her
Journal, fhe confidered it as a rough Draft only,
to be revifed and digefted if Opportunity offered;
and as the Opportunity appears never to have
offered to her, it is publifhed as it remains,
without Alteration by others. We have thus
a Narrative of 'the Events worth remembering
while fhe was at *Court*,' and the Impreffions
obtained of them on the Inftant by a very clever
Woman. Nor can it be queftioned for a Moment that they are precifely what they purport
to be—rough and hurried, but authentic Memo-
randa of Events which came under her daily
Obfervation.

There is Evidence in the Diary itfelf to fhow
that the Writer was an accomplifhed and ob-
fervant Perfon. Yet, apart from this, the Sum
of her perfonal Memoirs is fcanty, and there is
not much to be told of her Life and its Inci-
dents. Her maiden Name was *Mary Clavering*,
and fhe was the Daughter of *John Clavering*,
Efq., of *Chopwell*, in the County of *Durham*,
who was himfelf of a younger Branch of the
ancient Northumbrian Family of *Clavering* of
Callalee and *Axwell*, a Race entertaining the
Jacobite Predilections which were then fo preva-
lent in the North of *England* and *Scotland*. She
herfelf was born in 1685, and fhe was married

in 1706 to *William* Lord *Cowper*, who had then
recently been made Lord Keeper of the Great
Seal, and who was fhortly afterwards named
Lord Chancellor. Her Introduction to her future Hufband arofe out of fome Law Bufinefs,
on which fhe had Occafion to confult him at
his Chambers, and their Marriage, which very
fpeedily followed, was for fome Time kept fecret, as the Readers of Lord *Campbell* will doubtlefs call to Mind. Lord *Cowper*, in a Letter to
his Wife of *December* 20th, 1706, as quoted by
Lord *Campbell*, fays, ' I am going to vifit my
Mother, and perhaps fhall begin to prepare her
for what fhe muft, I hope, know in a little
Time.' Lady *Cowper* herfelf alludes to the Se-
crecy which attended her Marriage in the Paffage
relating to Lady *Harriet Vere*, and her Defigns
on the Heart of the *Chancellor*, on Pages 33–4
of the prefent Diary. Yet no fufficient Reafon
is given for this Concealment, either by Lady
Cowper or any other Perfon. She appears, from
her Portrait by Sir *Godfrey Kneller* (an Engraving
from which is prefixed to this Volume), to have
been poffeffed of confiderable perfonal Attractions,
and there is a further direct Teftimony to her
Beauty in one of the curious little Books of the
Day, a *Hiflory of the Kit Cat Club*, which contains fome Verfes in honour of ' Miftrefs *Mary*

Clavering,' as one of the ' Toafts ' of the Club,
by Earl *Rivers*.

There is alfo Evidence that fhe was well-read,
and of a ftudious Difpofition, in a numerous
Collection of Books belonging to her, and now
in the Library at *Panfhanger*, many of them
on rather abftrufe Subjects, and which contain,
in addition to her Name, copious Annotations in
her Handwriting. We find from her Diary that
fhe was in the Habit of tranflating into French
her Hufband's Memorials, that they might be
intelligible to the Hanoverian King. We can
fee, from various Paffages in this Diary referring
to her Hufband and Children, that fhe was an
exemplary Wife and an attached Mother. Although fhe was evidently the Object of much
Admiration at the Court of *George I.*, fhe preferved an unfullied Reputation, and fhe appears
to have been held in efpecial Regard by her
Hufband, whofe Letters to her up to his Death,
on the 10th of *October*, 1723, are quoted in this
very Senfe by Lord *Campbell*. She did not long
furvive this Event, for fhe herfelf died three
Months later, aged thirty-nine, on the 5th of
January, 1723-4.

At the Date of the Commencement of her
Diary, then, fhe muft have been in her twenty-
ninth Year, and until this Time, which corre-

fponds nearly with the Acceffion of *George I.*, we can find but few Traces of her Occupations or Exiftence. Neverthelefs, fhe appears to have been a frequent Correfpondent of *Sarah* Duchefs of *Marlborough*, and to have been an active Agent for the Hanoverian Succeffion, fiding always with the Politics of her Hufband rather than with the Predilections and Opinions of her Jacobite Kinfmen. She herfelf tells us in her Diary, that for the four Years previous to its Commencement fhe had kept a conftant Correfpondence with the Princefs *Caroline*, and had received many, and thofe the kindeft, Letters from her. Whence their Intimacy may have arifen we are not informed, but it is evident that Lady *Cowper* had founded upon it the Expectation—very reafonable in her Cafe, as the Event proved—that when the *Princefs* came to *England* fhe would be attached to her Court and Service. After a little Delay and Uncertainty, the Intelligence that fhe had been named a Lady of the Bedchamber was conveyed to her by Baron *Bernftorff* in perfon, and in this Capacity fhe commenced the Diary, of which all that remains is now prefented to the Reader.

The firft Portion of this Diary—that from which Extracts were, as we ftated, made by Lord *Campbell*—extends from *October* 1714 to

October 1716. But at this latter Point there is a Break of four Years, up to 1720, when a still more rough and fragmentary Document is appended. This closes on the 10th *July*, 1720, and it is the last Instalment of its Kind. Both Portions, however, of the Diary may be said to cover a Crisis of extreme Importance to our constitutional *Status*, and pregnant with Peril to the Hanoverian Line. The First comprises the Rebellion of 1715, and the Second the Reconciliation of *George I.* and the Prince of *Wales* after that Series of Quarrels which had shaken the public Confidence in their Dynasty. On the First of these Occurrences Lady *Cowper* gives us many additional Details to the Information we possessed already; but on the Second she is not so explicit as to alter the Impressions which are currently received. It is well known that the Jealousy of the *Prince* entertained by the *King* commenced long before the violent Quarrel which occurred at the Christening of Prince *George William*, the Son of the Former; and Lady *Cowper* merely takes up the Negotiations at a Stage when the Flagrancy of the Scandal made a Reconciliation imperative. She was interested in the Result to a great Degree in a personal Sense, for there is Reason to infer that Lord *Cowper* had lost the Favour of the *King* by

his Adherence to the Side of the *Prince*, and that
he had refigned the Great Seal in confequence in
April 1718. An undated Letter of the *King* to the
Prince, which is given in Appendix D, appears to
refer to an earlier Stage of this Family Feud,
which, but for the oftenfible Reconciliation which
followed, might have fatally endangered the Hanoverian Succeffion. Lady *Cowper*, in her Diary,
defcribes the Negotiations and final Arrange-
ments for this happy Refult, the Rejoicings with
which the Event was celebrated by all the Friends
of the Houfe of *Hanover*, and the Fears that had
been entertained that fuch a Difunion between
Father and Son might eventually terminate in
the Succefs of the *Pretender*.

It remains only neceffary to ftate the Reafon
for the fragmentary Condition in which Lady
Cowper's MSS. have reached us. After Lord
Cowper had quitted Office, a Year or fo before
his and his Wife's Death, that is to fay, in 1722,
' Reports were fpread about that he had coalefced
with the Tories, and was even plotting with the
Jacobites—Reports for which there was not the
flighteft Colour.' When a Difcovery was made
of *Layer's* Confpiracy, in 1723, to reftore the
Stuarts by a French Invafion, and *Layer* was examined in the *Tower* by a Minifterial Committee
of the *Houfe of Commons*, he thought to ingra-

tiate himfelf with the Government of the Day, and perhaps obtain a Pardon, by implicating fome of the difcontented Whig Lords, and, amongft others, imputed Complicity to Lord *Cowper*. The Calumny, on Examination, proved to be utterly unfounded ; but before the Imputation had been removed, Lady *Cowper* herfelf had taken unneceffary Alarm, and deftroyed a confiderable Portion of her Diary and Correfpondence. The Circumftances are thus detailed in a Memorandum by her Daughter, Lady *Sarah*.

In the News Letter, written to the Poftmafter at *Hertford*, is the following Article, dated *September* 4th, 1722 :—' It is reported that the Lord *Cowper* offered to be Bail for the Bifhop of *Rochefter*, which was fo highly refented by a certain Perfon of Diftinction, that he moved for a Warrant to fearch His *Lordfhip's* Houfe. This Letter was fent immediately to my Mother at *Cole Green*, by Mrs. *Bowde*, who kept the Poft and Coffee-houfe at *Hertford* ; and though the firft Part of the Article was notorioufly falfe, and the Report to be defpifed, yet my Mother had fo many Intimations and Hints fent her by different Hands of a Defign to attack my Father, and try to involve his Character, in the Examination then on Foot relating to the Plot, that fhe took Fright for fome Papers fhe had drawn up by way of Diary (a Part of which only remains), and for Papers belonging to the *Prince* and *Princefs*, which I have fince heard fhe had in her Hands, relating to the Quarrel in the Royal Family, and not being able to place them in Safety in fuch a Hurry, fhe burned fuch as fhe thought would do moft Harm if difcovered, by which many curious Scraps of fecret Hiftory are probably loft ; and, Circumftances confidered, I wonder fhe had the Courage to preferve the *Princefs's* Letters, and fo much of her own Diary as is yet remaining.

'The latter End of *December* my Mother grew much weaker and extremely ill. She loft her Appetite entirely, and at Times her Memory, fo that fhe would fpeak of my Father as if living, afk for him, and expect him Home. When fhe recollected his Death, it feemed to be with fo lively a Grief, as if it had juft then happened. In fhort, fhe had really what is often talked of, but feen in very few Inftances—a broken Heart. She died the 5th of *February*, 1724, four Months after her Hufband.'   .

It appears, from a further undated Memorandum of Lady *Sarah*, that the Princefs of *Wales*, then become *Queen*, had fome Anxiety in refpect of feventy Letters written to Lady *Cowper*, and fuppofed by her to be ftill in Lady *Sarah's* Poffeffion. As to this Impreffion on the Part of Queen *Caroline*, it is to be noted that Lady *Sarah* obferves :—' All that I have to add on the Subject is, that I was once told by a Perfon of much Penetration, who is conftantly with the *Queen* (though I believe little in her Favour), that by feveral Things the *Queen* had faid unguardedly, fhe apprehended the great Caufe of Her *Majefty's* Anger and Averfion to me was, that fhe thought I had fome Papers in my Hands that fhe wifhed to have only in her own. If there were any fuch, they were, as I faid before, committed to the Fire, and I have None the *Queen* can be in any Uneafinefs about, unlefs fhe feels fome from my retaining Expreffions of Friendfhip fhe never felt, and Promifes I have Caufe to think fhe has no Intention to perform.'

The concluding Expreffions of this Statement would feem to imply that Lady *Cowper* was herfelf aggrieved by fome Slight, real or imagined, on the Part of Her *Majefty*, and this muft have occurred fubfequent to Lord *Cowper's* Refignation of Office. Thus we have a faint Image of the Life of an amiable and affectionate Woman clofing prematurely in Sorrow and Gloom. Her Bereavement by the Death of her Hufband accounts chiefly and confeffedly for the State of Proftration into which fhe fank ; but there is ftill a little Myftery furviving her Death, there

is ftill a Tag of her Story unravelled, and we
have not the Facilities to follow out the Clue.
As we have no further Light to throw upon this
obfcure Paffage, we muft leave it as it ftands,
with the Diary itfelf, to the free and candid
Conftruction of the Reader.

Diary of Lady COWPER.

1714.

THE perpetual Lies that One hears have determined me, in fpite of my Want of Leifure, to write down all the Events that are worth remembering whilft I am at *Court*; and although I find it will be impoffible for me to do this daily, yet I hope I fhall be able to have an Hour or two once a Week: and I intend this only for my own Ufe, it being a rough Draft only, which, if *God* blefs me with Health and Leifure, I intend hereafter to revife and digeft into a better Method.

I believe it will be neceffary, in the firft Place, to recolleƈt what paffed in order to my coming into the *Court*: and to give a better Light in that Matter, I muft tell that for four Years paft I had kept a conftant Correfpondence with the *Princefs* now my Miftrefs;[1] I had received many, and thofe

---

[1] *Caroline* Princefs of *Wales*, Daughter of the Margrave of *Anfpach*, born in 1683, married in 1703 to the Eleƈtoral Prince of *Hanover*, afterwards *George II.* Lord *Chefterfield* fays of her: 'She would have been an agreeable Woman in focial,

the kindeft, Letters from her. Upon the Death
of the *Queen*, after fhe had done me the Honour
to anfwer my Letter of Congratulation, I wrote
another Letter to offer her my Service, and to
exprefs the perfect Refignation I had to whatever fhe would think fit to do, were it to choofe
or refufe me. This Letter fhe anfwered, telling
me fhe was entirely at the *Prince's* Difpofal, and
fo could give me no Promife; but that fhe did
not doubt the *Prince's* Willingnefs to exprefs his
Friendfhip to me upon all Occafions. By the
whole Letter I took it for granted that fhe had fo
many Importunities upon that Subject, that fhe
could not take me into her Service, and therefore
I refolved not to add to the Number of her Tor-
mentors, and never mentioned the Thing any
more. I was the more confirmed in my Opinion
when I faw myfelf treated with fuch Marks of
Diftinction, and at the fame Time two new Ladies made, and I had heard Nothing; but I knew
that the Neceffity of Affairs often forces Princes
to do many Things againft their Inclinations, and
I daily received fo many diftinguifhing Marks
of the *Princefs's* Favour that I had great Reafon

if fhe had not aimed at being a great One
in public, Life. She profeffed Art inftead
of concealing it, and valued herfelf upon
her Skill in Simulation and Diffimulation,
by which fhe made herfelf many Enemies,
and not a Friend even among the Women
neareft to her Perfon; Cunning and Per-
fidy were the Means fhe made Ufe of in
Bufinefs.' It muft, however, be remem-
bered that Lord *Chefterfield* was a hoftile
Witnefs. During the Reign of *George I.*
the Princefs of *Wales* maintained a
fplendid Court, and became very popular.
She held a Drawing-room every Morning, and had a Reception at Night twice
a Week. Her country Refidence was
Richmond Lodge. Speaker *Onflow* fays:
'She was a very wife Woman in what fhe
knew; was an excellent Wife and Mother,
had a high Senfe of Religion, and carried
her State and Dignity with Eafe and
Decency.'

to be fatisfied. Things ftood in this Manner till the Coronation, which was *October* 20, 1714.

I went thither with Lady *Briftol*,[2] who had ftill a greater Mind to be a Lady of the Bed-chamber than I had; fhe told me I was to be one, but durft not then tell me fhe had heard it from the *Princefs* herfelf. When we came from the *Hall* into the *Abbey* (for we faw every Part of the Ceremony), the Peereffes' Places were fo full, that we and feveral other Ladies went to the Bifhops' Benches at the Side of the Altar. I fat next the Pulpit Stairs on the back Bench, and feveral Ladies coming by me to go nearer the Altar, at laft my Lady *Northampton*[3] came pulling my Lady *Nottingham*[4] by the Hand, which Laft took my Place from me, and I was forced to mount the Pulpit Stairs. I thought this rude, but did not fuppofe there had been any Defign in it, though we had both been talked of for being Governefs to the young Princeffes,[5] and fhe, I believe, had really folicited for it, and apprehended I had done fo too, notwithftanding I had never thought of it. However, her Ill-breeding got me the beft Place in the *Abbey*, for

[2] *Elizabeth*, only Daughter and Heir of Sir *Thomas Felton*, Bart., of *Playford*, County *Suffolk*; married in 1695 to *John Hervey*, created, in 1714, Earl of *Briftol*.

[3] *Jane*, Daughter of Sir *Stephen Fox*, married in 1706 to *George* fourth Earl of *Northampton*.

[4] *Anne*, fecond Wife of *Daniel* fecond Earl of *Nottingham*, and only Daughter of *Chriftopher* Vifcount *Hatton*, whofe Eftates defcended to her Son, the Earl of *Winchelfea* and *Nottingham*. She was the Mother of thirty Children.

[5] *Anne*, afterwards Princefs of *Orange*, and the Princeffes *Amelia* and *Caroline*.

I faw all the Ceremony, which few befides did,
and I own I never was fo affected with Joy in
all my Life ; it brought Tears into my Eyes,
and I hope I fhall never forget the Bleffing of
feeing our holy Religion thus preferved, as well
as our Liberties and Properties.

My Lady *Nottingham*, when the Litany was to
be fung, broke from behind the Reft of the Company, where fhe was placed, and kneeled down
before them all (though none of the Reft did),
facing the *King*, and repeating the Litany.
Everybody ftared at her, and I could read in
their Countenances that they thought fhe over-
did her High Church Part.   But to return to my
Place.   The Lords that were over againft me,
feeing me thus mounted, faid to my Lord, that
they hoped I would preach; to which he anfwered
that he believed I had Zeal enough for it, but
that he did not know that I could preach ; to
which my Lord *Nottingham*[6] anfwered, 'No, my
Lord ? Indeed you muft pardon me.   She can,
and has preached for thefe laft four Years fuch
Doctrines as, had fhe been profecuted in any
Court for them, you yourfelf could not defend
her.'   This he faid with fuch an Air, that my
Lord fpoke of it to me.   That, joined to what
my Lady *Nottingham* had done that Day, and

* *Daniel Finch*, fecond Earl of *Not-*
tingham, had held feveral high Offices,
and on the Acceffion of *George I.* was
made Prefident of the Council, but retired
from public Affairs in 1716 ; was one
of the Heads of the High Church Party ;
and wrote a Reply to *Whifton*, for which he
was thanked by the Univerfity of *Oxford.*
Died in 1730.

fome other little Paffages that had happened, opened my Eyes, and fhowed me how that Family maligned me, and helped to perfuade me that it was impoffible the *Princefs* could think of me.

At the Coronation, my Lord *Bolingbroke* for the firft Time faw the *King*. He had attempted it before without Succefs. The *King* feeing a Face he did not know, afked his Name, when he did him Homage; and he (Lord *B.*) hearing it as he went down the Steps from the Throne, turned round and bowed three Times down to the very Ground. The Ladies, not walking in the Proceffion, had no gold Medals.

One may eafily conclude this was not a Day of real Joy to the Jacobites. However, they were all there, looking as cheerful as they could, but very peevifh with Everybody that fpoke to them. My Lady *Dorchefter*[7] ftood underneath me; and when the *Archbifhop* went round the Throne, demanding the Confent of the People, fhe turned about to me, and faid, ' Does the old Fool think that Anybody here will fay no to his Queftion, when there are fo many drawn Swords?' However, there was no Remedy but Patience, and fo Everybody was pleafed, or pretended to be fo.

I went to the Chapel in the Morning, and

---

[7] *Catherine Sedley*, Daughter of Sir *Charles Sedley*, Miftrefs of *James II.*, who created her Countefs of *Dorchefter* for Life. She married Lord *Portmore*, and died at *Bath* in 1717. She is reported to have faid, ' I wonder for what Qualities *James II.* choofes his Miftreffes. We are none of us handfome, and if we have Wit, he has not enough of it himfelf to find it out.'

1714. when it was done, to the Drawing-room; and
the *Princefs* feeing me, called to me, and faid,
' Did Lady *Effex Robartes*[8] deliver my Meffage
to you?' To which I anfwered, that I had
not feen her fince her Royal Highnefs had
fpoke to her laft Night at the Opera. 'Then,'
faid fhe, ' I will tell you myfelf that you have
made a Conqueft;' and feeing me blufh, fhe
laughed, and faid, ' I am refolved to fhame you,
or rather to do you Honour. 'T is Mr. *Bernftorff*,[9] who never was in love in his Life before;
and 't is fo confiderable a Conqueft, that you
ought to be proud of it; and I, to pleafe him,
have ordered him to make you a Compliment
from me.' And with that fhe went out of the
Room.

When I came to the Bottom of the Stairs, I
found Mr. *Bernftorff's* Man, who defired me to
name an Hour for him to come to me. I named
Four; and Mr. *Bernftorff* came punctually, to tell
me that he had Orders from the *Princefs* to offer
me to be *une Dame du Palais*. I was very glad to

[8] Youngeft Daughter of *Robert* Vifcount *Bodmyn*, and Granddaughter of
John Robartes, Earl of *Radnor*. The
Name of *Effex* borne by her Aunt and
herfelf was probably given in Honour of
Lord *Effex*, the Parliamentary General
under whom her Grandfather commanded a Regiment of Horfe at *Edge-
hill*.

[9] The *King's* German Minifter.
George I.'s principal Favourites were,
Baron *Bothmar*, Baron *Bernftorff*, and Mr.
Robethon. During the whole of his

Reign they exercifed the greateft Influence in all Appointments to public
Stations, Baron *Bernftorff* efpecially fo.
He was the Minifter whom the *King*
moft confulted on foreign Affairs, and
he himfelf afpired to a Seat in the Englifh *Houfe of Lords*. See *Coxe's Memoirs
of Sir Robert Walpole*, i. 153, &c. He
was Anceftor of the prefent able and
popular Pruffian *Ambaffador* in *London*
(Count *Bernftorff*), and his Countrymen
feem to have entertained a very high
Opinion of him.

hear this, and told him that I wifhed it mightily, but that I had never made any Application for it after the Letter I have already mentioned, becaufe I would not add to the Number of the *Princefs's* Perfecutors; upon which he made me a thoufand Compliments, both from the *Princefs*, the *Prince*, and himfelf, and ordered me to go the next Day to kifs the *Princefs's* Hand. I gave him at the fame Time a Treatife[1] on the State of Parties, which I had tranfcribed and tranflated for my Lord, in French and Englifh, to give the *King*.

In the Morning, by Eleven, I waited upon the *Princefs*. I found the Duchefs of *St. Albans*[2] in the outward Room upon the fame Errand. She went in firft and kiffed the *Princefs's* Hand, and I followed. The *Princefs*, when I had done it, took me up and embraced me three or four Times, and faid the kindeft Things to me—far beyond the Value of any Riches. There were prefent the Duchefles of *St. Albans* and *Bolton*,[3] Mrs. *Clayton*,[4] Mrs. *Howard*,[5] the

---

[1] This Treatife is given at length in the Appendix to Lord *Campbell's* Life of Lord *Cowper* (*Lives of the Chancellors*).

[2] *Diana de Vere*, eldeft Daughter and eventually fole Heirefs of *Aubrey*, twentieth and laft Earl of *Oxford* of that Family. She was married in 1694, and died in 1742.

[3] *Henrietta Crofts*, natural Daughter of *James* Duke of *Monmouth* by *Eleanor*, Daughter of Sir *Robert Needham*.

[4] Wife of *William Clayton*, afterwards Lord *Sundon*. Introduced by the Duchefs

of *Marlborough* to the *Princefs*, fhe became a Woman of the Bedchamber and Miftrefs of the Robes. She is faid to have obtained her Influence in confequence of having difcovered the Secret of a phyfical Infirmity which the *Princefs* took extraordinary Pains to conceal. *Horace Walpole* terms her an abfurd pompous Simpleton, but Lord *Hervey's* Opinion of her is highly favourable.

[5] Daughter of Sir *H. Hobart*, of *Blickling*, born in 1688, married to *Charles Howard*, afterwards Earl of *Suffolk*. She

1714. Governefs, and two or three of the foreign Ladies. The *Prince* alfo faluted the Duchefs of
St. Albans and me upon our being declared;
and we both waited that Night in the Drawing-
room.

October 26,   *October* 26 and 27 paffed without Anything
27.   remarkable, unlefs the Duchefs of *Shrewfbury*[6]
being named a Lady of the Bedchamber Extraordinary deferves to be thought fo. She had
folicited the *King* for it, who had afked the
Princefs three Times to do it, and fince had told
her it would be an Obligation to him. The
Princefs faid to me afterwards that the Duchefs
of *Shrewfbury* was not her own Choice, nor can
Anybody reafonably believe fhe could be, all the
World knowing that her Brother had forced the
Duke to marry her after an Intrigue together;
which made a Lady fay that the *Duke* had been
tricked out of the beft Marriage (meaning the
Duchefs of *Somerfet* when Lady *Ogle*),[7] and in-
to the worft in Chriftendom. The Duchefs of
Shrewfbury had fome extraordinary Talents, and it
was impoffible to hate her fo much as her Lord,
though fhe was engaged in the fame ill Defign.
She had a wonderful Art at entertaining and

went to live in *Hanover*, and became
Lady of the Bedchamber to the *Princefs*
on the Acceffion of *George I.* She
married, fecondly, *George Berkeley*, and
died in 1767.

⁶ Daughter of the Marquis *Paleotti*,
of *Bologna*, and defcended, by her Mother,
from Sir *Robert Dudley*, natural Son of

Dudley, Earl of *Leicefter*. She abjured
the Romifh Faith in order to be married
to the Duke of *Shrewfbury*, who was a
Proteftant.

⁷ The great *Percy* Heirefs, Widow of
Lord *Ogle*, married to the proud Duke
of *Somerfet*.

diverting People, though ſhe would ſometimes exceed the Bounds of Decency. She had a great Memory, had read a good deal, and ſpoke three Languages to Perfeſtion ; but then, with all her Prate and Noiſe, ſhe was the moſt cunning, deſigning Woman alive, obliging to People in Proſperity, and a great Party-woman, as I may ſay from Experience, for after a little Diſpute at *Sacheverel's* Trial, and my Lord's laying down the Seals, ſhe forbore viſiting me, or ſpeaking to me when ſhe met me anywhere, till the *King's* coming to the Crown.

Then our Acquaintance was renewed by supping together at Madame *Kielmanſegge's* [8] about a Month ago ; but it was ſhyly till now, for a Converſation happening at Supper, when ſpeaking of the King of *France's* Eating, ſhe was counting twenty Things upon her Fingers that he had eat at a Time.[9] She was ſaying, 'Sire, il mange ceci et cela ;' on which I ſaid, ' Sire, Madame la *Ducheſſe* oublie qu'il a bien plus

---

[8] Counteſs *von Platen,* Wife of General *Kielmanſegge,* who died in 1721, created on his Death Counteſs of *Darlington. H. Walpole* ſays of her : ' I remember as a Boy being terrified at her enormous Figure. The fierce black Eyes, large and rolling beneath two lofty arched Eyebrows, two Acres of Cheeks ſpread with Crimſon, an Ocean of Neck, that overflowed, and was not diſtinguiſhed from, the lower Part of her Body, and no Part reſtrained by Stays. No Wonder that a Child dreaded ſuch an Ogreſs.' She died in 1724.

[9] *St. Simon* ſays : ' Toute l'Année il mangeait une Quantité prodigieuſe de Salade. Ses Potages, dont il mangeait Soir et Matin de pluſieurs, et en Quantité de chacun ſans Préjudice du Reſte, étaient pleins de Jus, et d'une extrême Force. Il mangeait de tout ſans Exception. Aux premières Cuillerées de Potage l'Appétit s'ouvrit toujours, et il mangeait ſi prodigieuſement et ſi ſolidement Soir et Matin, et ſi également encore, qu'on ne s'accoutumait point à le voir.'

mangé que cela.' 'Qu'a-t-il mangé donc ?' faid
the *King*. 'Sire,' anfwered I, 'il a mangé et dévoré
fon Peuple ; et fi la Providence n'avoit pas conduit
votre Majefté au Trône, au Moment qu'elle l'a fait,
il nous auroit mangé auffi.' On which the *King*
turned to the *Duchefs* and faid, ' Entendez-vous,
Madame, ce qu'elle dit ?' And he did me the
Honour to repeat this to feveral People, which
did not at all ftrengthen my Intereft with her
Grace. But upon coming into the Bedchamber
all old Quarrels are laid afide for the Eafe and
Quiet of our Miftrefs.

The Duchefs of *St. Albans* and I waited in
the Drawing-room, as we had done every Night,
to kifs the *King's* Hand upon our Preferment,
and this was the firft Day we came there. He
had forgot that he had feen the Duchefs of
St. Albans before, fo he faluted her without Hefi-
tation; but when I was prefented, he faid five
or fix Times, ' Oh ! je l'ay vue; elle eft de ma
Connoiffance ;' and at laft the Duke of *Grafton*[1]
told him it was upon my being made a Lady
of the Bedchamber. So then he faid, ' Ouy
dà, je le ferai avec Plaifir,' and I was faluted.
This Day was paffed in Difputes amongft us
Servants about the *Princefs's* kiffing my *Lady
Mayorefs*, and quoting of Precedents ; but Queen
Anne not having kiffed her when fhe dined in
the City, my Miftrefs did not do it either.

---

[1] *Charles* fecond Duke of *Grafton*,   Duchefs of *Cleveland*, was at this Time a
K.G., Grandfon of *Charles II*. and the   Lord of the Bedchamber.

We went to my *Lord Mayor's*[2] Show, four
of us in the Duchefs of *Shrewfbury's* Coach, and
two with the *Prince's* Lords in one of the *King's*
Coaches. We ftood at a Quaker's, over againft
Bow Church. I thought I fhould have loft the
Ufe of my Ears with the continual Noife of
Huzzas, Mufic, and Drums; and when we got
to the *Hall* the Crowd was inconceivably great.
My poor Lady *Humphreys* made a fad Figure in
her black Velvet, and did make a moft violent
Bawling to her Page to hold up her Train
before the *Princefs*, being loath to lofe the Privilege of her Mayoralty. But the greateft Jeft
was that the *King* and the *Princefs* both had
been told that my *Lord Mayor* had borrowed her
for that Day only; fo I had much ado to convince
them of the Contrary, though he by Marriage is
a Sort of Relation of my Lord's firft Wife.[3] At
laft they did agree that if he had borrowed a
Wife, it would have been another Sort of One
than fhe was.

This Day was the *Prince's* Birthday. I never
faw the *Court* fo fplendidly fine. The Evening concluded with a Ball, which the *Prince*
and *Princefs* began. She danced in Slippers[4]
very well, and the *Prince* better than Anybody.

[2] The *Lord Mayor* Sir *William Humphreys*, created a Baronet in 1714, when the
King and Prince of *Wales* dined at *Guild-
hall*. He was very active in fuppreffing
Jacobite Libels and fending the Hawkers
to Prifon, for which he received the
King's Thanks. He was alfo Member
of Parliament for *Marlborough*.

[3] *Judith*, Daughter of Sir *Robert
Booth*. Died April 1705, leaving a Son,
who died young.

[4] That is, the *Princefs* danced in low-
heeled Shoes, which was not, at that
Time the fafhionable Ufage.

My Lord and I fupped at the Duke of *Shrewf-bury's*[5] with my Lord[6] and Lady *Wharton*[7] and Madame *Kielmanfegge,* to wait upon the. *King.*

Supped at my Lady *Brifol's*, to wait upon the *King.* The Duchefs. of *Bolton* was there, the Dukes of *Kent*[8] and *Grafton*, Duchefs of *Shrewfbury,* Madame *Kielmanfegge,* and. myfelf. I never faw the *King* in better Humour: than this Night. He faid a World of fprightly Things. Amongft the Reft, the Duchefs of *Shrewfbury* faid to him, ' Sire, nous fommes en colère con-tre votre Majefté de ce que vous ne voulez. pas vous faire peindre ; et voici votre Médaille qui donnera votre Effigie à la Poftérité, où vous avez un Nez long comme le Bras.' ' Tant mieux,' faid the *King* ; ' c'eft une Tête à l'Antique.' But though I was mightily diverted, and there was a great deal of Mufic, yet I could not avoid being uneafy at the Repetition of fome Words in French which the Duchefs of *Bolton* had faid by Miftake, which convinced me that the two foreign Ladies were no better than they fhould be.

Mr. *Bernftorff* made me a Vifit. I defired him to take care of Sir *David Hamilton's*[9]

---

[5] *Charles* Duke of *Shrewfbury*, to whom Queen *Anne* on her Death-bed delivered the Lord Treafurer's Staff, was at this Time Lord Chamberlain. He died in 1717.

[6] *Thomas* fifth Baron and firft Marquis, one of the Leaders of the Whig Party, Father of the Duke of *Wharton*.

[7] *Lucy,* Daughter of *Adam Loftus* Lord *Lifmore.*

[8] *Henry de Grey*, Duke of *Kent*, K.G., lived in great Splendour at *Wreft*, in *Bedfordfhire* ; was at this Time a Lord of the Bedchamber ; was made, in 1716, Lord Steward of the Houfehold, and in 1718 Lord Privy Seal.

[9] Phyfician to Queen *Anne* and *George I.* He left fome curious Memoirs relative to Queen *Anne*, which are ftill in MS.

being made Firſt Phyſician, which he promiſed to do. Went out to carry the *Princeſs* all my Lord *Bacon's* Works, which ſhe had bade me get her. The Day proved fine, and ſhe ſhowed our Engliſh Ladies that ſhe could walk as well as ever the Princeſs *Sophia*[1] had done.

I brought the *Princeſs* a Book that Madame *Kielmanſegge* had ſent me to give her, and after preſenting it I underſtood by Mrs. *Howard* that there was a mortal Hatred between them, and that the *Princeſs* thought her a wicked Woman. She alſo told me that her ſending it to me was a Deſign to perſuade the *Princeſs* that ſhe was very well with me, in order to ruin my Credit with her; 'For,' added ſhe, 'if it had not been ſo, ſhe would have ſent it either by the Duchefs of *Bolton* or *Shrewſbury*, that are ſo well with her; but ſhe never ſtuck a Pin into her Gown without a Deſign.' *Piloti* told me that ſhe was the Daughter of the old Counteſs of *Platen*, who was Miſtreſs to the *King's* Father, and had cauſed the Separation.[2]

This Day the Duchefs of *St. Albans* made Groom of the Stole,[3] and Duchefs of *Shrewſbury* made a Lady in Ordinary, as we are all.

---

[1] The Mother of *George I.* *Toland,* who accompanied the Earl of *Maccleſfield* on his Miſſion to *Hanover* with the Act of Succeſſion in 1700, ſays: 'She (the Electreſs *Sophia*) is the moſt conſtant and greateſt Walker I ever knew. She perfectly tires all thoſe of her Court who attend her in that Exerciſe.'

[2] *Eliſabeth von Meiſſingen,* Counteſs of *Platen,* Miſtreſs of the *Elector,* Father of *George I.,* was ſaid to have been the Cauſe of the Separation between the *King* and his Wife *Sophia Dorothea,* of *Zell,* by her Inſinuations and Intrigues.

[3] 'Though an Office ſomewhat incongruous in Name, that of "Groom of the

1714. My Birthday. Pray *God* grant that the Reft of
my Life may be paffed according to His Will and
in His Service.

Nov. 15.   I came into Waiting. I was ill when I came
in, and continued fo the whole Week. The
Princefs told me fhe had feen the Treatife on the
State of Parties, already mentioned; and com-
plimented me mightily upon it. In the Evening
I played at Baffet as low as I could, which
they rallied me for; but I told my Miftrefs I
played out of Duty, not Inclination, and having
four Children, Nobody would think ill of me if
for their Sakes I defired to fave my Money, when
I did not do Anything that was mean, difhoneft,
or difhonourable ; for which fhe commended me,
and faid fhe thought the principal Duty of a
Woman was to take care of her Children.[4]

Nov. 17.   Dr. *Clarke*[5] came in this Morning and prefented the *Princefs* with his Books. This Day
fhe expreffed a Diflike to my Lady *Briftol's*

Stole" is ufually combined with the Duties
of the Miftrefs of the Robes when a
female Sovereign is on the Throne, as
was the Cafe in the Reign of Queen
Anne. The Stole is a narrow Veft, lined
with crimfon Sarcenet, and was formerly
embroidered with Rofes, Fleur-de-lis, and
Crowns ; but the Office of Groom is a
Sinecure.'—*Dodd's Manual of Dignities,*
p. 138. For further Particulars fee
The Book of the Court, edited by *W. J.
Thoms,* p. 346, and the Letter of the
Duchefs of *Marlborough,* printed in Appendix A.
    [4] She did not always act up to this
moral Sentiment. See *Pope's* farcaftic

Lines : 'And all her Children bleft,' &c.
    [5] *Samuel Clarke,* D.D., the great Con-
troverfialift, Rector of *St. James's,* publifhed a Work in 1712, entitled, ' *The
Scripture Doctrine of the Trinity* which
involved him in endlefs Controverfy, and
laid him open to the Imputation of not
being quite orthodox, and on the Death
of Sir *Ifaac Newton* he was offered, but
refufed, the Place of Mafter of the *Mint.*
He died in 1729. *Voltaire* characterifes
his logical Powers and tedious Manner
by calling him ' un Moulin à Raifonne-
ment.' He was in high Favour with the
Princefs, who repeatedly attempted, but in
vain, to induce him to accept a Bifhopric.

Project of attacking the Duchefs of *Shrewfbury*
in the *Houfe of Commons* about her being a Fo-
reigner, and confequently incapable of having any
Place about the *Princefs*.

The Duchefs of *Bolton* afked me to go to her   *Nov. 18.*
Houfe to meet the *Prince*, and play at Cards
with all the Ladies of the Bedchamber. But
I was in Waiting : the Duchefs of *St. Albans*
fupped out alfo that Night where the *King* was.
She had been made Groom of the Stole the
Week before, and fo the Duchefs of *Shrewfbury*
had come into her Place ; and now Lady *Briftol*
laboured to get in, in the fame Manner that the
Duchefs of *Shrewfbury* had been before. But fhe
has fince had a direct Denial.

She fpoke to me to give an ill Character of
Mrs. *Coke*[6] to the *Princefs*, which I refufed to
do, faying that I knew no Ill of her, fo that it
would be barbarous to flander any one without
Caufe. She replied that I might fay fhe told me
that fhe was an ill Woman ; that her Behaviour
at her Houfe was fcandalous ; that fhe had feen
my Lord Berkeley[7] give her a Letter ; and that

---

[6] Mrs. *Coke* was the Daughter of Mr. *Hale*, and the fecond Wife of the Right Honourable *Thomas Coke*, M.P. for *Derby-fhire*, and Vice-Chamberlain to Queen *Anne*, the Sir *Plume* in *Pope's Rape of the Lock*. As Mifs *Hale*, Mrs. *Coke* had been one of the Maids of Honour to Queen *Anne*, and fhe was, at all Events, a Woman of remarkable Beauty. *Swift* fpeaks of her as fuch in his *Journal to Stella*, Auguft 1711 : 'Mr. *Coke*, the Vice-Chamberlain,

made me a long Vifit this Morning, but the *Toaft*, his *Lady*, was unfortunately engaged.'

[7] *James* third Earl *Berkeley*, a diftin-guifhed naval Officer. He was Firft Lord of the *Admiralty* in 1718 and 1727, and K.G. In the Heat of the Quarrel be-tween *George I.* and his Son, Lord *Berkeley* propofed to carry off the *Prince* to *America* and keep him there.

Sir John Germaine,[8] and Lady *Betty* had both
told her that the laſt Child Mrs. *Coke* had
was actually Lord *Berkeley's*. I anſwered that I
thought it was much properer for her to ſay this
to the *Princeſs* than me, becauſe ſhe could ſpeak
of her own Knowledge, which I could not; but
ſhe ſtill inſiſted that ſhe had private Reaſons of
her own not to do it, which ſhe was obliged not
to tell me, but that I ſhould do a great Service to
the *Princeſs* if I would ſay this to her. But I refuſed, and ſaid, if there were any private Reaſons
to conceal, I was ſure that was Reaſon enough
for me not to do it, for I did not know what I
was about, and ſo would not meddle in it. I
have ſince learned, from undeniable Teſtimony,
that Lady *Briſtol* had ſpoken to the *Princeſs* to
be Miſtreſs of her Robes, and that ſhe anſwered
her that ſhe did not deſign to have any, but
that if ſhe was obliged to take one, the *Prince*
had made her promiſe it ſhould be Mrs. *Coke*:
and yet this was before my Lady *Briſtol* put me
upon this hard Service.

Nov. 19. In the Morning, whilſt I was in Waiting,
came in my Lady *Nottingham*. We had juſt
before been talking of Dr. *Smaldridge,*[9] Biſhop

---

[8] Of *Drayton*, County *Northampton*,
which he got from his firſt Wife, the
divorced Ducheſs of *Norfolk*. Lady
Betty was Siſter of Lord *Berkeley*. She
inherited her Huſband's Eſtates, and be-
queathed them to Lord *George Sackville*,
who took on that Account the Name of
Germaine.

[9] *George Smaldridge*, a Friend and
Aſſociate of *Atterbury*, Biſhop of *Rocheſ-*
ter, to ſeveral of whoſe Preferments he
ſucceeded. Conjointly with *Aldrich*,
they publiſhed a famous Diſcourſe on
Church Government. He died in 1719.
He was a great Favourite of the Princeſs
of *Wales*, who ſettled 300*l.* a Year on his
Widow.

of *Briſtol*, who had been praiſed to the *Princeſs*
as the greateſt Saint upon Earth; but till this
Morning ſhe had never known that he was one
of Dr. *Sacheverel's* Speech-makers, and that he
had waited upon him all the Time of his Trial.
When my Lady *Nottingham* came in, the *Princeſs* addreſſed herſelf to her, and ſaid : ' We have
been talking of Dr. *Smaldridge*.' Upon which
the other launched out in his Praiſe; and ſays
my Miſtreſs: 'Here's Dr. *Clarke* ſhall be one
of my Favourites; his Writings are the fineſt
Things in the World.' Says the *Counteſs*:
' Yes, Madam, his firſt Writings; but his laſt
are tainted with Hereſy.' And ſo ſhe ſaid abundance upon that Subject; and in ſpeaking of
his Scripture Doctrine of the Trinity, that Part
relating to *Athanaſius's* Creed, which ſhe called
the Teſt of Religion, ſhe quoted Dr. *Smaldridge*
as an Authority againſt Dr. *Clarke*. Mrs. *Clayton*
was by, and ſaid that Dr. *Smaldridge*, whatever
he had ſaid to the *Counteſs*, yet had ſaid to her
that every private Chriſtian was not obliged to
believe every Part of the Athanaſian Creed. Not-
withſtanding this, Lady *Nottingham* defended
her Opinion of Dr. *Clarke's* being a Heretic as
well as ſhe could ; and I ſaid to her : ' Madam,
I have read theſe Books, and I really ſee no Cauſe
to accuſe him of Hereſy, which is a heavy Charge;
but I ſuppoſe your Ladyſhip is better acquainted
with them than I am. Since you can accuſe
him, pray quote a Paſſage out of his Books.' To

* c

which fhe anfwered, drawing herfelf up as if fhe had been afraid of Something: ' Not I, indeed. I dare not truft myfelf with the Reading fuch Books. I 'll affure you I never looked into them.' ' What, Madam ?' faid I, ' Do you undertake to condemn Anybody as a Heretic, or to decide upon a Controverfy, without knowing what it is they believe and maintain ? I would not venture to do fo for all the World.' This Difpute happening before the *Princefs*, will hardly be a Step to making her Governefs to the young *Princeffes*, which fhe had afked to be ; nor do I believe that Dr. *Smaldridge* will have Power to do fo much Harm as he has done, or defigns to do, for I am told for a Certainty that he and my Lord *Nottingham* are the Hopes of the Tories, and that the one in the Church, and the other in the State, had undertaken to fet all Things upon the right Foot, as they call it. I am perfuaded that Lord *Nottingham's* Heart was never with the Whigs, though it was againft the laft Miniftry ; and it was this Hatred to Lord *Oxford* that made him play the Part he did, joined with his Refent-ment at not being brought into Place, for the *Queen* had a mortal Averfion to him, becaufe of his Rapacioufnefs ; and long before thefe Times, after the *Queen* had turned him out from being Secretary of State, fhe wrote a Letter to my Lord *Godolphin*, to tell him fhe would part with her Crown rather than make Ufe of my Lord *Nottingham* again, he was fo overbearing and greedy of Places for himfelf and Family. Lord *Oxford* was even with him, for he hated him as much as he was hated, and defpifed him withal, calling him '*Spintext*,' and always ridiculing him. In the Evening the *King* was in the Drawing-room. The Duchefs of *St. Albans* put on the *Princefs's* Shift, according to *Court* Rules, when I was by, fhe being Groom of the Stole.

This Day I read to the *Princefs* the original Affidavits concerning the Riots at three feveral Places on the Coronation Day, which gave an Account of the Affronts offered to the *King*. The Pretence was, that the other Side would have burnt the *Pope* and *Pretender*; that they had Notice that *Sacheverel's* Image was to be burnt, and the Word was given, ' *Sacheverel* for ever !' as I believe it was all over *England*; and in fome of thefe Places they added, ' D——n King *George* !' 'T is certain the Hopes of the Tories ran very high, and that all Endeavours imaginable were ufed to get a Tory *Parliament*, not a Night paffing but fome fcandalous Pamphlet or other was cried about upon fome of the Whigs; and I remember one Night I bought my Lord's Speech to the *King* and Council in vindication of the Duke of *Ormond*.[1] Thefe Things did a great deal of Harm among the common People ; but what clinched the Nail was, that this Week every one, or almoft all the Lords in Office,

---

[1] An imaginary Speech.

received the *Pretender's* Declaration[2] by the foreign Poft, which fpoke fo openly of the late *Queen's* good Intentions towards him, that at firft People were of Opinion it had not been genuine; but about a Week after, Mr. *Prior*[3] fent over Notice from *France* that fuch a Thing was come out, and that at firft he thought it had been only a Story raifed by the Englifh Nuns and Irifh Priefts (both famous at *Paris* for lying), but that he found it was authentic, and that he was trying to get a Copy, which he would fend away by a fpecial Meffenger as foon as he got it. Thefe Things I believe have helped to convince the *Court* that though 't is reafonable to give the Tories very good Words, yet they are not to be trufted, notwithftanding their Pretence of un-limited and paffive Obedience. The *Court* went to the Opera. The Duke of *Shrewfbury* had been in a great Grief for a Report that was in Town that the *Duchefs* had told the *Princefs* that Gentlemen's Wives had kiffed her Hand when fhe firft came into *England*. To be fure, Nobody had ever done it, unlefs it might be fome belonging to the *Duke's* Family, though the *Princefs* fays fhe told her fo. The Duke of *Bolton* was by, who had told Madame *Kielmanfegge* of it, and fhe that very Day whifpered it to the Duchefs of *Shrewfbury*, then by. She expreffed

[2] There is an Analyfis of this Document, with Extracts, in *Tindal's Continuation of Rapin*, vol. iv. pt. ii.

p. 409, folio edition, 1747.
[3] *Matthew Prior*, the Poet, then
Minifter Plenipotentiary in *Paris*.

a world of Refentment, and was very angry at
thofe that had mentioned it; and in that fhe was
in the Right, for certainly Nobody fhould repeat
a Converfation out of a Princefs's Chamber. This
Night the *Prince* and *Princefs* went to the Opera,
which was ftark Nought.

I went to Chapel, which concluded the Service
of my Week. I received a thoufand Marks of
my Miftrefs's Favour, as embracing me, kiffing
me, faying the kindeft Things, and telling me
that fhe was truly forry my Week of Waiting was
fo near out. I am fo charmed with her good Nature and good Qualities, that I fhall never think
I can do enough to pleafe her. I am fure, if
being fincerely true and juft to her will be any
Means to merit her Favour, I fhall have it, for I
am come into the *Court* with Refolution never
to tell a Lie; and I hope I find the good Effects
of it, for fhe repofes more Confidence in what I
fay than in any others, upon that very Account.
A great Buftle was heard this Day at the Chapel.
It was the Countefs of *Nottingham*, who was
going out before Church was done (like a true
High Churchwoman), to take her Place behind
the *Princefs's* Chair-back in the Drawing-room,
preferring to make her Court to an earthly rather than to a heavenly Power. I was ill from
ftanding fo long upon my Feet, for which Reafon
I did undrefs me as foon as I came Home, and
ftayed within for two Days, to recover myfelf.

I dined, undreffed, at Mrs. *Clayton's*, with the

1714. Duchefs of *Marlborough*, Countefs of *Piquebourg*, and Lady *Effex Robartes*. The *Duchefs* gave me a Pattern for Embroidery for the next Birthday.

Nov. 25. I went to *Court* in the Morning, and found the *Prince* had been ill of a Surfeit. In the Afternoon Monfieur *Bernftorff* came. My Lord tried to have kept Mr. *Monkton* in the Commiffion of Trade, for the Honour of the *Houfe of Lords*, he having been turned out fingly by the laft Miniftry, for being a Witnefs before the *Houfe of Lords* againft them the laft Year ; but it was all refolved before, and fo he was fhamefully put out.[4] He (Mr. *B.*) told me they began to find out the Earl of *Nottingham* and the Bifhop of *Briftol*, and that their Reign was at an end. After he was gone I went to *Court*. The *Prince* was in Bed ; but, notwithftanding, all the Ladies of the Bedchamber that were attending were called in, and Tables were placed, and we were all fet to play at Ombre with the Lords of the *Prince's* Bedchamber, and, for a Miracle, I won eight Guineas.

Nov. 26. We all went to *Court* twice. In the Evening, not knowing any Order to the contrary, I called for a Table and Cards, and played at Ombre. I fince begged my Miftrefs's Pardon, and told her that it was through Ignorance I had been guilty, for Mr. *Coke*,[5] the *King's* Vice-

---

[4] He had been Commiffioner of Trade and Plantations from 1706 to 1713.
[5] The Right Honourable *Thomas Coke*, of *Melbourne*, *Derbyfhire*, Vice-Chamberlain to Queen *Anne* and *George I.* His Daughter and Heirefs married Sir

Chamberlain, had told me that we that were her
Servants were to fet a good Example to the
Reft by playing, and that fhe might be fure I
fhould be the Laft that would break any Rule
fhe made.   She told me fhe readily believed me,
and that the Tables and Chairs were taken out
of the Drawing-room becaufe People ufed to fit
down before her, but that Anybody might play
in the outward Room that would.

Both Days I was fick and ftayed at Home.
Befides, I thought I had fome Reafon to appre-
hend *Nancy's*[6] having a Return of her Convulfion Fits; fo I partly ftayed to watch her.   I
gave her fome of my Aunt's Convulfion Powder,
and I thank *God* my Fears have been groundlefs.
Mrs. *Clayton* ftayed and fupped with me.

I went to *Court* to enquire of my Miftrefs's
Health, who had been out of Order, and I found
her gone a walking.   I ftayed till fhe came back.
She had walked to *Kenfington*, and the Coaches
brought them back again.   She thanked me for
drinking her Health with Mrs. *Clayton* at Supper
the Night before.   I told her I never failed at my
Meals drinking hers and my Mafter's; upon which
the *Prince* faid he did not wonder he had fuch
good Health fince he came into *England*, fince
I took fo much Part in it.   I told him that before
his coming hither, I and my Children had conftantly drunk his Health by the Name of *Young*

Matthew Lamb, Father of the firft Vif-   [6] Lady *Anne Cowper*.
count *Melbourne*.

1714. *Hanover Brave,*[7] which was the Title Mr. *Con-greve*[8] had given him in a Ballad. This made him afk who Mr. *Congreve* was, and fo gave me an Opportunity of faying all the Good of Mr. *Congreve* which I think he truly deferves.

Nov. 30. This Day was employed in packing, for re-moving from *Ruffell Street* (where I had a de-lightful Houfe, with the fineft View backwards of any Houfe in Town) to the Houfe in *Lincoln's Inn Fields*, where I had lived before, when my Lord had the Seals, and which my Lord *Har-court* lived in whilft he was Chancellor. I wrote a Letter as earneft as I could make it to my Lord *Halifax*,[9] at the Defire of my Sifter *Liddell*,[1] to get her Hufband put into the Commiffion of the *Salt Office*, which I fent the next Morning.

Dec. 1. My Lord *Halifax* came in to fee my Lord, and defired him to tell me that he had all the Concern in the World that he could not do what I defired in relation to my Brother *Liddell*, for the Commiffion had been long before the *King*, but that he had fo great a Mind to ferve me, that the Place of Treafurer of the *Stamp*

---

[7] From the Song by Mr. *Congreve* on the Battle of *Oudenarde*, beginning, 'Ye Commons and Peers:'—

'Not fo did behave
Young *Hanover* brave
In this bloody Field, I affure ye;
When his War-horfe was fhot
He valued it not,
But fought ftill on Foot like a Fury.'

[8] *William Congreve*, the celebrated Dramatift. The *Prince's* Queftion, 'Who Mr. *Congreve* was?' gives us the Meafure of the Ignorance of the two firft Princes of the Houfe of *Hanover* refpecting Everything Englifh.

[9] *Charles Montague*, Earl of *Halifax*, K.G., the Poet, Wit, and Statefman, died in 1715.

[1] *Anne*, youngeft Daughter of *John Clavering*, Efq., of *Chopwell*, Wife of *Henry*, Son of Sir *Henry Liddell*.

Duties (which was vacant by Mr. *Frankland's*
dying) was at my Service, if I would accept of
it. My Lord anfwered that I fhould be infinitely obliged to him for it, and, when Lord
Halifax was gone, came up and told me of it.
I own I was never more overjoyed in my Life
than with the Thoughts of being able to do
my Sifter this Service. I wrote to my Sifter to
tell her, and to know if I had her Confent and
my Brother's for writing to my Lord *Halifax*
to thank him and accept. They were both at
Supper at my Coufin *Waite's*, and my Brother
in coming Home called at Mr. *Freeke's*, where
his Father was, and from thence wrote me a   '
Letter of Thanks, and that he gladly accepted
the Favour. To clinch the Matter, I fat down and
wrote a Letter of Thanks to my Lord *Halifax*,
accepting the Place.

In the following Morning my Coufin *Waite*   *Dec. 2.*
and my Sifter *E. Clavering* came to make me a
Vifit. This Laft brought a Meffage from my
Sifter *Liddell* to give me many Thanks for the
Trouble I had taken about her Hufband's Affair,
but withal to tell me that there was a great
Security which muft be given to the Government before he could enter upon it, fo that fhe
was forry he had accepted it, for it was utterly
againft her Confent. I was a little nettled at
this Meffage, but made no other Anfwer than
that I thought that Sir *Harry Liddell* and
Mr. *Freeke*, who had advifed him to accept it,

had more Wit than my Sifter. My Coufin *Waite* at the fame Time defired me to fpeak to my Lord *Halifax* to get her Hufband into the *Wine Licenfe*, which I begged Pardon for re-fufing to do the Day after he had given me a Place. In the Afternoon came Mrs. *Darcy*, to defire me to fpeak to the *Princefs* to make Mrs. *H. Howard*[2] a Bedchamber Woman. She urged that Mrs. *Howard* had had a Promife of it from *Hanover* in the Princefs *Sophia's* Time, in a Let-ter from her to Lady *Frederica Schomberg*.[3] I faid I had a Friend of my own (Mrs. *Kreinberg*) that had put in for the Place, and that I had pro-mifed to help her if it was in my Power. Mrs. *Darcy* anfwered me that I could afk for two, if I pleafed, as well as for one. I fmiled, and faid I was not thorough-paced Courtier enough yet to come up to thofe Notions, and fo I defired to be excufed. I would not have undertaken this Affair for all the World.

My Aunt *Allanfon* came in the Evening to fee me. I told her of my Sifter *Liddell's* Beha-viour to me, which fhe juftified mightily, faying the Place was but a poor 300*l.* per Annum, that there were Taxes to be paid out of it, and a new War might break out, and then there muft be four Shillings in the Pound; that there

---

[2] On the Acceffion of *George I.*, Mrs. *Henrietta Howard*, afterwards Lady *Suf-folk*, was appointed one of the Bed-chamber Women to the Princefs of *Wales*. See the Preface to the *Letters*

of Lady Suffolk, edited by Mr. *Croker*. [3] *Frederica*, fecond Daughter of *Mein-hardt* Duke of *Schomberg*; married, firft, the Earl of *Holdernefs*, and fecondly, the Earl *Fitzwalter*. She died 1751.

were no Perquifites (which is falfe), and urging highly my Duty to do all I could for my Rela- tions. I told her fince my Relations were fo hard to pleafe, after I had taken all thefe Pains, they fhould get the next Place themfelves, for this was fo difcouraging that I would meddle no more for Anybody. From hence high Words arofe, and fuch as plainly fhowed me that after all I have done for my Family, I am thought but ' an unprofitable Servant;' which I think a little hard, after I have got a Place for my Uncle *Allanfon* from my Lord, which brings him near a thoufand Pounds a Year. My Lord, in both Times of his being Chancellor, has let him officiate, though my Lord fays that he opens the Bufinefs fo ill that he can never underftand what he reads, but is forced to read all the Briefs himfelf; whereas when *Dupper*, who is now his Deputy, brings Anything, my Lord is never at that Trouble. When my Aunt was gone, I told my Lord how I had been ufed by my Friends. He was mightily difpleafed, particularly with my Aunt, whofe Treatment he refented fo much, that he would have taken away the Commiffioner- fhip, had I not foothed him, and told him I did them good for Confcience Sake. But it is hard to meet with the Return I do from my Relations.

I removed to my new old Houfe in *Lincoln's* *Inn Fields.* As I went into the Door, came a Letter from my Lord *Halifax*, to tell me that the *King*, by Monfieur *Bernflorff*, had ordered

1714. him to put Another into the Place he had given
my Brother; that he had fent *Robethon*[4] to ex-
poftulate, and tell him it was given to me. I
fealed the Letter up, and fent it to my Sifter,
who did richly deferve this Turn. My Brother
wrote to me to make a great many Expreffions,
and to tell me he was afhamed to defire me to
purfue this Matter any further, fince I had had
fo much Trouble already in it; but, however,
faid enough to let me know he was quite of another Mind than his Wife.

Dec. 4. In the Evening Monfieur *Bernftorff* came o
bring me my Place, which the *King* refufed to
meddle with as foon as he heard who it was for;
faying, ' Laiffez-la lui ; je n'y veux pas toucher :
elle l'aura, elle l'aura ;' which obliging Expreffion
was more than the Thing itfelf, though I fuppofe my Relations would have liked 10*l.* a Year
Addition much better.

Dec. 6. I waited upon the *Princefs* in the Morning,
and told her how good the *King* had been to me ;
that I was fure it muft be from my having the
Honour to be about her Perfon that I had received
fuch a Favour, having no Merit of my own. In
the Evening I went to the Drawing-room, and
thanked the *King*. The Room was exceffive
hot, and I got a great Cold coming out, for my
Chairmen had left me. In the Evening went

* Private Secretary of *George I.*, and
one of his principal Favourites ; had
great Influence in the Difpofal of Places
and Patronage. He was of French Ex-
traction, and broken Fortunes, and had
been Private Secretary to *William III.*
In the *Macpherfon Papers* he appears as a
frequent Correfpondent of *Bothmar.*

out to fup at Madame *Montandre's*,[5] to wait upon 1714.
the *King*. There was Nobody there but Madame
Kielmanfegge, Lady *Dorchefter*, Madame *Tron*[6]
the Venetian Ambaffadrefs, myfelf, and Mr.
Methuen,[7] who makes fweet Eyes at Madame *K.*
At Supper Madame *Tron* had a Letter from her
Hufband, ordering her to come Home. He's
very jealous; but now fhe has got into a free
Country, fhe fays fhe will live and go about like
other People; and he, not liking her to do this,
beats her very often. That's the only Thing
fhe fears, for if fhe can but efcape Beating, fhe
values Nothing, which has got her the Name of
' La Beauté fans Souci.'

   Bernftorff came, and made Complaints of my *Dec.* 8.
Lord *Halifax's* infupportable Pride to his fellow-
Minifters (which he has fome Reafon for fhowing, having been very ill ufed by fome of them in
the difpofing of Places), of his Familiarity with
my Lord *Oxford* and others (which he utterly de-
nies), and to defire all Quarrels may be made up
(which he promifes to do). The Report of his
Intimacy with Lord *Oxford* has no other Foundation than my Lord *Dupplin's*[8] not being yet
out of his Place, which is given to my Lord *Not-*

---

[5] Wife of *Francis de la Rochefaucald*, Marquis de *Montandre*, who came to *England* with *William III.*, and ferved in all the Wars of that Monarch and of Queen *Anne*.

[6] Signor *Tron*, Venetian Ambaffador, had his firft Audience of the *King November* 18, 1714, to congratulate him on his Acceffion. There is a Palace of this Name at *Venice*.

[7] *Paul Methuen* was, at different Times, Ambaffador to *Spain*, Comptroller of the Houfehold, and Secretary of State. He was Son of the Negotiator of the *Methuen* Treaty with *Portugal*.

[8] *Thomas* Vifcount *Dupplin* became Earl of *Kinnoul* in 1758.

1714 *tingham* for his Son-in-law, Sir *Roger Moſtyn*,[9] a rank Jacobite. My Lord *Halifax* refuſed to put Sir *Roger* into the Place till an Account is made up that is depending between him and the Government, which they are doing with all the Expedition imaginable.

Dec. 11. *Bernſtorff* came in the Evening, by Appointment, to try to get my Lord to make the Matter up among the Whig Lords, and to tell my Lord *Halifax* that the *King* heard he would not do his Part in the *Treaſury* againſt the old Miniſters for their Detection in the enſuing Seſſions of *Parliament*; and by that he would think he was in Friendſhip with my Lord *Oxford*. My Lord willingly undertook it, and my Lord *Halifax* as willingly promiſed to do his Part. This Lie probably came from my Lord *Nottingham*, who harangues the *King* every Day for an Hour and Half (concluding always with his Hand upon His Breaſt, and theſe Words: 'Sir, I have done my Duty and diſcharged my Conſcience, after having laid the Truth before your Majeſty. If your Majeſty will not follow my Advice, I have Nothing to do but to ſubmit with Reſignation to your Majeſty's better Judgment'), and who is angry with Lord *Halifax* for not admitting his Son-in-law, Sir *Roger Moſtyn*, into his Place. I was ill at Home. Lady *Eſſex Robartes* came in the Evening to take her Leave of me, ſhe being

---

⁹ Third Baronet. Married Lady *Eſſex*   *tingham*; made a Teller of the *Exchequer*
Finch, Daughter of *Daniel* Earl of *Not-*   in 1714.

to begin her Cornifh Journey[1] to-morrow Morning, which fhe will be about twelve Days in
performing. She undertakes it with great Fear.

Mr. *Benfon*[2] came in the Evening, much mortified with being left out of the *Board of Trade*,
where Mr. *Chetwynd* had got in by Madame
Kielmanfegge's Intereft, he having given her (as
he told me he is well affured) five hundred
Guineas down, and is to pay her a Penfion of
200*l.* per Annum as long as he has the Place;
and I have fince learnt from another Hand that
he gave her alfo the fine Brilliant Ear-rings which
fhe wears, it being certain fhe never had any fuch
Jewels abroad.

At Home all Day. Mrs. *Tuttle* came to fee
me in the Morning. She told me that my Relations took it ill of me that I did not go oftener
to them; that my Aunt expected I fhould have
got her a Place about the *Princefs*, and my Uncle
another in the *Salt Office*. How People judge
of their own Merit! This Day a Man was fent
to *Newgate*, that on Saturday laft had come
into the Court at *St. James's*, and made two or
three Paffes with his Sword at the Colours, re-
viling the *King* and his Title. He was an Irifh

---

[1] To *Lanhyderoch*, near *Bodmin*, now
in the Occupation of Mr. *Robartes*.

[2] *Robert Benfon*, of *Bramham Park*,
Yorkfhire, M.P. for *York*, was a Lord of
the *Treafury* from *Auguft* 1710 to *April*
1711, and Chancellor of the *Exchequer*
from *May* 1711 to 1713. He was fub-
fequently created Lord *Bingley*, and was
Ambaffador to *Madrid*, and Treafurer of
the Houfehold, 1729-30. *John Chetwynd*, whom he feems to have thought
more fortunate than himfelf on the Occafion above mentioned, was appointed,
and remained one of the Commiffioners
of Trade and Plantations from 1714 to
1728.

1714.   Papift, and had formerly been a Servant to *Wilks*,[3]
the Player, who had turned him out of the Playhoufe, upon a Complaint made of him by the
Duke of *Argyle*[4] for talking in a like Manner.

Dec. 15.   *Bernftorff* dined here.   I hope the Matter of
the Whigs is amicably fettled.   Lord *Nottingham*
and his Brother are well known, and 't is promifed that they fhall never be able to do Harm.
The *King* is as we wifh upon the Subject of
Parties, and keeps my Lord's Manufcript by
him, which he has read feveral Times.   I have
prevailed for Sir *David Hamilton* to be fole Phyfician to the *Princefs.*

Dec. 16.   Mrs. *Clayton* dined here.   She told me that
the Duchefs of *Bolton* made great Intereft for
Mrs. *M. Oglethorpe* to be a Maid of Honour (if a
Woman can be fo that has had feveral Children).
The *Princefs* is mightily obliged to her Grace for
the Recommendation, for the *Oglethorpes* have
always been Spies to *France,* and this very Woman took a Journey thither the Day after the
Queen was buried: and to be fure fhe had always been a Spy upon the Whigs, her Mother
having turned her out of Doors upon pretence
of her being a Proteftant and a Whig.   So fhe
harboured herfelf with thofe who were really fo;

<hr />

[3] Was defcended from a good Family in *Worcefterfhire*, and Grandfon of Judge *Wilks*. He firft appeared on the Stage in *Ireland,* but ultimately obtained great Succefs in *England.*

[4] *John*, fecond Duke, ferved under *Marlborough*, and was Commander-in-chief in *Scotland* in 1715. Commemo-rated by *Pope* : —

‘ *Argyle*, the State's whole Thunder born
   to wield,
  And fhake alike the Senate and the
   Field.’

Died in 1743, without male Iffue.

particularly, fhe was always at my Lady *Mohun's*,[5] where all the libertine Whigs were frequently, and fhe certainly did a world of Harm that way.

This Morning I fent early to Baron *Bernftorff*, to defire to fee him. He had requefted me to give him Notice if Mrs. *Oglethorpe* was recommended to my Miftrefs, and withal to give him Notice of another Piece of Intelligence, which was, that Mrs. *Kirk* (Widow of that Mr. *Kirk* who killed *Conway Seymour*[6]) was recommended by the Duchefs of *St. Albans* for a Bedchamber Woman. I told him what both thofe Ladies were ; that Mrs. *Kirk* had managed all the Intrigue between Lady *Mary Vere*[7] and the Duke of *Ormond*, took care of the Child, was Manager of all the Intrigues of the *Oxford* Family, had an ill Reputation as to herfelf, and had been the Duke of *Somerfet's* Miftrefs. *Bernftorff* took down their Names, and promifed to fpeak about them.

I could have told him a good deal more of this laft Lady, if it had been fit for me to do fo ; but I never opened my Mouth in relation to what 1 know of her upon my Account in my whole Life, and therefore it won't be amifs to fet down here, by way of Memorandum, what

---

[5] *Charles*, fifth and laft Lord *Mohun*, killed in a Duel with the Duke of *Hamilton* in 1712, married, firft, *Charlotte Mainwaring*, Niece of *Charles* Earl of *Macclesfield*, and fecondly, *Elizabeth*, Daughter of Dr. *Thomas Lawrence*, and Widow of Colonel *Griffith*. The Latter is of courfe the Lady *Mohun* mentioned above.

[6] For an Account of their Duel, fee *Macaulay*, vol. v. p. 240.

[7] *Aubrey de Vere*, twentieth and laft Earl of *Oxford*, died 1702, leaving Iffue *Diana*, Wife of the firft Duke of *St. Albans*, and *Mary* and *Henrietta*, who both died unmarried.

fhe formerly did towards making me unhappy. But I thank *God* I have efcaped that Snare.

My Lord being a Widower when the late *Queen* gave him the Seals, it was no Wonder the young Women laid out all their Snares to catch him. None took fo much Pains as Lady *Harriet Vere*, whofe Poverty and ruined Reputation made it impoffible for her to run any Rifk in the Purfuit, let it end as it would. She had made feveral Advances to my Lord by Mrs. *Morley*, her Kinfwoman, and finding Nothing came of it, they immediately concluded my Lord muft be pre-engaged to Somebody elfe; fo they fet a Spy upon him, and found that he had country Lodging at *Hammerfmith*, where he lay conftantly, and upon Enquiry they found I was the Caufe of this Coldnefs to Lady *H.* Upon this, they fettled a Correfpondence under a feigned Name with him; and in thofe Letters (which were always fent by a Fellow dreffed up in Woman's Clothes, who could never be overtaken) they pretended to be fome great Perfon, that threatened him, if he married me, to hinder the Paffing of his Title. The firft of thefe Letters came the Day before I was married. However, it did not hinder our Marriage, though my Lord thought it advifable to keep it a Secret;[6] and fo he re-

---

[6] There were, perhaps, other Reafons for his keeping the Marriage fecret for a Time, as in a Letter, quoted by Lord *Campbell*, from the *Chancellor* to his newly-married *Wife*, *December* 30, 1706, he fays: 'I am going to vifit my Mother, and, perhaps, fhall begin to prepare her for what fhe muft, I hope, know in a little Time.'

moved the next Day to *London*.   His Corref-
pondents, feeing they had made him leave the
Place, thought it would be no hard Matter to
break the Match; and from that Time to the
Beginning of *January*, which was almoft four
Months, my Lord had a Letter every Day, fome
of whole Sheets of Paper, filled with Lies about
me: to fay I was a mean Wretch; that I was
Coquette, and fhould be more fo; that my playing fo well was, and would be, a Temptation to
bring all the Rakes in Town about me; that it
had been fo thus far of my Life; and that I was
treated fo familiarly by the rakifh Part of the
Town, that one Night, at a Play, my Lord
Wharton[7] had faid to my Lord *Dorchefter*,[8]
' Now that the Opera is done, let's go and hear
Molly Clavering play it over again' (which was
all a plain Lie, for I never did play in any public
Company, and only at Home when Anybody that
vifited my Aunt *Wood*, with whom I lived, afked
me; and for thofe two Lords, I had never been in
a Room with either of them in my whole Life).
Thefe are only Specimens of what Lies they invented to hurt me.   At laft, when they thought
they had routed me, by the ill Impreffions they
had falfely given of me, upon a Day when my
Lord was at the *Houfe of Lords*, one Mr. *Mafon*,
of the *Houfe of Commons*, came to him, and told

---

[7] *Thomas* Earl, and afterwards Marquis, of *Wharton*, was one of the Leaders
of the Whig Party and a Man of profligate Character.

[8] *Evelyn Pierpoint*, Marquis of *Dorchefter*, created Duke of *Kingfton* in 1715,
Father of Lady *Mary W. Montague.*

him that Mrs. *Weedon* (a Client of my Brother's, that had a foul Caufe in the *Court of Delegates*) defired to fpeak with him. My Lord at firft refufed; but at length fhe teafed him fo much that he confented to fee her; and by her Appointment, and faying fhe had a very fine Lady to recommend to him (which gave him a Thought he fhould find out his Correfpondent), he waited upon her at Mrs. *Kirk's*, which was the Place appointed. He had fome little Jealoufy before he went that the fine Lady was Lady *Harriet Vere*, for fhe and Mrs. *Kirk* had always been in a Hackney Coach every Sunday for at leaft a Month, to ogle him and pafs and repafs his Coach when he went and came from the Chapel. He found he was right; for there fhe was, fet out in all her Airs, with her Elbow upon a Table that had two wax Candles on it, and holding her Head, which fhe faid ached. There fhe difplayed herfelf, and fo did her two Artificers, and not a Word faid of the Caufe. This Interview brought on feveral others, and thofe Vifits to my Lord from Mrs. *K.* and Mrs. *W.*, to try to make this Match. They told him that the *Queen* had promifed Lady *H.* 100,000*l.* when fhe married. He faid upon that Score he durft not prefume to marry her, for he had not an Eftate to make a Settlement anfwerable to fo great a Fortune; and at laft they preffed him fo much, that he owned he was engaged to me, and that it would be barbarous to ruin an innocent

young Woman, who had no Fault but receiving
his Vifits fo long. They could not agree with
him that it was barbarous, for it was only ferving
me in my own Kind, for I was contracted to
Mr. *Floyd*, whom I had left for him. My Lord
faid they were miftaken in that Affair (which
he knew full well). However, this did not dif-
courage them; and once, when he feemed to
yield, he brought Mrs. *Kirk* to confefs the Pains
they had been at to bring this about, and fhe
mentioned particularly the Letters, which were
contrived and writ at her Houfe, and copied
afterwards by Lady *H. V.* herfelf. As foon as
my Lord had got this Confeffion, he wrote to
Lady *H.*, in anfwer to a Love-letter from her (for
fhe pretended to be terribly in love with him),
to excufe himfelf, and fay that he refolved to
marry me, for now he was affured that he had
met with a wife whofe Conduct was unble-
mifhed, for that the greateft Enemy I had in
the World had been writing every Day an Invective againft me, which was duly fent to him; and
that now all the Letters were laid out before him
he did not find Anything I was accufed of, but
of playing the beft upon the Harpfichord of any
Woman in *England*, which was fo far from being
a Fault, that it was an Argument to him that I
had been ufed to employ many of my Hours
alone, and not in the Company of Rakes, as they
would fuggeft. But they thought that there was
Hope, fince they did not believe we were actually

1714.   married, and my Lord could never get quit of their Importunity till he owned our Marriage to them, though it was before he owned it publicly; and even after that, both Mrs. *K.* and Lady *H. V.* wrote frequently to him. This I had not inserted, but as a Juftification for my endeavouring to hinder her coming into the *Princefs's* Bedchamber.

Dec. 18.   Lord *Halifax* dined here. After Dinner, I went to wait upon the little *Princeffes*, who are Miracles of their Ages, efpecially Princefs *Anne,*[9] who at five Years old fpeaks, reads, and writes both German and French to Perfection, knows a great deal of Hiftory and Geography, fpeaks Englifh very prettily, and dances very well.

Dec. 22.   I went to *Court* in the Morning, which was the firft Time of my going out. Sir *D. Hamilton* came in the Afternoon. He told me that Mrs. *Danvers,* at the next Door, had afked him how he could bear ever to fee me, becaufe I fpoke ill of the *Queen.* I defired him to tell her that if fhe faw me herfelf fhe could take no Offence at me, for though I fpoke freely of the *Queen,* I fpoke mighty well of thofe that killed her. Mrs. *Danvers* had been many Years Dreffer to the late *Queen,* both when fhe was Queen and after. She was generally pretty well wed to her own Party, but a Bear to all the Whigs after the Change of the Miniftry. She had good Senfe,

* *Princefs Royal,* eldeft Daughter of *George II.,* afterwards Princefs of *Orange.* The late King of *Holland* was her Great-   grandfon. There was once a Queftion, originating with the Duc de *Bourbon,* of her marrying *Louis XV.*

a great deal of Cunning, and was the violenteſt Jacobite in the World, and a good deal truſted by them. She had made great Profeſſions to me the firſt Time my Lord was Chancellor, but neither ſhe nor Mrs. *Hartſtongue* ever came near me after; which ſhe was told of by a Friend of mine, to whom ſhe anſwered that ſhe had Something elſe to do. After the happy Change, ſhe took a Houſe next to mine in *Lincoln's Inn Fields*, and told Sir *David Hamilton* that ſhe intended to be my very good Neighbour, and ſee me every Day. I bid Sir *David* tell her ſhe would find herſelf miſtaken, for now I had Something elſe to do. Having named her Daughter, it will be right to ſay that ſhe married an Iriſh Biſhop, who hoped to have been made an Engliſh Biſhop by marrying one of the *Queen's* Dreſſers; but, I don't know how it happened, he miſſed his Aim, and got only one of the frightfulleſt, diſagreeableſt Wives in the Kingdom. Her Mother had perſuaded the *Queen* to make her Daughter a Dreſſer, that ſhe might be ſure that ſhe was about her after her Death. The Ducheſs of *Marlborough* had refuſed to meddle in it, ſo Mrs. *Danvers* applied herſelf to Lady *Maſham*, who undertook it upon condition that ſhe would bear a Part in getting the *Ducheſs* out of the *Court*, which they did effectually; and Mrs. *Danvers* and her Daughter played their Part notably on that Occaſion. It was about a Year after the young One was made Dreſſer that this reverend Prelate was ſmitten

1714.   with her Beauty and married her. I fhall only
tell two little Stories as a Specimen of him. The
one was, that, at a Chriftening, after he had
baptifed the Child, he brought the Bafin of Water
that had been ufed on that Occafion to the Lady
of the Houfe, faying, ' This, Madam, is fanctified
Water ; pray let it be put into Bottles. I affure
you it is a fovereign Remedy for fore Eyes.' The
other, while he was in *Ireland*, a Sea Captain
came to wait on him, whom, according to his
Cuftom, he entertained mighty well (for he might
have been a Roman Prelate for his Luxury).
After Dinner he would needs fhow the Tar his
Library, which the Other did not care for, ex-
cepting himfelf becaufe he did not underftand
Books ; but the *Bifhop* infifting upon it, they rofe,
and he followed the *Bifhop*, who carried him into
the fineft Cellars, and the beft filled, the *Captain*
had ever feen ; and then, turning to him, he faid,
' How do you like my Library ?' The Other
replied, ' Ah ! this is Something like a Library.
I affure your Lordfhip it is one of the fineft I
ever faw ; though I defire to remark to your
Lordfhip that moft of the Books are in Quarto.'

Dec. 23.   I went to the Backftairs in the Evening. In
the outward Room was a great Difpute upon
what the *Princefs* was to give at Chriftenings.
She had been Godmother to Mrs. *Harcourt's*
Child, and the *Prince* Godfather, and they had
fent thirty Guineas between them, which our
Ladies thought too little ; though, upon Informa-

tion, I find King *Charles II.* never gave more on fuch an Occafion than five Guineas to a Commoner's Nurfes, ten to a Baron's, twenty to an Earl's, and fo raifed five Guineas in every Degree. 'T is true Things are altered fince that Time (for now People of Quality fometimes give fifteen Guineas); but it is our Folly has increafed this, as it has every other Expenfe. This Day the Bifhop of *London* [1] waited on my Miftrefs, and defired Mrs. *Howard* to go in to the *Princefs*, and fay he thought it his Duty to wait upon her, as he was *Dean* of the *Chapel*, to fatisfy her in any Doubts or Scruples fhe might have in regard to our Religion, and to explain Anything to her which fhe did not comprehend. She was a little nettled when Mrs. *Howard* delivered this Meffage to her, and faid, 'Send him away civilly; though he is very impertinent to fuppofe that I, who refufed to be Emprefs [2] for the Sake of the Proteftant Religion, don't underftand it fully.'

This Day our Miftrefs and all her Servants received at the *Chapel*. I was pleafed with the *Princeffes'* Behaviour, which was the devouteft in the World.

[1] Dr. *Robinfon*, Dean of *Windfor* and Bifhop of *Briftol*, removed to *London*, *July*, 1714, ftrongly oppofed to Dr. *Clarke's* Views. He was Privy Seal in 1711 for a fhort Time, and one of the Plenipotentiaries for the Peace of *Utrecht*.

[2] She had refufed to marry the Archduke *Charles*, afterwards Emperor, because he was a Roman Catholic. *Gay* fays, in his *Epiftle to a Lady*, in fpeaking of her :—

'The Pomp of Titles eafy Faith might fhake ; She fcorned an Empire for Religion's Sake.'

I waited upon the *Princefs* to afk her Leave to go into the Country for three or four Days. The Duchefs of *Shrewfbury* and I had changed our Weeks, and fhe waited for me. This Day Monfieur *Robethon* procured the Grant of the *King* of Clerk of the *Parliament*, after Mr. *Johnfon's* Death, for Anybody he would name. He let my Brother *Cowper*[3] have it in Reverfion after Mr. *Johnson* for his two Sons for 1,800*l.*

[1] *Spencer Cowper*, M.P. for *Truro*, and one of the Managers on *Sacheverel's* Trial, was made a Judge in 1727. His two Sons, *William* and *Ashley Cowper*, held this lucrative Appointment in fuc-cefsion from 1716 to 1788; and their Nephew, the late *Henry Cowper*, of *Tewin Water*, was Deputy Clerk of the *Parliaments* from 1785 to 1825.

1715.

THIS was Twelfth Night, and such a *Jan.* 6. Crowd I never saw in my Life. My Miſtreſs and the Ducheſs of *Montague*[4] went halves at Hazard, and won 600*l.* Mr. *Archer*[5] came in great Form to offer me a Place at the Table ; but I laughed, and ſaid he did not know me if he thought that I was capable of venturing two hundred Guineas at Play—for None ſit down to the Table with leſs. In this great Crowd One may eaſily imagine there was a world of ſhouldering and hunching People. The Venetian *Ambaſſadreſs*, who I believe had been uſed to cry out to her Huſband, when he beat her, to take care of her Face, met with a good deal of it, and ' Prenez garde à mon Vizaze !'[6] was her Cry all Night long, and ſo loud, that the *King* heard her, and, turning to Somebody that ſtood behind him, ſaid, ' Entendez-vous l'*Ambaſ-*

---

[4] Daughter of the Duke of *Marl-borough*.
[5] *Thomas Archer*, Eſq., was Groom Porter of all His Majeſty's Houſes in *England* and elſewhere.
[6] The Italian Pronunciation of *Vi-ſage*.

1715. *ſadrice ?* Elle vous abandonne tout le Reſte du Corps, pourvu que vous ayez ſoin du Viſage.'

Jan. 7.   I aſked Leave from the *Princeſs* to be abſent at Night, for the *King* ſupped at *Montague Houſe,*[7] and the *Duchefs* would not ſuffer me to deny being with her, no more than the Duchefs of *Marlborough* would. Before I went out in the Evening I had a Preſent from the *King* of two Wild Boars' Heads ; one of which he had cut of, and found it ſo very good, that he ſaid it was the beſt he had ever eat, and bade Mr. *Lowman* ſend it to me, and ſay he had been my Taſter. This, I preſume, is a great Addition to the Preſent, and puts me in mind of the King of *France,*[8] who always ſups publicly ; and when he has a Mind to make a great Compliment to Anybody, he bites a Bit of Sweetmeat with his Gums (for he has no Teeth), and ſends the Reſidue to thoſe he would oblige. But to return to our Supper. The *King* was very grave. The Duchefs of *Shrewſbury*, Madame *Kielmanſegge*, and I very weary. A very ſhort Supper ; and about one o'Clock the *King* went to ſee the Houſe, and then the Duchefs of *Shrewſbury* and I ſlipped away.

Jan. 8.   In the Evening the Groom of the Stole and I waited upon the *Princeſs* to Lady *Berkeley's,*

[7] The Houſe mentioned in the Text was built by the Duke of *Montague.* It was in *Great Ruſſell Street, Bloomſbury,* on the Site of the *Britiſh Muſeum.* The Fields behind *Montague Houſe* were the great Rendezvous of Duelliſts.

[8] *Louis XIV.* This Story is hardly compatible with the *Grand Monarque's* Reputation for good Manners.

where fhe chriftened the Child with the *King* and Lady *Betty Germaine.* She gave thirty Guineas to the Nurfe.

At *Court.* My Miftrefs complained of Lord *Halifax.* I have fpoken to my Lord to bid him go and juftify himfelf at *Court.*

I received at *St. Giles's* [9] with my Lord, in order to take the Oaths.

I took the Oaths appointed in the *Court of* *Chancery,* with the Duchefs of *St. Albans* and Mrs. *Brett,* [1] the Seamftrefs. We afterwards went to *Court.* I dined at the Duchefs of *Marlborough's,* and from thence I waited upon the *Princefs* to the Playhoufe in *Drury Lane,* [2] and afked Leave to come Home direftly from thence, having had a hard Day's Work.

Bernftorff was here. The Duke of *Bucking-* *ham,* [3] upon what Confideration I know not, has refufed his Penfion, and Lord *Strafford's* [4] is at an End. About the Middle of laft Month Lord *Strafford* put his Papers into Lord *Townfhend's* [5] Hands, by the *King's* Orders; upon which his

[9] The prefent Church was finifhed in 1734. The Church at which *Lady Cowper* received the Sacrament was built in 1628, and confecrated by Archbifhop *Laud.*

[1] Probably the *Ann Brett* who became Miftrefs of *George I.* fhortly before his Death.

[2] The fecond Theatre defigned by *Wren,* and opened in 1674.

[3] *John Sheffield,* Duke of *Buckingham,* of fome Note as a Wit and Statefman, was favoured by *James II., William,* and *Anne,* and is reported to have fought the Hand of the Laft in Marriage. Died 1721.

[4] *Thomas Wentworth,* Lord *Raby,* created Earl of *Strafford* in 1711, Grand-nephew of the famous Earl of *Strafford,* was Minifter in *Holland,* and one of the Plenipotentiaries at the Peace of *Utrecht.* Was included in the Impeachment by *Parliament* of *Oxford* and *Bolingbroke.* Died in 1739.

[5] *Charles,* fecond Vifcount, was *George I.'s* Secretary of State on his Acceffion. He was Brother-in-law and at this Time the Friend of *Walpole.*

1715. Wife, who had fancied herſelf with Child, miſ-
carried, as ſhe had reſolved to do as ſoon as my
Lord's Buſineſs was talked on, and as I had been
told by her Mother-in-law (in Confidence) ſhe
would do. I ſpoke to get Mr. *Rowley* made
Maſter of the Mechanics, which Mr. *Bernſtorff*
promiſed me. He alſo promiſed me to get
Madame *Selnave's* Penſion continued, and her
Suit made an End of in the Iſland of *St.
Chriſtopher's.*

Feb. 14. The *Princeſs* told me that my Lord *Halifax*
had been with her, and had juſtified himſelf,
very much to her Satisfaction. There was a
Drawing-room in the Evening, and the Ducheſs
of *Roxburgh*[6] told the Counteſs of *Buckenburg*[7]
that the Play the *Princeſs* was to go to the next
Day was ſuch a One as Nobody could ſee with a
good Reputation. It was *The Wanton Wife.*[8] I
had ſeen it once; and I believe there were few
in Town had ſeen it ſo ſeldom, for it uſed to be
a favourite Play, and often beſpoke by the Ladies.
I told this to the *Princeſs*, who reſolved to venture going upon my Character of it.

Feb. 15. Went to the Play with my Miſtreſs; and, to
my great Satisfaction, ſhe liked it as well as
any Play ſhe had ſeen; and it certainly is not
more obſcene than all Comedies are. It were to

⁶ *Mary*, Daughter of *Daniel* Earl of
Nottingham, and Widow of the Marquis
of *Halifax*. Died in 1718, and was buried
in *Weſtminſter Abbey*.
⁷ Counteſs of *Lippe* and *Buckenburg*

(or, in French, *Piquebourg*), one of the
Ladies of the Princeſs of *Wales*.
⁸ By *Betterton*; but better known as
The Amorous Widow.

be wifhed our Stage was chafter; and I cannot but hope, now it is under Mr. *Steele's* [9] Direction, that it will mend.

I waited both Morning and Evening. At Night there was a Ball, which is to be every *Wednefday.* This Fatigue was abundantly too much for me. The Duchefs of *Roxburgh* told me fhe heard Sir *H. St. John* [1] is to be made an Earl for Life, and defired me to try to prevent it.

I came mighty ill to *Court*, and the Duchefs of *Shrewfbury* had fo much Humanity as to wait out my Week for me. As I was going through the Rooms, I met Baron *Bernftorff.* I told him that my Lord had ordered me to fpeak to him to hinder Mr. *Burgefs* from going Governor to *New England.* [2] He is the moft immoral Man in the World; was tried for the Murders of two Men, and was fo common a Swearer that the People, who are rigid Puritans, and left the Kingdom before the Civil Wars, to enjoy their own Way of Worfhip in Peace, would look at his being fent as a Judgment upon them. I

---

[9] Sir *Richard Steele*, on the Acceffion of *George I.*, was made 'Surveyor of the Royal Stables and Governor of the *King's* Comedians.'

[1] Father of Lord *Bolingbroke*, 'a Man of Pleafure that walks about the *Mall*,' fays *Swift*, 'and frequents *St. James's Coffee-houfe* and the Chocolate-houfes,' was created Vifcount *St. John*, and died in 1742, on the verge of ninety. On hearing of his celebrated Son's Elevation to the Peerage, he faid, 'Ah! *Harry.* I always faid you would be hanged, but I find you will be beheaded.'

[2] Colonel *Elifha Burgefs*, appointed Governor of *Maffachufetts* in 1715. Had been a Fellow-foldier of General *Stanhope*, the new Secretary of State; but the Agent of *Maffachufetts*, being then in *London*, advanced 1,000*l.* to induce him to relinquifh his Appointment in favour of *Samuel Shute.*

1715. alfo did afk him about Sir *Henry St. John.* He told me the Thing was true. I gave him all the good Reafons I could againft it, and 't is certain, if it fhould be done, fuch a Mark of Favour will infallibly damp the Profecution the *King* is driving on againft my Lord *Bolingbroke* in the next Seffions of *Parliament.* I'm told, from good Hands, that Mr. *Bothmar* [3] is to have the Advantage of doing it.

From this Time I was confined to the Houfe till the Birthday, during which Time Peace was made at *Bernftorff's* among the Whig Lords. *Bernftorff* had told the *King* that I would be Caution for my Lord *Halifax's* Behaviour, which I chid him for, becaufe 't is fufficient to anfwer for One's own Actions, without bearing the Burthen of other People's Faults. I am forry to think what may be the Confequence of thefe Divifions. I am fure it muft do a great deal of Harm, and it is a Rock we have already fplit upon.

Feb. 28. Lady *St. John* [4] and Madame de *Gouvernet* [5] fupped here. The Firft fhowed me a Letter from Lord *Bolingbroke* to his Father, with Profeffions

[1] Was Hanoverian Minifter at the *Hague,* and an active Agent in the *Elector's* Tranfactions with *England.* He figures in the Hiftory of *Marlborough's* Campaigns, and exercifed great Influence in the Difpofal of Crown Offices on the Acceffion of *George I. Townfhend* vehemently declared of him, 'He has every Day fome infamous Project or other on Foot to get Money.' His Character is alfo defcribed in a Letter from *Craggs* to

Schaub in the *Hardwicke Papers.*

[4] Second Wife of Sir *Henry St. John.*

[5] *Elie Bénoit* fays, 'A la Révocation de l'Edit de *Nantes,* la Marquife de *Gouvernet* obtint avec beaucoup de Peine la Permiffion de fe retirer en *Angleterre,* où une de fes Filles était établie.' The Head of the ancient Family of *La Tour du Pin* in *France* bears the Title of Marquis de *Gouvernet.*

of his Innocence in refpect of the *Pretender* (a 1715.
Copy of which I have taken),[6] but I believe it
won't ferve his Turn.

This Day Madame *Selnave* was with me to *March* 8.
thank me for her Affair being ended to her Satif-
faction.

I do not pretend to fet down the Occurrences
of this Month with the greateft Regularity, becaufe many of the Dates of Things are out of my
Head; but I think it will be good to fet them
down as well as I can, for a Help to my own
Memory hereafter.

I was now at *Kenfington*, where I intended to *October*.
ftay as long as the Camp was in *Hyde Park*, the
Roads being fo fecure by it, that One might
come from *London* any Time of the Night without Danger, which I did very often, for the
Rebels were up in *Northumberland*,[7] and I was
mightily folicited from my Friends at *Newcaftle*
to procure them fome Affiftance, which I effectually did by Baron *Bernftorff*, to the great Vexation of Lord *Townfhend* and Mr. *Walpole*, who
at that Time were for palliating Everything, and
beating down the Report of the Rebellion, thus
making it plain beyond Contradiction. I alfo
had two other Affairs to folicit; one in which
my Lord *Cowper* was engaged, the other by the
Commands of the *Princefs*, which I did faithfully.
The Firft was a Place for Lord *William Pawlet*,
who got it (a Teller's Place), the Other for Mr.

<hr>

⁶ See Appendix B.   ⁷ See Letters in Appendix C.

Clayton. As I loved Mrs. *Clayton* very much, I did what I could for Mr. *Clayton.* The Place he aimed at was that of Secretary to Mr. *Walpole's* Office. But Mr. *Walpole* [6] had a Mind *Horace Walpole* fhould have it, and fo had Lord *Townfhend.* Mr. *Clayton* had folicited very much for it, and was helped by the *Prince* and *Princefs,* who fpoke about it to Lord *Townfhend,* Mr. *Walpole,* and Baron *Bernftorff.* But firft I fhould tell that when the late Earl of *Halifax* was alive, and hated by his old Friends, Mr. *Walpole* came to Mr. *Clayton* and put him upon afking it of Lord *Halifax;* but he dying foon after, and the Earl of *Carlifle* [7] coming into his Place, Mr. *Walpole* put Mr. *Clayton* upon afking it again of Lord *Carlifle,* who had taken the Office to re-fign it foon after Mr. *Walpole.* At the fame Time he preffed Mr. *Clayton* to afk for the Place, and fwore to him by *God* that if ever he came into Lord *Carlifle's* Office he would make him take it. When Mr. *Walpole* was put into Office, Mr. *Clayton* found him a little cold; fo was Lord *Townfhend;* which Mrs. *Clayton* perceiving, de-fired me to fpeak of the Matter to Baron *Bern-ftorff.* I did fo, and he affured me there was no Danger, for he had fpoke to Mr. *Walpole* and Lord *Townfhend,* and they had promifed that the Place fhould be given to Mr. *Clayton.*

About this Time an old Hatred broke out

betwixt the Duke of *Somerſet* [8] and Lord *Townſ-* *hend*. The Duke of *Somerſet's* aſſiſting Sir *William Windham* [9] was made the Pretence, and he was turned out, without acquainting the *Prince* or Lord *Cowper* with it. They had done a world of Things to force Lord *Cowper* to quit, who was their Superior in Everything, becauſe they were afraid of his Honeſty and Plaindealing. But to return to Mr. *Clayton*: I told Mrs. *Clayton* what Baron *Bernſtorff* had ſaid to me. She fell a laughing, and ſaid, when Mr. *Walpole* and Lord *Townſhend* promiſed that Mr. *Clayton* ſhould have the Place, they knew that *Horace Walpole* was on the Sea, they having ſent for him to give him this Office, for Mr. *Clayton* was with Mr. *Walpole* this Morning, who told him, ' I know you have a great Intereſt with the *Prince* and *Princeſs*; but that ſhan't do, for no Intereſt in *England* ſhall hinder my giving this to. *Horace Walpole*, who I can deny Nothing to he has a Mind to have.' Mr. *Clayton* made a low Bow, and ſaid, ' Sir, I had never thought of it, if you yourſelf had not put me upon it, and I not only had your Promiſe confirmed by your Oath, but both you and Lord *Townſhend* have promiſed it over and over to the *Prince* and *Princeſs*; and after

[8] *Charles Seymour,* 'the proud' Duke of *Somerſet*, K.G. (*Collins's Peerage* ſays), reſigned his Appointment of Maſter of the Horſe on the Committal of his Son-in-law, Sir *W. Windham*, to the *Tower*, he having a Promiſe that if Sir *W.* ſurrendered he ſhould not be impriſoned.

[9] Chancellor of the *Exchequer* in the Tory Government of Queen *Anne*, and afterwards Leader of the Jacobite Party in the *Houſe of Commons*. His Son, Lord *Egremont*, ſucceeded to Part of the Duke of *Somerſet's* vaſt Eſtates.

1715.   fome more fuch Difcourfe they parted, and Mr.
Walpole had been fo afraid that Baron *Bernftorff*
would fpeak to the *King* for it, that he got a
Warrant of the *King* to give him Power to nominate a Secretary of the *Treafury*, which was a
Thing uprecedented, it being ufual for the *King*
to nominate in fuch Cafes.   The *Prince* and
Princefs then engaged to get another Place for
Mr. *Clayton* : it was one that Lord *Townfhend*
defigned for Colonel *Selwyn*,[1] fo that many Dif-
ficulties arofe about it.   The *Princefs* fent me
feveral Times to Baron *Bernftorff*, which Lord
Townfhend and Mr. *Walpole* perceiving, they
grew enraged[2] to the laft Degree, and faw it
was from me that fome of the Oppofition came ;
and being already afraid of my Lord *Cowper*, they
let out all their Malice in a great Degree, being
helped by Lord *Sunderland*,[3] who hated Lord
Cowper of old, for differing with him in *Parliament* about a Thing in which Lord *Sunderland* was manifeftly in the Wrong, and for which
the late *Queen* would have difcharged him, if
my Lord *Cowper* had not mightily interceded
for him.
      Baron *Bernftorff* came foon after this to fee

---

[1] Colonel *John Selwyn*, of *Matfon*, in
Gloucefterfhire, Member of Parliament,
and Father of *George Selwyn*.
   [2] It is not furprifing that they were
offended, when they difcovered this Attempt to take the Patronage of their
feveral Departments from them.
   [3] *Charles* third Earl of *Sunderland*,
Son-in-law of the Duke of *Marlborough*,
under whom he ferved both in a military
and diplomatic Charaĉter.   He was Secretary of State to Queen *Anne*, and difplayed Vigour in the Suppreffion of the
Sacheverel Riots.   From 1717 to 1721
he was at the Head of the Government.
His fecond Son inherited the *Marlborough*
Dukedom.

Lord *Cowper* and me. My Lord was called out to the Duke of *Somerfet*. When he was gone, Baron *Bernftorff* began to talk of the Duke of *Somerfet's* being out. I told him it was faid in Town that his Place was to be given, after a Time, to the Duke of *Newcaftle*.[4] I faw he was not very well pleafed that I had come out with it, and by his Manner I thought I could fee it was true. When he was going away, he faid, ' Milord eft beaucoup trop vif, et vous êtes beaucoup trop vive de votre côté. Les Miniftres fe plaignent fort de milord *Cowper*. Ils difent qu'il leur reproche trop fouvent les Fautes qu'ils ont pu commettre.' I faid, ' Je fuis fâché, Monfieur, que vous croyez cela. Notre feul But eft de bien fervir le *Roi*.' He faid again, ' Je vous dis que vous êtes trop vifs tous les deux. Croyezmoi, cela ne vaut rien, cela tourne toujours en Ruine.' And for fear I fhould not have heard thefe laft Words, he faid, with great Violence, ' Je vous dis que cela tourne toujours en Ruine.' One may guefs what Effect this had upon me, for I fincerely believe it was the firft Time that an Englifh Lady that had Bread to put into her Mouth had been fo treated on fuch an Occafion. I knew from whence all this Storm came, and plainly faw our Enemies had got the Better. The Duke of *Somerfet* repeated to my Lord all the Converfation he had with Lord *Townfhend* upon

---

[4] *Thomas Pelham*, created in 1714 Duke of *Newcaftle*, famous for his long Tenure of Office under *George II*.

his Difmiffion. Lord *Townfhend* came to the
Duke of *Somerfet*, and with a forrowful Air told
him he was forry to fay that the *King* had fent
him to tell his Grace that he had no further
Occafion for his Services. The Duke of *Somerfet*
then faid, ' Pray, my Lord, what is the Reafon
of it?' Lord *Townfhend* anfwers, ' He did not
know.' Then fays the Duke of *Somerfet*, ' By
G——! my Lord, you lie. You know that the
King puts me out for no other Caufe but for the
Lies which you, and fuch as you, have invented
and told of me.'⁵ He further afked Leave to
wait upon the *King*; but next Morning had a
Meffage not to come till he was fent for. Lord
Cowper had advifed the Cabinet Council againft
this Step, when the Queftion was raifed, fo they
did not acquaint him with it when it was done.
The Caufe they gave out was, that the Duke of
Somerfet had been with Sir *William Windham* at
Sir *Edward Northey's*⁶ Chambers, to confult with
him if the Proofs againft Sir *William Windham*
amounted to Treafon, before he furrendered himfelf; but I have fince heard that they had only
a Sufpicion of its being fo, from the Duke of
Somerfet's Coach being feen waiting in the Street

---

⁵ We muft remember that this is the
Duke of *Somerfet's* Account of the Converfation. It is not very probable that
Lord *Townfhend*, who was a man of violent and irafcible Temper, and who once
drew his Sword upon his own Brother-
in-law, Sir *Robert Walpole*, would have
permitted fuch Language to be held to
him with Impunity.

⁶ Sir *E. Northey*, a famous Lawyer.
Swift, in *The Bundle of Sticks*, fays :—
' Difpatch, or elfe that Rafcal *Northey*
Will undertake to do it for thee.
And be affured the *Court* will find him
Prepared to leap o'er Sticks or bind
them.'

where Sir *E. Northey* lives, for the *Duke* was going to Mr. *Lechmere's* [7] Chambers. My Lord fell ill again the Saturday following, and continued fo a great While, which occafioned a Report that he was going out of his Place. Some faid he had not Health to keep in. Others more truly faid, ' The Lords of the Cabinet Council were jealous of his great Reputation, and had a Mind to have him out, fo were refolved to weary him out of it ;' which laft Report was true, for they had refolved among themfelves, without acquainting Baron *Bernftorff*, to put my Lord Chief Juftice *Parker* [8] into his Place. I kept Houfe all this Time, and faw Nobody, and had enough to do to keep my Lord *Cowper* from giving up ; and I am fure the Difputes and Arguments we had upon that Subject were wholly the Occafion of his ftaying in ; and it was at leaft three Weeks before I could prevail.

The Month ending with the Solemnifation of the *Prince's* Birthday, which fhould have been folemnifed the 30th, if it had not been Sunday, I went privately to wifh them Joy, my Lord being very ill, fo I faw them alone in the Bedchamber. The *Prince* afked me what Lord *Cowper* faid to the Duke of *Somerfet's* being put

---

[7] *Nicholas*, afterwards Lord *Lechmere*, Solicitor-General in 1714, Chancellor of the Duchy of *Lancafter* in 1717, and Attorney-General in 1718. He was one of the Managers againft *Sacheverel*, and died of Apoplexy while at Table at *Camden Houfe* in 1727.

[8] Afterwards Earl of *Macclesfield*. Succeeded Lord *Cowper* as Chancellor in 1718. He fupported the *King* againft the *Prince* and *Princefs*. This they never forgave, and the Refolution for his Impeachment originated at *Leicefter Houfe*.

out. I faid he knew Nothing of it. He faid,
'No more did I; for I oppofed it once when it
was named, and fo they kept it from me.' I faid
that was my Lord *Cowper's* Cafe. The *Prince*
faid a thoufand kind Things of Lord *Cowper*, and
fo did the *Princefs*; and the *Prince* bade me tell
him he wifhed he would not lay Things fo much
to Heart; that he looked upon him as an old
Courtier, or elfe he had imparted fome of his
Experience to him, which was, when the *King*
fided with what he thought not right, to endea-
vour to prevent it; and when he could not, to
go on cheerfully. 'And tell him, when I come
to be King, all Things fhall go to his Mind; and
in the Meantime, whenever he has a Mind to
take the other Pull in the Cabinet Council, I
am ready to keep his back Hand.' The *Princefs*
made as many Expreffions as the *Prince* had
done; but by fome Words the *Princefs* let drop,
I perceived that fhe had been talked to by Baron
Bernftorff, for meddling with what had been
doing.

November.   Baron *Bernftorff* came to fee us twice in the
Beginning of the Month; but I did not fee him
alone, nor open my Lips of any News at all.
The 16th came the News that the Rebels had
furrendered to the *King's* Forces at *Prefton*.[9]   I
am fo unfortunate as to have a great many Relations among them, though moft of them are

---

[9] *Prefton*, in *Lancafhire*, where the   *Carpenter* and *Wills*, and were nearly all
Rebels were defeated by Generals   taken Prifoners.

Roman Catholics. Mr. *Foſter*,[1] one of my Couſins, Knight of the Shire for *Northumberland*, was their General. The Meſſengers had been down in the Summer to take him up; but he had hid himſelf at my Couſin *Fenwick's*, of *Bywell*, ſo they did not get him. I conjecture that it was for the Sake of his Uncle[2] and Aunt that he was made General, and not at all from the Fitneſs of the Thing, for he had never ſeen an Army in his Life. The Concern and Agitation of Mind which my Lady *Crewe*[3] had, for fear the Meſſenger ſhould take him up, killed her, for ſhe fell into Convulſions and died in four Days.

The Surrender of theſe Priſoners filled the Town with Joy, which was augmented by the News of a Victory in *Scotland*.[4] The Illwill which was borne the Duke of *Argyle* made it to be mightily leſſened, and even reported to have been none at all, but rather a Defeat; but the Conſequences ſhowed plainly that he had the Advantage, for the Rebels diſperſed after it, and they had not above 1,500 Men together, till the *Pretender* came to them. It will be neceſſary to ſay a Word or two of the Duke of *Argyle* as a

---

[1] *Thomas Foſter*, M.P. for *Northumberland*, choſen to be General of the Rebels not ſo much on account of his Poſition or Abilities as becauſe he was a Proteſtant. He proclaimed the *Pretender* at *Warkworth*. He was taken Priſoner at *Preſton*, and ſent to *London*, but eſcaped from *Newgate*.

[2] Lord and Lady *Crewe*.

[3] Wife of *Nathaniel Crewe*, Lord *Crewe*, and Biſhop of *Durham*.

[4] Battle of *Sheriffmuir*, in *Perthſhire*, between the Duke of *Argyle* and the Earl of *Mar*, indeciſive in its immediate Reſults, but of which the *Duke* reaped the whole Advantage. The right Wing of the Highlanders broke and cut to Pieces *Argyle's* left Wing, while the Clans on the left of *Mar's*, though conſiſting of *Stewarts*, *Mackenzies*, and *Camerons*, were completely routed.

further Light to what fhall follow. There had been a long Time a Mifunderftanding and Hatred between the Duke of *Marlborough* and him. Each Side almoft openly avowed it, or at leaft made no Secret of it, though both gave different Reafons. The Duke of *Argyle* faid that the Duke of *Marlborough* hated him to that Degree, that in one of the Battles he had put him upon the moft defperate Service there was, to get rid of him, which the Duke of *Marlborough's* Friends faid was falfe, but that he, *Argyle*, left his Place [5] and was forced to be brought back to it ; but the Duke of *Marlborough* was fure that when Queen *Anne* changed her Miniftry, the Duke of *Argyle* had gone to the *Queen* and told her that the Army would follow any General as well as they would the Duke of *Marlborough*, and fo laid the Foundation of the *Queen's* putting out the *Duke*.

Lord *Townfhend*, Baron *Bernftorff*, Mr. *Walpole*, and Lord *Sunderland*, were all afraid of the Duke of *Argyle*, whofe Favour with the *Prince* made them fear that one Day he would get the Better of them; fo, to leffen his Reputation, he had been fent to *Scotland* with very few Troops, and even thofe that were to go to him, by the fecret Orders of the Duke of *Marlborough*, were fo long

---

[5] Thefe abfurd Charges of Cowardice againft the Heroes of a hundred Fights were frequent in thofe Days of virulent Party Spirit. *Swift* has the Impudence to accufe the Duke of *Marlborough* himfelf of Want of Courage. The Duke of *Argyle* commanded twenty Battalions of Infantry at *Oudenarde*, and greatly diftinguifhed himfelf at *Lille* and *Ghent*. He was at this Time Groom of the Stole to the Prince of *Wales*.

a coming, that the Earl of *Mar* had Time to ftrengthen himfelf. This made the Duke of *Argyle* fly out prodigioufly. He complained loudly of the Miniftry, and his Animofity at laft grew fo high, that he made himfelf to be more in the Wrong even than they had been.

The Talk continued that my Lord *Cowper* was to be turned out. Mrs. *Clayton* came one Night and faid, fhe heard Lord *Cowper* was going to lay down. I anfwered, ' He is, they fay, going to be turned out. And they need not have given themfelves that Trouble : if they had but hinted to my Lord that they were weary of him, he would have laid down. They know he has done that once already,[6] which is more than ever will be faid of them, and upon Occafion he can do fo again.' She repeated this to the *Prince*, who fent away immediately for Baron *Bernftorff*, and chid him for giving in to any fuch Thing. About this Time Mademoifelle *Schutz*[7] came over to ftay with Baron *Bernftorff*. She was a pretty Woman, and had good Qualities, but withal was fo affuming, that fhe had made herfelf mightily hated at *Court*. We had been long and familiarly acquainted, fo that I faw her often ; but the *Prince* had expreffed fo great a Diflike of her to me, that I was in a good deal of Pain how to carry myfelf between them. She now

---

[6] In 1711.
[7] Niece of Baron *Bernftorff*, and probably related to Monfieur *Schutz*, who was Hanoverian Minifter at the Court of Queen *Anne*.

told me that Baron *Bernflorff* was very angry
with me; that I had not treated him like a
Friend; that I had not given him an Opportunity of feeing me alone for the laft four Times
he had been to fee me. I muft own that after
what had paffed at the laft Vifit at *Kenfington* I
thought they muft both be befide themfelves to
talk to me in that Manner. However, at her
Requeft, I agreed to fee Baron *Bernflorff* on the
Friday following.

Baron *Bernflorff* came as he had appointed.
The Sum of his Bufinefs was firft to complain of
Want of Friendfhip in me, that I had entertained
a Thought that he was confenting that my Lord
fhould be put out of his Place. I faid I heard it
was defigned by the Miniftry. Then he complained that I fhould have let him know. I faid,
coldly, that I knew he had fo much other Bufinefs, that I did not care to trouble him with
Anything concerning me. He made a world of
Expreffions upon this Point, and faid how little
capable he was of fuffering us to be injured; that
the Place of Lord *Cowper* was fure, and that
Nothing could take it from him but *God*, and
that the *King* had all the Kindnefs imaginable
for him. I faid I was very little attached to the
Place; that One muft be fond of a Thing before
One can fear to lofe it, and that it was too pain-
ful a Place to be fond of. Baron *Bernflorff* complained that my Lord *Cowper* was peevifh and
difficult, and that the *King* had told him fo;

that he had excufed my Lord *Cowper* to the
King, but that he defired I would try to foften
him, and make him compliable. I faid I muft
beg Leave to fay I was furprifed to hear this Complaint, becaufe it was the furtheft Thing from
his Character in the World, and I fancied he
muft have miftook the *King*. He hummed and
hawed, and faid a great deal upon this which I
cannot remember, and then went away. I told
my Lord what the *Baron* had faid of him, who
protefted folemnly to me that he was fo far from
being confcious of having been guilty of what
Baron *Bernftorff* accufed him, that he did not
fo much as know what he meant by faying it;
and by a great many concurring Circumftances
I dare be pofitive that it was Lord *Townfhend*,
and not the *King*, that had complained of Lord
Cowper; and that this was a political *Fineffe* of
the *Baron's* to make my Lord fubmit to Lord
Townfhend, who grew at laft fo great a Favourite
with Baron *Bernftorff* that he became wholly
governed by him.

The 5th I went into Waiting. The *Princefs* December.
was extremely kind to me. The Coming of the
Pretender into *Scotland*[8] began to be talked of,
though it did not happen fo foon as was expected.
This Week the Prifoners were brought to Town
from *Prefton*. They came in with their Arms

---

[8] He landed at *Peterhead* on December 22, 1715, and on *January* 2, 1716,
made his Entry into *Dundee* and *Perth*;
but on the Approach of the Duke of *Argyle* retreated to *Montrofe*, and em-
barked for *France*. His Flight may be
faid to have terminated the Rebellion of
1715.

tied, and their Horfes (whofe Bridles were taken off) led each by a Soldier. The Mob infulted them terribly, carrying a Warming-pan⁹ before them, and faying a thoufand barbarous Things, which fome of the Prifoners returned with Spirit. The Chief of my Father's Family¹ was amongft them. He is above feventy Years old. A defperate Fortune had drove him from Home in hopes to have repaired it. I did not fee them come into Town, nor let any of my Children do fo. I thought it would be an infulting of the Relations I had here; though almoft Everybody went to fee them.

I forgot in the laft Month a ftrange Offer made me by Mademoifelle *Schutz* from Baron *Bernftorff*, which was to let *Tom Forfter* efcape, if I had a Mind to it, upon the Road.²

---

⁹ In allufion to the Story invented by the Enemies of *James II.*, that the Infant *Pretender* had been brought into the Palace in a Warming-pan.

¹ *Clavering* of *Callalee.*

² He effected his Efcape from *New-*gate, probably with the Connivance of the Government, a few Days before the Time appointed for his Trial, and died in *France* in the early Part of the Reign of *George II.*

1716.

THIS Month uſed to be uſhered in with New Year's Gifts from the Lawyers, which uſed to come to near 3,000*l.* to the Chancellor. The Original of this Cuſtom was, Preſents of Wine and Proviſions, which uſed to be ſent to the Chancellor by the People who practiſed in his Court. But in proceſs of Time a covetous Chancellor inſinuated to them that Gold would be more acceptable; ſo it was changed into Gold, and continued ſo till the firſt Time my Lord had the Seals: Everyone having blamed it that ever had the Seals, but None forbidding it. *Jan.* 17.

The Earl of *Nottingham*,[3] when Chancellor, uſed to receive them ſtanding by a Table; and at the ſame Time he took the Money to lay it upon the Table, he uſed to cry out, 'Oh, tyrant Cuthtom! (for he liſped)—my Lord forbade the bringing them.[4] I ſtayed at Home till the Middle

[3] *Heneage Finch*, firſt Earl of *Nottingham*, Lord Chancellor in 1675. The *Amri* of *Dryden*.

[4] 'The preſent Lord Keeper did another Thing of a great Example. On the firſt Day of the Year it was become a Cuſtom for all thoſe who practiſed in *Chancery* to offer a New Year's Gift to the Lord who had the Great Seal. Theſe grew to be ſo conſiderable that they

1716.   of the Month, and when I did go out was very weak.

Feb. 1.   I ftayed at Home all Day.   Mr. *Horneck,*[5] who wrote *The High German Doctor,* came here. He is juft made a Solicitor of the *Treafury,* a Place worth 200*l.* per Annum.   He told me that Sir *Richard Steele* had no Hand in writing the *Town Talk,* which was attributed to him ; that it was one Dr. *Mandeville*[6] and an Apothecary of his Acquaintance that wrote that Paper ; and that fome Paffages were wrote on purpofe to make believe it was Sir *R. Steele.*   I alfo faw Mr. *Woodford,* who told me old Mr. *Craggs* had fupped with him the Night before ; and that he got out of him a Confirmation that Lord Chief Juftice *Parker* was to be made a Peer, and to be Privy Seal in the room of the Earl of *Sunderland,* who was to be made fome great Thing in the *King's* Clofet.   I believe that Baron *Bernftorff* had not been let into the Secret when he told me of his being to be a Peer.

Feb. 2.   I went to wait upon the *Princefs,* who received me very gracioufly.   She was writing, in her

amounted to 1,500*l.* a Year.   On the New Year's Day (1706), which was his firft, he fignified to all who, according to Cuftom, were expected to come with their Prefents, that he would receive none, but would break that Cuftom.   He thought it looked like the infinuating themfelves into the Favour of the Court ; and that if it was not Bribery, yet it came too near it and looked too like it.   This contributed not a little to the raifing his Character.   He managed the *Court of Chancery* with impartial Juftice and great Difpatch, and was very ufeful to the *Houfe of Lords* in the promoting of Bufinefs.'—*Burnet's Hiftory of the Reign of Queen Anne.*

[5] *Philip Horneck,* Author of an *Ode to the Earl of Wharton.*

[6] Author of the Fable of *The Bees,* publifhed in 1714.

Clofet, to Madame d'*Orléans*.[7] She afked me after News, and expreffed a very great Diflike to Lord *Townfhend* and Mr. *Walpole*, feeming to infinuate they would ruin all. I took that Opportunity of afking her if fhe continued in the Refolution of being a Tory. She told me that till I could give her convincing Arguments that a Whig was more than a Tory for the *King's* Prerogative. I faid I hoped to do fo. I called upon Lady *St. John* on my Way Home, who is the moft melancholy and afflicted Woman for the Lofs of her Son[8] that I ever faw in my Life. The Earl of *Nottingham* takes great Pains to infinuate the Tories into the *Princefs's* Favour. The fame Game is played by Lord *Finch*. What the *Prince* and Baron *Bernflorff* told me, the Difpute he raifed about the High Steward of *England*, was done with ill Intention; for he knew if it had paffed the *Houfe of Lords* it would have been rejected by the *Houfe of Commons*; and he hoped the Quarrel would have put off the Trials.

I went to vifit Madame *Robethon*.[9] Mr. *Robethon* came in to us, and brought Sir *William Gordon*[1] in with him. He was foliciting Succours

[7] *Charlotte* of *Bavaria*, Mother of the *Regent*, Duke of *Orleans*, was the moft voluminous and *moft improper* Letter-writer in *Europe*.

[8] *George St. John*, eldeft Son of Sir *H. St. John* by the fecond Marriage, was Secretary to the Englifh Plenipotentiaries at *Utrecht*. Died at *Venice*, 1716.

[9] Madame *Robethon* was one of the *Hanover* Ladies of lower Rank; a remarkable Squatnefs of Perfon and a croaking Voice obtained for her the Name of Madame *Grenouille*.

[1] Sir *William Gordon*, of *Upton* and *Earlfton*, who diftinguifhed himfelf greatly in the Battles of *William III.*, was made Governor of *Fort William* in *Scotland*, honoured (1706) with a Scotch Baronetcy, and died in *December* 1718. See *Burke's Peerage* and *Baronetage*.

1716. for the Earl of *Sutherland*,[2] who he said would
be fwallowed up by Lord *Mar*,[3] who it was fure
would retreat towards *Murray* at the Approach of
the Duke of *Argyle*. Mr. *Robethon* let fall fome
Words which fhowed plainly he did not think
fo well of the Miniftry as he had done before. I
fuppofe they have got Something done againft
the Confent or without the Privity of the foreign
Miniftry. I own I laugh to fee the Beginning
of a Quarrel, after fo much Love and Fondnefs
undeferved. I went afterwards to wait upon the
Princefs. I found three or four of the Ladies
in the Dreffing-room. The *Princefs* had ordered
my Lord *Winchefter*[4] to let me have fix Tickets
for the Mafquerade at *Montague Houfe*, which he
was pleafed to difpofe of otherwife ; fo I had but
two, that the *Prince* had got for me with much
Ado.

Feb. 4.   I was two Hours alone with the *Princefs*. She
told me fhe found Baron *Bernftorff* was not near
fo fond of Lord *Townfhend* and Mr. *Walpole* as
he had been ; but, in my Opinion, he tells her
this to pacify her, and to get at her real Senti-
ments. She told me alfo that Lord *Anglefey*[5] was

[2] *John*, fifteenth Earl, performed ufe- ful Service againft the Rebels in *Scotland* by marching againft *Invernefs*, and pre- venting the Troops of the Earl of *Seaforth* from joining the Earl of *Mar's* Army.

[3] *John*, eleventh Earl, Secretary of State for *Scotland* in 1706. In 1715 he commanded the Army of the *Pretender*, and proclaimed him King by the Title of *James VIII*. He commanded at the

Battle of *Dumblain* or *Sheriffmuir*, and took Credit for a Victory, but eventually fled to *France*, and died in 1732.

[4] *Charles* fecond Duke of *Bolton* was Marquis of *Winchefter* at this Time.

[5] *Arthur Annefley*, fifth Earl of *Anglefey*, one of the Lords Juftices on the Death of Queen *Anne*, was Vice-Trea- furer of *Ireland* and High Steward of the Univerfity of *Cambridge*. Died in 1737.

put out, and Lord *Sunderland* into his Place. She feemed difpleafed at it; and faid it was becaufe the *Parliament* of *Ireland* fell upon him; and that it was unworthy in the Miniftry to fall upon him too, becaufe he had done Services in ill Times. To which I replied, it was true that he had done Good in one Vote (which was to ferve a Purpofe of his own), but that it was not done from a Principle of Honefty, for on the next Occafion, which was ftill of greater Confequence than the Former, he voted with his old Friends again, notwithftanding the Affurances he had given to the Contrary : that I fhould have thought the Miniftry needed not to have ftayed for this Occafion of putting out Lord *Anglefey*, he having given them a much better Caufe before, when he made that flaming Speech about the Shaking of the *King's* Sceptre,[6] juft before the Rebellion broke out : that it fuited ill with the *King's* Honour to keep him in after it. The *Princefs* faid, ' Why was it not done then ?' I replied, I wifhed it had; but upon the Whole I begged her to content herfelf, for fhe might depend upon it that the Earl of *Anglefey* was a very ill Man, and that fhe would find him fo. The *Princefs* faid that the Duke of *Argyle* was mightily in the Wrong for behaving himfelf fo ill as he did. I endeavoured to appeafe her upon that Subject,

---

[6] On the Vote of the *Commons* for fending the Earl of *Oxford* to the *Tower* (*July* 12, 1715). For the Debate eli- cited by this Expreffion of Lord *Angle-fey*, fee *Parl. Hift.* vol. vii. c. 107.

by telling her that he did not begin, but was
ufed unreafonably. She faid he had a great
many good Qualities, but fome Faults that covered them; that he was an inveterate Enemy,
and apt to take Stories too lightly up; that he
had oppofed my being about her, and, in order to
it, had told her that I had an Intrigue with the
King. I anfwered that he did very ill to do fo,
for I could anfwer that I would not have an
Intrigue with the greateft Man that ever was
born, and that I hoped fhe believed it as firmly
as I did, and did not want to have Arguments
ufed to prove it, for I thought that was a forry
Virtue that wanted Arguments for its Defence.
She fell a laughing, and replied, ' You have juft
now faid what I faid the Beginning of this
Winter to Madame *Kielmanfegge*; and I will
tell you the Story, but you muft not repeat it.'
Madame *Kielmanfegge* had been told that the
Prince had faid that fhe had intrigued with all
the Men at *Hanover.* She came to complain of
this to the *Princefs*, who replied, fhe did not
believe the *Prince* had faid fo, it not being his
Cuftom to fpeak in that Manner. Madame
Kielmanfegge cried, and faid it had made her defpifed, and that many of her Acquaintance had
left her upon that Story; but that her Hufband
had taken all the Care he could to vindicate her
Reputation; and thereupon fhe drew forth out
of her Pocket a Certificate under her Hufband's
Hand, in which he certified, in all the due Forms,

that fhe had always been a faithful Wife to `1716.`
him, and that he had never had any Caufe to fufpect her Honefty. The *Princefs* fmiled, and faid
that fhe did not doubt it at all, and that all
that Trouble was very unneceffary, and that it
was a very bad Reputation that wanted fuch
a Support. I believe it is the firft Certificate
of the Kind that ever was given. The moft of
what I can gather from the Converfation of
To-night is, that Lord *Nottingham* and the Duchefs of *Roxburgh* take mortal Pains to make the
Princefs think well of the Tories.

I dined at Madame *Gouvernet's* with Baron 　*Feb. 6.*
Bernftorff and others of his Relations. From
thence I went to the Play, which was *The Cob-*
bler of Prefton[7]—the Poet's Night. One might
fee the good Effects of the News which came
Yefterday that the Rebels had abandoned *Perth*,
and the *King's* Forces taken Poffeffion of it; for
there was not a Word that was loyal but what
met with the greateft Acclamations.

February 7 was the mafquerading Day. I could
not go to *Court* till paft feven o'Clock, becaufe
my poor youngeft Boy was not well. When I
got there, I found Sir *John Germaine* fhowing the
Princefs his Rarities, confifting of Seals and Re-
liefs. She had not Time to fee them all this
Evening, fo many of the Mafquers came in to
fhow themfelves. There was a Drawing-room

---

[7] A Farce in two Acts, by *Charles*　Subject (*Le Braffeur de Prefton*), was given
Johnfon. A pretty Opera on the fame　at *Paris* in 1846.

1716. for the *King*, who was not there. I was told
Everything was in great Order and Magnificence,
and that the Entertainment could not have coft
lefs than five or fix hundred Pounds. Monfieur
d'*Iberville*⁸ fays amongft his Cronies that the *Pretender's* Retreat from *Perth* is all a Feint, and
was concocted in *France* only to prolong the
Time till the Regent of *France* can fuccour him
openly.

Feb. 8. I waited in the Morning for the Duchefs of
Bolton, who had been at the Mafquerade. The
*Archbifhop*⁹ came to wait upon the *Princefs*, and
brought with him the Miffionaries of the King
of *Denmark* that were going to the *Eaft Indies*.
They had with them a Boy, a Native of that
Country. He fhowed the *Princefs* the Manner
of their Writing, which is upon narrow and long
Palmetto Leaves. He held an iron Pencil in his
right Hand, and by the help of a Notch made
in the Thumbnail of the left Hand, he guided
the Pencil and wrote as he ftood without laying
the Leaf down upon Anything, but holding it
in his Hand all the Time. This Boy was an
olive-black ; his Hair was as black as Jet, but it
was long, and not like Wool. The *Archbifhop*
gave me a Book printed in the Malayan Character, fuch as this Boy wrote. I dined with Mrs.
Clayton, where I found the Countefs of *Dorchefter*,

---

⁸ Envoy Extraordinary from *France*,   correfponded with the Adherents of the
fent to *George I.* with the Notification of   *Pretender*.
the Death of *Louis XIV.* in 1715. He   ⁹ Dr. *Wake*, Archbifhop of *Canterbury*.

who was in her Airs. I think fhe had a Mind to perfuade me to go Home and advife my Lord to hang himfelf; at leaft her Difcourfe feemed to point at it, for fhe ran on much in his Praife, beyond that of others, and then faid People were miferable that were engaged with Fools. ' That,' faid fhe, ' made the wife *Achitophel* hang himfelf; for you can't be fo weak as to be- lieve that it was becaufe *Abfalom* would not follow his Advice. No; he was a wife Man, and was engaged with Fools: *Abfalom* was fo great a One himfelf, that *Achitophel* faw he was a King Nobody could ever make Anything of, for he would liften to no Advice, and the Reft he was joined with were fuch Fools, they were not capable of receiving good Advice, and he knew *David* to be a wife Man, and One that would not only lay the Blame of what was done againft him upon *Achitophel*, but would even make him accountable for the Advice he had given; and from all this he might reafonably conclude that if he did not hang himfelf, *David* would hang him, fo he chofe wifely to have the doing of it himfelf.' Juft as fhe had faid thefe Words, Monfieur *Schutz* brought in Word that an Ex- prefs was arrived from the Duke of *Argyle*, who was got into *Dundee*. Soon after, the *Prin- cefs* called me in to fee the Remainder of Sir *John Germaine's* Rarities. They were the Col- lection of the late Earl of *Peterborough*,[1] Father

---

[1] *Henry* fecond Earl of *Peterborough.*

1716. to the famous Duchefs of *Norfolk*, who was divorced, and afterwards married Sir *John Germaine*. Amongft other Things, he fhowed us the Dagger of King *Henry VIII.*, which he always wore and is pictured with.

Feb. 9. The Day of the Trials. My Lord was named High Steward by the *King*, to his Vexation and mine; but it could not be helped, and fo we muft fubmit, though we both heartily wifhed it had been Lord *Nottingham*. The Form of the Attendance was this from hence. The Servants had all new Liveries; ten Footmen; four Coaches with two Horfes, and one with fix; eighteen Gentlemen out of Livery, and Garter at Arms and Ufher of the Black Rod in the fame Coach; Garter carrying the Wand. I was told it was cuftomary to make fine Liveries upon this Occafion, but had them all plain. I think it very wrong to make a Parade upon fo difmal an Occafion as that of putting to death One's Fellow-creatures; nor could I go to the Trial to fee them receive their Sentences, having a Relation among them, my Lord *Widdrington*.[2] The *Prince* was there, and came home much touched with Compaffion. What Pity it is that fuch Cruelties fhould be neceffary!

Feb. 10. I went to *Court* in the Afternoon. The *Princefs* heard a Caufe that kept her an Hour.

---

[2] *William* Lord *Widdrington*, Great-grandfon of the Lord *Widdrington* killed on the *King's* Side in 1651, was one of the Lords impeached with the Earl of *Derwentwater* for a Share in the Rebellion. He was fentenced to Death, but afterwards pardoned.

It was a Difpute between the Ladies of the Bedchamber and the Lord Chamberlain and Vice-Chamberlain, in which I believe the Ladies were in the Wrong. It was about the two Officers above mentioned coming into the Bedchamber, which has been a Right always pretended to by them, and always contefted by the Ladies.

My poor *Spencer* [3] pretty well, for which I *Feb. 11.* heartily thank *God.* This Morning, before I went out, I bought a Parcel of fmall Rubies and Emeralds of *Mizan.* Two Letters from Mademoifelle *Schutz.* 'T is very troublefome to be writing thus at every Turn. I wifh fhe had as much Occupation as I have. I dined at Mrs. *Clayton's* with my Lord and Lady *Halifax,*[4] Lady *Dorchefter*, and Lady *W. Pawlet.* Great Complaints of the Preamble to the Land Tax Bill[5] cooked up by Mr. *Lechmere* and Lord *Coningfby.*[6] 'T is a defamatory Libel upon the late *Queen* and all her Miniftry, the laft all deferving to be hanged for what they have done. It is very injudicious for a Houfe of Commons to brand any

[3] Her fecond Son, afterwards Dean of *Durham*, and Author *inter alia* of a Work entitled *A Differtation on the Diftinct Powers of Reafon and Revelation.*

[4] *George* fecond Earl of *Halifax* married, firft, *Richarda*, Daughter of *Richard Saltenftall*, of *Chippen Warden*; and, fecondly, *Mary*, Daughter of *Richard* Earl of *Scarborough*.

[5] For the Queftions involved in this Preamble, and the Difcuffion which enfued, almoft involving a Difpute between the two Houfes of Parliament, fee *Tindal's*

Continuation of Rapin, vol. iv. part. ii. p. 488, folio edition, 1747.

[6] A Friend of the Duke of *Marlborough*, Paymafter of the Forces in 1704; created an Earl in 1719. He conducted the Impeachment of Lord *Oxford*. His Daughter married Sir *C. Hanbury Williams*.

' Here lies Lord *Coningfby* : be civil.
The Reft *God* knows, and perhaps the Devil.'
Alfo ' Coningfby Harangues.' Vide *Pope.*

1716. People they have before them in a judicial Way, before they come to their Trials, and my Lord *Halifax* faid, if it was paffed in the Manner in which it has paffed the *Houfe of Commons*, it will be a Reproach upon this Parliament never to be blotted out. My Lady *Dorchefter's* Wit makes Amends for her Uglinefs. She has always more to fay for herfelf than Anybody. Sir *Ifaac Newton*[7] and Dr. *Clarke* came this Afternoon, to explain Sir *Ifaac's* Syftem of Philofophy to the *Princefs*. I could not ftay to hear them, having left my Lord not well. I am delighted beyond Meafure to hear my Lord's Speech (at the pronouncing Sentence) fo commended by Everybody, but I efteem Nobody's Commendation like Dr. *Clarke's*, who fays 't is fuperlatively good, and that it is impoffible to add or diminifh one Letter without hurting it.[8]

Feb. 12. The News holds good that the *Pretender* and Lord *Mar* are gone; that my Lord *Drummond*[9] went after them to the Veffel, on board which they were, in an open Boat. The Veffel is of *St. Malo's*, of ten Guns. Lord *Tinmouth*[1] was left behind by miftake. Earl Marifchal[2] all this

---

[7] Sir *Ifaac Newton* was at this Time feventy-five Years of Age. He died in 1727.

[8] The Speech is given in Lord *Campbell's* Life of Lord *Cowper*.

[9] *James* fecond Duke of *Perth*, of *James II.'s* Creation, was at the Head of the Plot to feize the Caftle of *Edinburgh* in 1715. Died at *Paris*, 1720.

[1] Son of the Duke of *Berwick*; had accompanied the *Pretender* from *France* to *Scotland*.

[2] *George Keith*, Earl Marifchal, one of the principal Supporters of the *Pretender*. At his Seat, *Fettereffo*, near *Aberdeen*, the *Pretender* met and conferred with the Rebel Lords. He entered the Service and became the Friend of *Frederick the Great*, under whom his Brother, Marfhal *Keith*, attained to great Renown. Mi-

While of their getting off was mounting Guard at the Head-quarters, and knew Nothing of the Matter. The *Squirrel* is in purfuit of this Veffel, and is a good Sailer.

Feb. 13.

Stayed at Home with my Lord, who is very ill. I was to dine at Baron *Bernftorff's*, but excufed myfelf. The Ladies that were there came here in the Afternoon. Mademoifelle *Schutz* is a very unreafonable Body, and would take no Hints that I wifhed to be alone, but took a Pleafure in ftaying, becaufe I was uneafy at it.

Feb. 14.

The News was confirmed Yefterday. The *Pretender* is gone. My Lord is fo ill, that he has a Mind to quit Office. I have made a Refolution never to prefs him more to keep his Place. I had a Letter from Mademoifelle *Schutz*, to offer to come to ftay with me all Day. I thank her for Nothing. I had too much of her Impertinence laft Night.

Feb. 15.

My Lord mighty ill, and ftill had a Mind to quit Office. I told him that I would never oppofe Anything he had a Mind to do ; and after arguing calmly upon the Matter, I offered him, if it would be any Pleafure done him, to retire with him into the Country, and quit too, and, what was more, never to repine at doing fo, though it was the greateft Sacrifice that could be made him. I believe he will accept.

Feb. 16.

Mademoifelle *Schutz* came. She had been in

lord Marifchal feems to have been beloved and efteemed by all who knew him.

the City to get a Suit of gold Ribbons. She had
a Mind to have me give her them, but I can't
help turning my deaf Ear to fuch unreafonable
People. She had a Mind alfo to have fome of
my Jewels; which is pretty impertinent, when I
am to be at the Birthday myfelf. Madame
Gouvernet offered me an emerald Necklace;
which I accepted rather becaufe it was offered me,
and I was afraid of difobliging her, than to make
myfelf fine (for I don't care one Farthing for
fetting myfelf out, and I hope always to make it
my Study rather to adorn my Mind than fet off
a vile Body of Duft and Afhes). Being thus provided of a Necklace, and Mademoifelle *Schutz*
hearing of it, fhe defired to borrow my fine
Pearl Necklace, which being of fo great Value,
I thought I had as good put it into my Hair; and
fo I told her I fhould be glad to accommodate
her, but that all the Jewels I had I fhould ufe,
and that I had fo few, that I was often forced to
borrow upon thofe Occafions myfelf. My Lord
ftill ill. I am out of my Wits to fee him fuffer,
which I declare is ten Times worfe than Death
to me, and would rather live with him all my
Life on Bread and Cheefe, up three Pair of Stairs,
than be all this World can make me and at the
fame Time fee him fuffer.

My Lord ftill ill. In my Perplexity, I told
Mrs. *Woodford* my Griefs, and bid her afk Mr.
Woodford's Advice; which fhe fays he gave very
kindly, and propofed that I fhould let him hint

to old Mr. *Craggs*[4] that my Lord *Cowper's* Office
was too hard for him; and propofed that old
Mr. *Craggs* having in the Days that the Miniftry
were cold to my Lord *Cowper* offered to Mr.
Woodford that if my Lord was weary he might
be Privy Seal; and that being now defigned for
Lord Chief Juftice *Parker*, who would certainly
come into my Lord *Cowper's* Place, he might
have the Privy Seal; and that the Reverfion of
Sir *John Shaw's*[5] Place fhould be added for two
Lives. Sir *David Hamilton* had a Letter from
my Lord *Carnwath*,[6] who is his fecond Coufin,
defiring to fpeak to him. He has had Leave, and
is gone To-night.

Mrs. *Woodford* came to fee me, not having *Feb. 17.*
refted well after I had told her the Night before
my Lord was better, and did not talk fo much
of quitting. His Illnefs, I really believe, proceeded from the Fall he had.

The Duchefs of *Marlborough* came in the
Evening. I faw her, though I was very ill. She
fays the Duchefs of *Roxburgh* is the greateft
Enemy that either my Lord or I have. The

---

[4] He is faid to have been a Footman to *Sarah* Duchefs of *Marlborough*, and was, at this Time, Poftmafter-General. He amaffed an immenfe Fortune, and was deeply implicated in the Frauds of the *South Sea Company*. He is fuppofed to have poifoned himfelf the Day before his Cafe was to come before the *Houfe of Commons*. His Eftate, valued at a Million and a Half, was confifcated. He died 1720, about a Month before his Son, who had been Secretary of State.

[5] Probably Sir *John Shaw*, fecond Baronet, whofe Father had obtained his Title for Services to *Charles II.*, and had been appointed one of the Farmers of the Cuftoms after the Reftoration.

[6] *Robert Dalzell*, Earl of *Carnwath*, was one of thofe who furrendered at *Prefton* to General *Carpenter*. He was condemned to Death, but was pardoned and releafed in 1717. His Title was reftored to his Defcendants in 1826.

78   *Diary of Lady* Cowper.

1716. Duchefs of *Roxburgh* is certainly an ill Woman. She does not care what fhe fays of Anybody to wreak her Malice or Revenge.

Feb. 18.   My Lord better, to my great Joy. No Talk of quitting To-day, though I fairly laid it in his Way. This Morning Mademoifelle *Schutz* came to fee me. She's always begging Something or other, and would have borrowed my Diamonds to put in her Hair, and at the fame Time faid, ' I make no Scruple in borrowing them from you, becaufe you are beft in your State of Nature, and always worft when you are dreffed out, your Jewels not becoming you.' Commend me to the Affurance of thefe Foreigners!

Feb. 19.   News of the *Prefton* Folks, by the Judges and People come up from thence, is, that the Country is very obftinate ; that they would not believe that the *King* durft hang any of them till the very Day of Execution came. Sad Pleadings : fome Sons drawn in by their Fathers, and Mr. *Shafto*[7] by his Son, who forced him to take Arms. Mrs. *Collingwood*[8] wrote to a Friend in Town to try to get her Hufband's Life granted to her. The Friend's Anfwer was as follows : ' I think you are mad when you talk of faving your Hufband's Life. Don't you know you will have five hundred Pounds a Year Jointure if he's hanged, and that you won't have a Groat if he's faved ?

[7] Mr. *Shafto* was tried and fhot at *Prefton* foon after the Battle.
[8] Mr. *Collingwood*, of *Eflington, North-umberland*, who was executed at *Liverpool*,

March 8, 1715, was the laft of the elder Branch of the Family of the famous Lord *Collingwood*.

Confider, and let me have your Anfwer, for I fhall do Nothing in it till then.' The Anfwer did not come Time enough, and fo he was hanged. They all pretend to know Nothing, and would have People believe this Affair was never concerted, and Nobody knows how he came into this Rebellion. *God* help them! 'T is a wrong Way to Mercy to come with a Lie in their Mouth.

I went to *Court*, my Lord being gone to a Committee at the *Cockpit*.[9] The *Princefs* told me fhe had fent for Amber out of *Germany*, for Boxes for her Ladies; but as fhe loved and ef- teemed me a hundred Times more than any of the Reft, fhe would make a Diftinction, and fo pulled out of a Drawer a fine gold Box, and gave it me with Words which far exceeded its Value. The *Princefs* is terribly vexed with Baron *Bern- ftorff*, that fhe fees fo bigoted to Lord *Townfhend* and Mr. *Walpole*. She told him he was an old Fool to be fo led by the Nofe by them. She chid the *King* alfo,[1] and told him he was grown lazy. He laughed, and faid he was bufy from Morning to Night. She faid, ' Sir, I tell you they fay the Miniftry does Everything, and you Nothing.' He fmiled, and faid, ' This is all the Thanks I get for all the Pains I take.' The *Princefs* has a great Mind to fave Lord *Carnwath*.

---

[9] The *Cockpit* at *Whitehall* ftood on the Site of the prefent *Privy Council Of- fice*, and at this Time, and for fome Years afterwards, Councils were held there.

[1] *George I.* always fpoke of her as ' cette Diableffe la Princeffe.'

1716.   She has defired me to get Sir *David Hamilton* to
go and fpeak to him, to lay fome Foundation with
the *King* to fave him ; but he will perfift in faying he knows Nothing. 'T is a thoufand Pities!
He's a Man of good Underftanding, and not
above Thirty. He has had his Education at *Oxford*, as One might guefs from his Actions.

Feb. 21.   My Lord is better. The Ladies of the con-
demned Lords brought their Petition to the
Houfe of Lords to folicit the *King* for a Reprieve.
The Duke of *St. Albans*[2] was the Man chofen
to deliver it, but the *Prince* advifed him not to
do fo without the *King's* Leave. The Archbifhop of *Canterbury* oppofes the *Court* ftrenuoufly
in the rejecting the Petition. Everybody in a
Confternation. 'T is a Trap laid to undo the
Miniftry. I went to the *Princefs*. She ordered
me to go to the *Archbifhop*, and talk with him.
Lord *Townfhend* came to the *Prince*, to beg of
him to help ; and he anfwered, ' C'eft une de vos
Sottifes, et à cette Heure vous venez me prier
de vous aider!' I went To-night to *Court*. The
Duchefs of *Bolton*[3] went with the Ladies, to make
believe fhe was one of the Royal Family : though
that won't do ; it 's too plainly writ in her Face
that fhe's *Penn's* Daughter, the quaking Preacher.[4]
The *Princefs* chid her, and fhe made all the Ex-

---

[2] Son of King *Charles II.* by *Nell Gwynne.* He diftinguifhed himfelf with the *Emperor's* Army at the Siege of *Belgrade,* and died in 1726.
[3] The Duchefs of *Bolton* was *Henrietta*

Crofts, natural Daughter to *James* Duke of *Monmouth* by *Eleanor,* Daughter of Sir *Robert Needham.*
[4] A fomewhat irreverent Defcription of *William Penn.*

cufes fhe could. She faid Lady *Derwentwater*[5]
came crying to her, when the *Duke* was not at
Home, and perfuaded her to go to plead for her
Lord.

I went this Morning to the Archbifhop of
Canterbury. He fays he's far from flying in the
King's Face, after all the Obligations he has received from him, and that he thought himfelf in
the right Way of ferving him; but if the *King* was
not of the fame Opinion, he would ftay at Home,
which was all he could do. I'm afraid, by his
Talk, that Bifhop *Gibfon*[6] influences him. The
Archbifhop told me he had been clofeted twice
about this, once by the *Prince*, and once by Lord
Townfhend, by Order of the *King*, which was a
Method he did not mightily admire, but had
given the fame Anfwers as to me. As I came
out, Sir *David Hamilton* followed me with a
Letter for the *Princefs* from Lord *Carnwath*. I
told her of it, and faid, if fhe had not a Mind to
receive it, I would take the Fault upon myfelf.
She took the Letter, and was much moved in
reading it, and wept, and faid, ' He muft fay
more to fave himfelf. Bid Sir *David Hamilton*
go to him again, and beg of him, for *God's* Sake,
to fave himfelf by confeffing. There is no other
Way ; and I will give him my Honour to fave

---

[5] *Anna Maria*, Daughter of Sir *John Webb*, Bart. She was the Mother of two Sons, who died young, and a Daughter, who married Lord *Petre*.
[6] Dr. *Edmund Gibfon*, then Bifhop of Lincoln, and of *London* in 1720, a pious and learned Divine. He offended *George I.* by denouncing Mafquerades, which his Majefty greatly enjoyed. Died in 1748.

1716.   him if he will confefs, but he muft not think
to impofe upon People by profeffing to know
Nothing, when his Mother [7] goes about talking
as violently for Jacobitifm as ever, and fays that
her Son falls in a glorious Caufe.' I fent for Sir
D. Hamilton, and gave him the *Princefs's* Orders.
The *Houfe* not up till Seven. The Petition received by a Majority of Five or Six.

Feb 23.   Lord *Nottingham* behaved fadly at the *Houfe*
Yefterday, faying he hoped the *King* would pardon the Prifoners if they confeffed; nay, he hoped
that he would pardon them though they did not
confefs. The Duke of *Bolton*, by Order of the
Houfe, waited upon the *King* with the Addrefs
of the Lords, to befeech him to reprieve fuch of
the Lords as fhould deferve it, for as long Time
as His Majefty fhall think fit. To which the
King returned this fhort Anfwer:—' I fhall always do what I think moft for the Honour of my
Government and the Safety of my Kingdoms.'
The Lords that had gone aftray the Day before
plainly fhowed by their Looks that they felt they
had played the Fool. Sir *D. Hamilton* has been
with Lord *Carnwath*, who confeffes to having
feen the *Pretender* when in *France*. He fays that
he went to *France* upon the Death of his Wife [8]
(whom he doted on), and waited upon Queen
Mary there, and told her he would have ftayed

[7] *Henrietta*, Daughter of Sir *William*   *Alexander* Earl of *Eglinton*. He was
Murray, Bart., of *Stanhope*.   married four Times.
    [8] Lady *Grace Montgomery*, Daughter of

at Home, but that he thought it more for the
Pretender's Service to take care of his Health, in
order to ferve him in his Expedition to *Scotland*.
She anfwered very obligingly. She was living
in a Convent, as fhe always is in Winter. She
was laid upon a Bed. He ftayed at a confiderable Town, pretending to travel, for two or three
Months, and then went to *Lorraine*, where he
addreffed himfelf to Mr. *Lesly*,[9] who procured a
Meeting with the *Pretender*. He went alone,
up a Pair of Backftairs. The *Pretender* opened
the Door to him, and led him into a Clofet,
where he had been writing. He had a great
Surtout on over his Clothes. (This was in
January 1714). The *Pretender* enquired after his
Family, and how they were affected. He faid
he depended upon his Friends in *Scotland*. The
Other faid he would do well to make fure
Friends in *England*; becaufe the Others were
not many of them Friends out of Principle, but
in order to redrefs fome Grievances, and that
thofe were not to be trufted, and that he wifhed
he would go to *Scotland*. To which the *Pretender* replied, ' I certainly will, if this Parliament
of *England* don't give me Encouragement and
Hopes of a Reftoration.' Lord *Carnwath* faw
the *Pretender* three Times, and believes he was
referved to him becaufe he did not bring with

---

[9] Probably a Relative of the Earl of
Rothes, or of the Scottifh Baronets *Leflie*,
Cadets of the fame Houfe, created Baronets in 1625, and who were zealous Ad-
herents of the *Stuarts*.

him a Letter from Queen *Mary*. He fays he often faw Mr. *Lefly* and Sir *Thomas Higgens*[1] during the three Days' Stay he made, and they told him that the Scheme at that Time was, if the Parliament of *England* did not do Something towards a Reftoration, then to engage the King of *Sweden*[2] to go to *Scotland* and eftablifh him there.

The *King*, the *Prince*, and *Princefs* all angry with Lord *Nottingham* for his Behaviour. Baron *Bernftorff* had the Affurance to tell the *Princefs* that the *Prince* had done a great deal of Harm in talking about the *King's* Prerogative in the *Houfe of Lords*; which is all a Banter, there being no Foundation for that Report. Mademoifelle *Schulenberg* in great Concern. She fays the *King* is more vexed by what happened in the *Houfe of Lords* than at Anything that has yet happened, infomuch that he faid he fhould be afhamed to fhow himfelf after this. He takes it defperately ill of Lord *Nottingham*, who enjoys 15,000*l.* a Year among himfelf and Friends from the *King's* Bounty. I carried the Gag which was brought from *Prefton* by Mr. *Carter* to *Court*, by Order of the *Princefs*. A great Number of them were found at the Houfe of one *Shuttleworth*, a Papift, afterwards hanged. He was famous for faying he hoped in a little Time to fee *Prefton* Streets running as faft with

---

[1] *Evelyn* fpeaks of Sir *Thomas Higgens*, who was Envoy of *James II.* at   *Venice* in 1686.
[2] *Charles XII.*

heretic Blood as they do with Water when it has rained twelve Hours. The Gags are really frightful. They go down the Throat a great Way, with a Bend, and under that there is an iron Spike that runs into the Tongue if it is ftirred, and the Ends have Screws that fcrew into the Cheeks. We fat up till paft Two, to do a pleafing Office, which was to reprieve four of the Lords in the *Tower*, though the Earl of *Nithfdale* [3] had made his Efcape ; but it was not then known, and fo he was reprieved with the Reft.

I did not go out To-day. Sir *David Hamil-ton* came to me, and told me he had been with my Lord *Carnwath*, who knew Nothing of his Reprieve till eight o'Clock this Morning. It was joyful News to him. Lord *Derwentwater* expected a Reprieve. The Folly of his Wife and Relations, in making the *Parliament* meddle, did him a great deal of Harm. He had treated the *Council* with a good deal of ill Manners and foolifh Cunning when he was examined about a Letter from the *Pretender*, which thanked him for tranfmitting Money fo generoufly, com-mending alfo his Uncle *Tom*,[4] and faying very hard Things of his Uncle *Will Ratcliffe*, with

---

[3] *William Maxwell*, Earl of *Nithfdale*, was taken Prifoner at *Prefton*, and con-demned to Death. He refided in *France* and *Italy* till his Death in 1744. Lady *Nithfdale* was a Daughter of the Marquis of *Powys*. There is a very interefting Letter from her to her Sifter, giving an Account of the Particulars of her Huf-band's Efcape, quoted by Mr. *Jeffe* in his *Memoirs of the Pretenders and their Ad-herents*.

[4] *Thomas Ratcliffe* was an Officer in the Army.

many Particulars, by fome of which the Miniftry had found out fufpected Perfons' Lodgings, and feized upon Papers of Confequence. When he was afked about the Letter, he denied Every-thing, and faid it was a Trick of his Uncle *Will* to do him a Mifchief. He was alfo the Firft to take up Arms. Thefe Things made him to be pitched upon as a Lord among the Englifh, as my Lord *Kenmure* [5] was among the Scotch, he having commanded the Forces by a Commif-fion from the Earl of *Mar*. They both fuf-fered this Morning, my Lord Vifcount *Kenmure* with great Courage and Intrepidity. He made no Speech, nor any Sign to the Executioner, but bid him take his own Time. The Earl of *Derwentwater* [6] was young, not yet thirty ; and Death at that Age, to One bred up in Soft-nefs and Eafe, is a dreadful Thing. It difmayed him at firft, but he recovered himfelf and read a Speech to the People, which he afterwards gave to the *Sheriff*. In it he declared that he died for his King, and was forry he had pleaded guilty, becaufe by that he had, in a Manner, owned the Title of a Perfon he did not think had any Right to the Throne ; but that his Friends had perfuaded him to it, as the beft

---

[5] *William Gordon*, Vifcount *Kenmure*, commanded the Rebels in the South-weft of *Scotland*. He was of a fingular good Temper, and too calm and mild for fuch a Poft, fays *Robert Patten*. He was beheaded with Lord *Derwentwater* on *February* 24, 1716.

[6] *James Radcliffe*, Earl of *Derwent-water*, poffeffed great Eftates and much Influence in the North of *England*. He was executed when only twenty-five Years of Age. *Smollett* fays, ' He was an amiable Youth, brave, open, generous, hofpitable, and humane.'

Means to fave his Life. A Poftfcript was added,
writ by another Hand (which he read alfo),
which faid that if the Perfon in poffeffion of
the Crown had given him his Life, his Honour
would have obliged him never to have borne
Arms againft him more. It was plain by the
whole Speech that it came out of a fpiteful
Prieft's Head. It was defigned by his Friends
that his Body fhould have lain about, to move
Pity, for they had not fo much as provided a Cof-
fin, fo it was wrapt up in a Piece of black Baize,
and put into a Coach. Fatal Neceffity, that it
fhould be neceffary for the Wellbeing of the
Community that our Fellow-creatures fhould
fuffer! *God* grant us Peace to heal all our Divifions, and to take away the Rancour we have
now among us! It is confirmed that Lord
Nithfdale is efcaped. I hope he'll get clear off.
I never was better pleafed at Anything in my
Life, and I believe Everybody is the fame.

Sir *D. Hamilton* cannot get into the *Tower* to
Lord *Carnwath*. They are more ftrictly kept
fince the Efcape. I was with the *Princefs*, who
had juft received a Letter from Madame d'Or-
léans ftuffed with Lies of the Jacobites, which
they wrote from *England* juft before the *Pre-*
tender got to *Lorraine*. The *Princefs* fays the
King and *Prince* are much difpleafed with Lord
Nottingham. She thinks Monfieur *Robethon* a
Knave, and Baron *Bothmar* another. Company
came in and ftopped our Converfation.

1716.
Feb. 26. Baron *Bernflorff* made a Vifit to my Lord Cowper upon two Subjects. The One to let him know that there fhould be no more Executions of the Peers in Prifon, and that the Miniftry were refolved to put out Lord *Nottingham*[7] and Lord *Aylesford.*[8] My Lord oppofed it at prefent, and thought it better to try them again, and put them out the next Occafion they gave; and if they gave none, then it was well it was not done. Baron *Bernflorff* faid it muft pofitively be done now, for if they did not take this Opportunity, they, may be, might not be able to do it when they would.

Feb. 27. Mademoifelle *Schutz* dined here, as did Lady *W. Pawlet.*[9] Mademoifelle *Schutz* fo impertinent, fhe made me quite peevifh. To-day my Lord *Nottingham* and my Lord *Aylesford* were put out of their Places.

Feb. 29. Monfieur and Madame *Robethon*, Lady *W. Pawlet*, and Madame de *Gouvernet* dined here. Mr. *Robethon* fpoke to me to propofe to my Lord *Cowper* to change his Place of Chancellor for that of Prefident of the Council. I have fpoke to him, and he refufes, and fays if they will

---

[7] *Daniel* fecond Earl of *Nottingham*, one of the Chief Secretaries of State, 1702-4, was Lord Prefident of the Council from 1714 to *February* 1715-16, when he retired, and 'loft a Penfion of 2,500*l.*, having given Umbrage to the *Court* by pleading in behalf of the condemned Lords.' *Collins' Peerage*, vol. iii. p. 400 (Edition 1812).

[8] *Heneage Finch*, created Earl of *Aylef-*

ford in 1714, and the fame Year appointed Chancellor of the Duchy of *Lancafter*, who refigned, or was 'put out' of, Office in *February* 1715–16.

[9] The firft Wife of Lord *W. Pawlet* was *Louifa*, only Daughter of the Marquis de *Monpouillon*, in *Holland.* His fecond Wife was *Anne*, Daughter and Coheir to *Ralph Egerton*, of *Betley.*

have him quit, he will do it, but he will not change. I reprefented to Monfieur *Robethon* it would be a great Difficulty to perfuade him to be Prefident of the Council, he not fpeaking the French Tongue. He replied, 'Pray ufe all your Art to get it done, or it will break all their Mea-fures, for fuch is their Scheme.'

The *Princefs's* Birthday. I am ill, but I muft *March 1.* go to wifh her many Years of Health and Hap-pinefs; which I unfeignedly do, for fhe's a moft charming, delightful Friend, as well as Miftrefs. She tells me that Baron *Bernftorff* had been with the *Prince,* to perfuade him to agree to make Lord *Cowper* Prefident of the Council; but the *Prince* abfolutely denied giving in to it, unlefs my Lord defired it, and infifted upon it, and fhe added that the Miniftry fhould never draw them into, or force them to give Confent to Anything that was againft my Lord *Cowper's* Inclination. I gave the *Princefs* a thoufand Thanks, and de-fired a Continuation of her Favour, and faid my Lord *Cowper* was ready to quit if they had Any-body better to put in his Room, but would never change that which he could acquit himfelf of with Honour for what he could not perform at all.

At *Court.* The Duchefs of *Roxburgh,* the *March 3.* Duchefs of *Marlborough,* and Lady *Townfhend*[1] with her. The Duchefs of *St. Albans* came in.

---

[1] *Dorothy,* Sifter of Sir *Robert Walpole.*

The Converſation was about the Diſcontent of the Duchcſs of *Cleveland*[2] that her Lord was not made Something. She wanted to turn out my Lord *Derby*[3] from being Captain of the *Beef-eaters,* and place His Grace in his Room. The Company laughed that the *Duchefs* ſhould take it into her Head to think him fit for Anything who is a natural Fool. The Duchcſs of *Marl-borough* turned to Lady *Townſhend,* and ſaid, ' That's no new Thing with her, for I dare ſay ſhe thinks him fit for Anything—to be in your Lord's Place, for example.' Lady *Townſhend* was nettled, and pulled up, as if it had been a violent Affront. The *Duchefs* added, ' Or in my Lord Chancellor's.' I was ſo merry with Lady *Townſhend's* offended Air, that I laughed, and ſaid, ' With all my Heart.'

March 6. At *Court.* An extraordinary Light[4] in the Sky, deſcribed to me ſince by Dr. *Clarke,* who ſaw it from the Beginning. Firſt appeared a

[2] *Anne,* Daughter of Sir *W. Pulteney,* of *Miſterton,* Wife of *Charles Fitzroy,* Duke of *Cleveland,* eldeſt Son of *Barbara Villiers,* Duchcſs of *Cleveland,* and *Charles II.*

[3] *James,* tenth Earl, ſerved under *William III.* in *Flanders* with ſome Diſtinction. Died 1735, without Iſſue male.

[4] In the *Hiſtorical Regiſter* for 1716 there is an Account of this Phenomenon. ' *March* 6. The ſame Evening, about eight of the Clock, was ſeen a ſtrange Phenomenon in the Sky. It appeared at firſt like a huge Body of Light, compact within itſelf, but without Motion ; but in a little Time it began to move and ſeparate, extending itſelf towards the Weſt,

when it ſeemed, as it were, to diſpoſe itſelf into Columns or Pillars of Flame. From thence it darted ſouth-eaſt with amazing Swiftneſs, and after many undulatory Motions and Vibrations, then appeared to be a continual Fulguration, interſperſed with green, red, blue, and yellow. Then it moved towards the North ; from whence, in a little Time, it renewed its wavy Motions and Coruſcations as before, which continued to be ſeen till paſt Three in the Morning.' Mr. *Gibſon,* the Antiquary, in his *Dilſton Hall, or Memoirs of the Earl of Derwentwater,* ſays that the Phenomenon has ever ſince been known as ' Lord *Derwentwater's* Lights.'

black Cloud, from whence Smoke and Light iſſued forth at once on every Side, and then the Cloud opened, and there was a great Body of pale Fire, that rolled up and down, and ſent forth all Sorts of Colours like the Rainbow on every Side; but this did not laſt above two or three Minutes. After that it was like pale elementary Fire iſſuing out on all Sides of the Horizon, but moſt eſpecially at the North and North-weſt, where it fixed at laſt. The Motion of it was extremely ſwift and rapid, like Clouds in their ſwifteſt Rack. Sometimes it diſcontinued for a While, at other Times it was but as Streaks of Light in the Sky, but moving always with great Swiftneſs. About one o'Clock this Phenomenon was ſo ſtrong, that the whole Face of the Heavens was entirely covered with it, moving as ſwiftly as before, but extremely low. It laſted till paſt Four, but decreaſed till it was quite gone. At One the Light was ſo great that I could, out of my Window, ſee People walk acroſs *Lincoln's Inn Fields*, though there was no Moon. Both Parties turned it on their Enemies. The Whigs ſaid it was *God's* Judgment on the horrid Rebellion, and the Tories ſaid that it came for the Whigs taking off the two Lords that were executed. I could hardly make my Chairmen ·come Home with me, they were ſo frightened, and I was forced to let my Glaſs down, and preach to them as I went along, to comfort them. I'm ſure Anybody that had overheard the Dialogue would have laughed heartily. All the People were drawn out into the Streets, which were fo full One could hardly pafs, and all frighted to death.

March 7. This Day the Lords had a further Reprieve for a Fortnight. Lord *Winton's*[5] Trial put off for a Week longer. The Town full of Lies of what was feen in the Air laft Night. Papers printed and fold that two Armies were feen to fight in the Air, that two Men with flaming Swords were feen to fight over *Lincoln's Inn Fields.* The Mob that went to Mr. *Linet's* Burial laft Night faid they faw two Men in the Sky fight without Heads. This *Linet* was Curate to the famous Dr. *Walton* of *Whitechapel,* who was fufpected to be a Jefuit, and upon a Quarrel with Dr. *Kennett*[6], Dean of *Peterborough,* had got an Altar-piece painted and fet up in his Church, where Dr. *Kennett's* Picture was drawn for *Judas Ifcariot,* and, to make it the more fure, had the Doctor's great black Patch put under the Wig upon the Forehead. But to return to *Linet* the Curate, he was a Jacobite, but forced by the late Act of Parliament to take the Oaths, or elfe quit his Preferment. He took them the Wednefday before, much againft his Will,

---

[5] *George Seton,* Earl of *Winton,* was a Man of very eccentric Character. He made his Efcape from the *Tower,* and died at *Rome* in 1749.

[6] Dr. *White Kennett,* Dean and afterwards Bifhop of *Peterborough,* a learned and able Divine, wrote an Anfwer to Dr. *Sacheverel's* Sermon. The Bifhop of *London* ordered the Picture mentioned here to be taken down. *Kennett* was held in great Odium by the High Church Party. He died in 1728.

and they choked him, for he actually died the next Day of no other Difeafe but fwearing to the Government.

A great deal of Pains taken to gather a Mob in Memory of Queen *Anne's* Acceffion to the Throne this Day; but it would not do.

At the Drawing-room. The *King* not there. Came away early. Loft my Chairmen and Servants; forced to borrow of the Duchefs of *Shrewf-bury*; and came Home in the firft Hackney I could get.

After the Evening Service, went to *Court*. The *Princefs* bid me ftay to fup with her. There were the Ducheffes of *Monmouth* [7] and *Rox-burgh* and Madame *Buckenburgh* in the Apartment. The Duchefs of *Monmouth* entertained us with Stories of King *Charles's* Court and Death as follows:—King *Charles* was taken ill in the Morning, as he was getting up. Sir *Edmund King*, one of his Phyficians, found him lying without Senfe or Motion, upon which he immediately bled him about Ten in the Morning.[8] He lay in the Fit till Seven at Night, at which Time, coming to himfelf, and ftaring violently about him, he afked, 'What is the Matter with me?' (for they, after trying all Tricks poffible, had clapped a hot Warming-pan

---

[7] Heirefs of *Buccleuch*, married when thirteen to the Duke of *Monmouth*, who was fourteen. She is highly fpoken of by contemporary Writers. *Dryden* ftyles her 'Patronefs of his poor unworthy Poetry.' Three Years after *Monmouth's* Execution fhe became the fecond Wife of *Charles* third Lord *Cornwallis*.

[8] See the Narrative in *Evelyn's Diary*.

upon his Head, which had brought him to himfelf) and 'What have you done to me?' The
Duke of *York* ftood at the Bed's Feet, near the
King's Head, which was turned that Way, and
cried out aloud to him, with great Hardnefs,
'You have had a Fit, Sir! You have had a Fit,
Sir!' But the *Duchefs* could not perceive that
the *King* heard him, for he immediately fell a
fnoring.[9] The Duchefs of *Portfmouth* was not in
the Room when the *Queen* was there, but at all
other Times, as were all the Ladies of that Office
to him. The Duchefs of *Portfmouth* had lately
been perfuading the *Princefs* that the *Queen* was
extremely fond of her, and that fhe took great
Care of her once, left fhe fhould mifcarry. The
Duchefs of *Monmouth* faid it was quite the Contrary, but that fhe never faw Anything that other
People could fee, and might miftake the *Queen's*
Contempt of her for Civility and Compliment.
She was fo blind that of a long Time fhe did
not perceive the *King's* Intrigue with Madame
Mazarin, long after it was public to Everybody
elfe. As foon as fhe perceived it, fhe went to
Everybody to complain that the *King* forfook her
for a Woman that had neither Beauty nor Merit
(according to her Opinion). The Duchefs of
Monmouth told us the *King* had long been weary
of the Duchefs of *Portfmouth*, but the Afcendant
that his Heart had given her over him at firft,

and then the Support fhe had from the Court of *France*, whofe Tool fhe was, hindered his quitting her, and the *Duchefs* gave fome Inftances which were good Proofs of the Truth of this Affertion; one of which was the Manner he fpoke to one of his Lords who was with him in the Duchefs of *Portfmouth's* Chamber, when the Doctors faid fhe could not live Half-an-hour, and that fhe had fent to the *King* to take her Leave of him, and recommend her Son to his Protection. The *King* ftood pretty careleffly at the Window, and this Lord came up to him, and lamented over the *Duchefs* (whom he thought dying) to the *King*. To which he replied, ' *God's* Fifh ! (that was his common Oath) I don't believe a Word of all this; fhe's better than you or I are, and fhe wants Something; that makes her play her Pranks over thus. She has ferved me fo often fo, that I am as fure of what I fay as if I was Part of her.' The, Duchefs of *Portfmouth* is going to *France* again. She had fome Hopes of getting Arrears of Penfion, which made her come over.

I went in the Evening to take my Leave of *March 12.* my Sifter *Cowper*,[1] who is going to *Hertford*. This Day poor Madame *Gouvernet* was taken ill of a Palsy. 'Tis a thoufand Pities. She is the moft charming, agreeable Woman in the World, without any of the ill Humours of Eighty, though of thofe Years.

[1] *Pennington*, Wife of *Spencer Cowper*, who lived at *Hertford Caftle*.

1716.

March 14. The Duke of *Bolton*, who, without the *King's* Leave, or giving me any Notice, had figned a Warrant to bid Mr. *Lowman* remove my Furniture out of the Lodgings at *Kenfington*, came in the *Houfe of Lords* to my Lord to excufe it, and fay it was a Miftake. I had got the *King* fpoke to about it, who had ordered him to leave me thofe Lodgings.

March 15, 16. Trial of my Lord *Wintoun*. My Lord *Cowper* High Steward. ' 'T is grinning Honour,' as Sir *John Falftaff* [2] calls it, for there is not one Farthing's Allowance for all the Expenfe. The *Commons* differ about fome imaginary Right they pretend to, fo the giving Sentence is put off till Monday. Lord *Nottingham* behaved fhamefully, fo did Lord *Aylesford*, infomuch that Lord *Harcourt* [3] was afhamed to fee them perfift fo much in the Wrong, and gave up the Matter.

March 17. Supped at *Court*. The *Princefs* very well and cheerful. The Duchefs of *Roxburgh*, the Duchefs of *St. Albans*, Madame *Buckenburgh*. The Duchefs of *Roxburgh* told us a ftrange Story, which Sir *Copleftone Bampfylde* [4] told to fome Mrs. *Price*, which Mrs. *Price* told Mrs. *Howard*, which Mrs. *Howard* told the Duchefs of *Roxburgh*, who told it us.

Sir *Copleftone Bampfylde* coming up to Town,

---

[2] 'I like not fuch grinning Honour as Sir *Walter* hath.'—*Henry IV*. Act v. Sc. 3.

[3] Simon Lord *Harcourt*, Lord Chancellor in the Tory Government of the laft Years of Queen *Anne's* Reign. The Patron and Friend of *Pope* and *Swift*.

[4] Sir *Copleftone Bampfylde*, Bart., M.P. for *Devonfhire* till his Deceafe in 1727.

at an Inn found a Scotch Pedlar, who offered him
twenty-four Ells of fine Holland fo cheap that
he bought it, and carefully put it up into his
Portmanteau himfelf, the Holland being tied up
in a Paper, and the Portmanteau made fecure.
As they were travelling upon fome great Plain
(perhaps *Salifbury Plain*), with his own Man
and a neighbouring Gentleman, a fudden Light
fhone round them, which frightened their Horfes
as well as them, fo that Sir *Coplefone* and his
Neighbour were thrown, and the Footman rode
away two Miles. When the Gentlemen got up,
they found their Man gone, and, talking to one
another of what happened, faw at a little Dif-
tance Something white, which they, going to
look at, found to be the twenty-four Ells of fine
Holland, ftretched out as for Whitening upon
the Ground. When the Man came back again,
they looked into the Portmanteau, and found it
faft, and the Paper and String which contained
the Holland whole ; but when they came to open
it, the Holland was gone, to their great Amaze-
ment. I think the Story wants a better Authority than any I have yet named to make it be
believed. Sir *Coplefone* is a drunken country Gentleman, and if he did not invent this (which
I am afraid he did), yet it may be a drunken
Fume ; and it feems to me he did not mightily
believe it himfelf, for he fays he has made the
Holland into Shirts, and expects that fome mur-

H

1716. dered Body will come and demand them of him one Day or another.

The Duchefs of *Roxburgh* is a great Believer in Ghofts. She is the moft credulous Woman alive, and this is not the firft Story of this Kind that I have heard her tell.

March 19. An Expedient found to keep the Peace between the two Houfes. My Lord *Winton* had fawed an iron Bar with the Spring of his Watch⁵ very near in two, in order to make his Efcape ; but it was found out. He received Sentence of Death, but behaved himfelf in a Manner to perfuade a world of People that he was a natural Fool or mad, though his natural Character is that of a ftubborn, illiterate, ill-bred Brute. He has eight Wives. I can't but be peevifh at all this Fufs to go Fool-hunting ; fure, if it is as People fay, he might have been declared incapable of committing Treafon.

March 20. At the Drawing-room. *George Mayo* turned out for being drunk and faucy. He fell out with Sir *James Baker,* and in the Fray had pulled him by the Nofe.

March 21. Baron *Bernftorff* made a Vifit to my Lord and me. He is afraid of ill People that influence the *Prince* and *Princefs* by telling Lies of the Whigs being againft the *King's* Prerogative. Defired me to ufe Endeavours to prevent it.

Before he went away, came in Mademoifelle *Schutz.* The Chariot was at the Door to carry

⁵ This gives us an Idea of the Size of Watches in thofe Days.

me out; but Mademoifelle *Schutz*, without afking if I could let her ftay, had fent away her Chairmen, and bid them not come till ten o'Clock. I told her I was forry I could not ftay fo long, but that I was obliged to go to *Court*. She faid, ' I 'll go with you ;' to which I faid, in a Fright, 'I hope you know Nobody goes into the Dreffing-room up the Backftairs but thofe that belong to the Bedchamber ?' This I faid becaufe fhe had come that Way, and had twice fent in her Name, and the *Princefs* had ordered them to bid her go the other Way. Hearing that I was to dine the next Day with Mrs. *Clayton*, fhe invited herfelf too. I never faw fuch Airs of Importance in my Life.

Dined with Mrs. *Clayton*, Mrs. *Wallop*,[6] Lady *Herbert*,[7] Mrs. *Dives*,[8] Mrs. *Howard*, Mademoifelle *Schutz*, Monfieur *Schutz*, &c. Mrs. *Clayton* in Raptures at all the kind Things the *Prince* had been faying of the Englifh,—that he thought them the beft, the handfomeft, the beft fhaped, the beft natured, and lovingeft People in the World, and that if Anybody would make their Court to him, it muft be by telling him he was like an Englifhman. This did not at all pleafe the Foreigners at our Table ; they could not contain themfelves, but fell into the violenteft, fillieft, ill-mannered Invective againft the Englifh that ever was heard, and Nothing could make

---

[6] Probably the Widow of *John Wallop*, Efq., whofe Son was created Vifcount *Lymington*, 1720, and Earl of *Portfmouth*, 1743.

[7] Mrs. *Herbert*, Sifter-in-law to Lord *Pembroke*, was a Bedchamber Woman to the *Princefs*, and Daughter of Speaker *Smith*.

[8] Niece of Lady *Sundon*.

1716. Monfieur *Schutz* believe that there was one handfome Woman in *England.*

April 1.   At the Communion with the *Princefs.* She
received it in the Drawing-room of her own
Apartment, whither fhe came out of her Bedchamber, where fhe had heard the Sermon.   Dr.
Dunfter[9] preached an intolerable dull Sermon, to
the Degree of an Opiate.   The Archbifhop of
Canterbury adminiftered the Communion.   He
gave (after the Prieft that was to help him) to
the *Princefs* in both Kinds, and then the Bread
to the Clergy firft, and fo round the Room, and
the Minifter gave the Cup.

In the Afternoon came in Mrs. *Clayton,* Lady
Powles, and Lord *Harborough.*[1]   Friday Night
Mr. *Mickelwaite* was fet upon by nine Footpads,
who fired at his Poftilion without bidding him
ftand, juft at the End of *Bedford Row,* in the
Road which goes there from *Pancras Church* to
Gray's Inn Lane.   His Servants and he fired at
them again, and the Pads did the fame, till all
the Fire was fpent, and then he rode through
them towards the Town, to call for Help, it being
dark, which they feeing they could not prevent,
ran away.   Near that Place, under the dead Wall
of *Gray's Inn Garden,* a Gentlewoman, coming
Home with her Son about half-an-hour after
Ten of Saturday Night, two Men met them, one
of whom ftruck the Lanthorn out of her Son's

* Probably the Rev. *Thomas Dunfter,*   [1] *Bennet,* firft Earl of *Harborough.* Died
D.D., Warden of *Wadham College.*   in 1732.

Hand, and ran away with his Hat and Wig. She 1716. cried out, 'Thieves!' and they fhot her immediately through the Head, and are not yet difcovered.

Two intercepted Letters from Monfieur d'*Uxelles*,[2] to Monfieur d'*Iberville* fhow that *France* is afraid of breaking with *England*. They are fetting Treaties on foot by the means of Monfieur *Devenvorde*,[3] whofe Vanity, the Letters fay, muft be firft worked upon, and then it muft be fhown him how much it is to be his private Intereft. The French hate the Earl of *Stairs*.[4]

Dine with Baron *Bernftorff* to meet my Lord *April* 2. and Lady *Sunderland*, who did not come. Took a Piece of Velvet of Mademoifelle *Schutz* for my Sifter *Betty*, at fix Francs the Dutch Ell. She borrows of me a lace Head for the 28th of *May*. (Commend me to a modeft Affurance! It lifts One out of many a Pinch, I find.) Monfieur *Robethon* came to Baron *Bernftorff* either drunk, or fo impertinent, there is no enduring him; but the *Princefs* always fays that Monfieur *Robethon* is the beft Man in the World, but he is infupportable when he pretends to be witty or pleafant. Mademoifelle *Schutz* fpeaks about the Earl of *Rochefter's*[5] Place, that it would be acceptable. Baron *Bernftorff* does not care to

[2] Marfhal d'*Uxelles*, then French Minifter for Foreign Affairs.
[3] Was appointed Ambaffador from the *States* to *England* in 1715. His Letters are among the *Hanover Papers*.
[4] *John* Earl of *Stair*, at this Time

Ambaffador at *Paris*, obtained from the *Regent* the Expulfion of the *Pretender* from the French Dominions.
[5] Grandfon of the famous Chancellor *Clarendon*. Was Joint-Treafurer of *Ireland* with *Arthur* Earl of *Anglefey*. Suc-

1716. conceal his Name. Lady *Sunderland* gone, for a
Cough and Sort of Hectic, to *Kenfington.*

April 4. Countefs of *Buckenburgh* faid, in a Vifit, that
the Englifh Women did not look like Women
of Quality, but made themfelves look as pitifully
and fneakingly as they could; that they hold their
Heads down, and look always in a Fright, whereas thofe that are Foreigners hold up their Heads
and hold out their Breafts, and make themfelves
look as great and ftately as they can, and more
nobly and more like Quality than the others. To
which Lady *Deloraine*⁶ replied, ' We fhow our
Quality by our Birth and Titles, Madam, and not
by fticking out our Bofoms.' The Countefs of
Buckenburgh fpeaks Englifh pretty well, but fometimes makes comical Miftakes; the other Night
fhe wanted to know what they call the Man of
a Goat (meaning a He-goat), and the Man of a
Sheep that is mentioned in the *Pfalms.*

April 6. Baron *Bernftorff* dined here with Lady *W. Powlett* and Mademoifelle *Schutz.* The Houfekeeper
forgot the middle Difh of the Deffert.

Baron *Bernftorff* fpoke to me to recommend to
my Lord that Part of the *Triennial Bill* which
related to *Scotland,* which was doing by Lord
*Iflay.*⁷ He faid he found that the Duke of *Argyle*
and Lord *Iflay* were doing all they could to draw

ceeded his Coufin in the Earldom of   the Prince of *Wales.*
Clarendon in 1723. He and his only   ⁷ *Archibald* Earl of *Iflay,* Brother of
Son, Lord *Cornbury,* died in 1753.   the Duke of *Argyle,* fucceeded him in
⁶ *Anne,* Wife of Lord *Henry Scott,*   the Title; was Keeper of the Privy Seal
created Earl of *Deloraine* in 1706. He   in *Scotland.*
was a Gentleman of the Bedchamber to

Everything to themfelves, firft by pufhing on a general Amnefty, and next by getting the *Trien-nial Bill* into their Hands with refpeét to *Scot-land*.

I dined with my Aunt *Allanfon*. After Dinner we went to Sir *Godfrey Kneller's*, to fee a Pic-ture of my Lord which he is drawing, and is the beft that was ever done for him. It is for my Dreffing-room, and in the fame Pofture that the dear Fellow watched me fo many Weeks in my great Illnefs. From thence I went to the *New Exchange*,[8] and bought a Teaboard, and came Home to wait upon my Spoufe, who came about an Hour after. As he came along, the People were pulling two Boys out of a Ditch, that had been ftript and flung there by Footpads.

In the Morning went to *Court*. The Duchefs of *Roxburgh* is not fo much a Favourite as fhe was. The *Princefs* refents her recommending Mrs. *Ballandine*,[9] and her great Friendfhip with Mrs. *Howard*. Brought Mrs. *Clayton* Home to dine with me. She, and Lady *W. Powlett*, and I, went to the Play together, for the Benefit of *Johnfon*, who is the beft Comedian this Day upon the Stage, and I believe as true and good a Player as ever was in any Age, for the Parts that he plays.

---

[8] The *New Exchange*, in the *Strand*, fo called in contradiftinétion to the *Royal Exchange*, was a Kind of *Soho Bazaar*, opened 1609, taken down 1737. See *Cunningham's Handbook of London*.

[9] *Mary Bellenden*, one of the Maids of Honour to the Princefs of *Wales*, was the Daughter of *John* fecond Lord *Bellenden*, and one of the moft beautiful Perfons of her Time. The *Prince* was very much in love with her, but fhe rejeéted his Ad-dreffes; and, in 1720, married Colonel *Campbell*, afterwards fourth Duke of *Argyle*.

1716.   The Play was *Love in a Tub*,[1] that took fo much
in the Reign of King *Charles II.*, that it was
acted for eighteen Nights together. Nothing
gives One a livelier Idea of the Diffolutenefs of
that Court than their Relifh for this Play.

April 14.   The Debate about the *Triennial Bill*[2] begun
To-day. The *Princefs* went to hear it.

Went a vifiting, and at Night at *Court*. The
Princefs in good Health—had been abroad. I
carried her fome clouted Cream.

Carried my Daughter to *Hyde Park*, then to
the Venetian Embaffy. News this Morning that
Tom Fofter had got out of *Newgate*. The Keeper
taken up. It appeared, when he was examined
before the Council, that he was confenting to it.

Bit in the Night—I'm afraid by a Bug : 'tis as
bad an Enemy as a Scotch *Highlander*. Sir *David Hamilton* here; he has been robbed by Footpads. He ordered me a little Oil of Elder to
anoint the Lid of my Eye where it was bit, and
I could not open it. Forced to keep at Home
To-day. Lady *Cowper*[3] in the Evening.

April 16.   This Morning I came into Waiting. The
Duchefs of *St. Albans* and I divide the Week ;
fhe waits in the Afternoon, and I in the Morn-

---

[1] By *Etherege*; but better known as
The Comical Revenge. As fuch it is men-
tioned in *Genefte* as being performed this
Night for the Benefit of *Johnfon*.

[2] A Queftion of Life and Death to the
Government. If the *Septennial Act*
had not paffed, a Jacobite Houfe of Commons would have been elected at this
Time. The Bill for the Septennial Election of the *Houfe of Commons* was propofed in the *Houfe of Lords*, April 10,
1716, by the Duke of *Devonfhire*, and
paffed by a Majority of 35. In the
Houfe of Commons it was carried by a
very large Majority.

[3] Mother of the *Chancellor*, Widow
of Sir *W. Cowper*, Bart., M.P. for *Hertford*. Died in 1719.

ing. The *Princess* did not go To-day to hear
the Debates. I hear that my Lord *Nottingham*
recapitulated all my Lord *Cowper* had faid (with
fo much Applaufe) the Saturday before, and he
and his Brother, with the Help of my Lord *Trevor*,[4] fell upon him in a moft furious as well as
unparliamentary Manner. The Truth is, they
were very angry that he had difcovered the Falfenefs of their Zeal for the Prerogative. However,
my Lord managed the Debate fo well againft all
the Three, that I believe they were heartily forry
they had meddled with him. I dined at Baron
Bernftorff's. Mademoifelle *Schutz* is fitting for
her Picture to one *Conftantine*, a French Refugee;
't is moft horridly done, and fo unfortunately like,
that Anybody may know it, and yet the ugieft
Thing in the World. I have one of the fame
Stamp. After Dinner went to Madame *Noftitz*,[5]
the Polifh *Envoy's* Lady, for the firft Time.
They have talked fo much of Lady *Sunderland's*
Death, that I have done Nothing but cry whenever I have been. The *Princess* gone out to take
the Air. It is twelve Weeks laft Saturday fince
fhe reckons herfelf with child.

Lady *W. Powlett* complains of Mademoifelle
Schutz, and fays fhe is fo importunate and troublefome, and always upon the Spunge. I fell
a laughing, and faid I was very glad it had come

[4] *Thomas* firft Lord *Trevor*, Solicitor-General in 1692, Attorney in 1695, Chief Juftice of the Common Pleas in 1701, Privy Seal in 1725, and Prefident of the Council in 1730.

[5] Count *Noftitz*, Envoy Extraordinary from the King of *Poland*, had an Audience of the *King*, November 17, 1714, to congratulate him on his Acceffion.

1716.

to Anybody's Share befides mine. Mademoifelle *Schutz* complains that I am always with
Mrs. *Clayton*, which fhe takes very ill.   At Lady
W. Powlett's, where we dined.   She had a great
Difpute about the Englifh, who fhe fays have no
Civility for Foreigners, they not always putting
the Foreigners firft, by which Argument fhe muft
hold it reafonable for her Chambermaid to go into
a Room before the Duchefs of *Somerfet*, becaufe
fhe's a Stranger.   The common People are no-
where what One would wifh them as to Civility,
but I can't help thinking that the People of
Fafhion have not only been civil to all the Strangers that came in with the *Court*, but have really
made a great Rout with them.   We have all
given Mademoifelle *Schutz* more Refpect and
Civility than was her Due, and a thoufand Times
more than any of her own Country do, they all
treating her *du haut en bas*, as the French call
it.   She was fo very impertinent in this Difpute
that Everybody was peevifh with her, and all the
Inftance fhe could give of their Want of Civility
was a Newfpaper calling the *Emperor's* Envoy
Mr. *Gallas* inftead of Count *Gallas*, nine Years
ago.   If it was not for her Uncle, Nobody would
endure her.

Old *Clavering* challenged by a Witnefs fet on
by Mrs. *Errington*.

April 19.

Everybody concerned for Lady *Sunderland*.
The Duchefs of *Marlborough* mightily afflicted,
but her Griefs foon wear off.   The *Duchefs* lived

as ill in Reality, though not in Appearance, with
Lady *Sunderland* as with any of her Children.
They all hated her, and though outwardly Lady
Sunderland carried it fair, yet it was in such a
Manner that the *Duchess* perceived it was for
Interest only, and despised her for it.

> *Restoration.*   Green Boughs.[6]   *May 29.*
> Thankfgiving.   Orange Ribbons.   Mob; Bon-   *June 7.*
> fires.
> *Pretender's* Birthday.   Guards; Roses.   *June 10.*
> Talk of the *Prince's* Regency.   Mademoifelle   *June 12.*
> *Schulenberg*[7] here about her Title.   My Lord's
> Opinion and *Lord Chief Justice's* all wrong.
> At *Court.*   Lord *Townshend* in Disgrace.   *June 19.*
> Mademoifelle *Schulenberg* at the *House of Lords*
> to take Oaths;—in what Manner treated.   My
> Lord makes Peace.
> Baron *Bernstorff* promises his Endeavours, but   *June 26.*
> fears the *King* will not come to Terms with the
> *Prince*, but will fee to put off the Going that
> Day to the *House.*   Goes to the *Princess*, then
> to the *Prince*, then to me ; fays he does not find
> the *Prince* pliant.   The *Prince* confents to what
> Lord *Cowper* does.   Lord *Cowper* goes with
> Baron *Bernstorff* to the *King.*   Lord *Sunderland*
> and Lord *Townshend* would have the *Prince*

---

[6] On the Anniverfary of the *Reftora-tion*, Perfons in oppofition to the Houfe of *Hanover* ufed to wear Oak-apples in their Hats, in allufion to the Efcape of *Charles II.*, and on *June* 10, the Pretender's Birthday, Rofes in their Button-holes.

[7] Was the Sifter of the Count of *Schulenberg*; was Maid of Honour to the Electrefs *Sophia*, Mother of *George I.*, and, in 1716, was created Duchefs of *Munfter*, and in 1719 Duchefs of *Kendal.* See Letters in Appendix E.

1716. brought to new Terms. Lord *Cowper* oppofes it. Lord *Sunderland* would have that Part relating to the *Prince* ftruck out of the Speech ;— carried againft Lord *Sunderland*. Baron *Bern-ftorff* comes to tell me all goes well. Then go to the *Princefs* to tell the Remainder of the News. Her Joy. At Night I go out with my Lord to take the Air, then to Mademoifelle *Schulenberg*, to wifh her Joy.

June 27. Baron *Bernftorff* here. Speaks of Peace. Go to the *Princefs*. The *Prince* angry. Go to the *Archbifhop*.[7] Mob to meet him at *Canterbury*.

June 28. Three Lords to be turned out. Reftrictions. Go to Mrs. *Clayton*. Hear there of a new Broil. They infift on new Terms. Lord *Cowper* dines with Lord *Townfhend*. The *King* angry ; infifts upon humbling the *Prince*, and making him part with *Argyle*, *Iflay*, &c. Will come to new Terms, or fend over for *D. E.*,[8] and make him Guardian of the Realm and Duke of *York*. I wifh to give Advice. They are all mad, and, for their own private Ends, will deftroy all.

Go into little *Princeffes*' Apartment. *Princefs* there, all in flame. To Lady *Effex Robartes*. Mademoifelle *Schutz* there : thinks Obedience in Children neceffary. Try to gain Lord *Townf-hend*. The *Prince* will fupport *Argyle*. Try to appeafe them. The *Prince* in an Agony ; fhakes me by the Hand ; refolved not to depart ; fends

---

7 Archbifhop *Wake*.

8 His Brother, *Erneft Auguftus*, after-   wards Duke of *York*, at this Time in   *Hanover*.

for Lord *Townſhend*; promiſed to give him good **1716.**
Words. Talk of Challenge ſent by the Dukc of
Argyle to Lord *Cadogan*.⁹ *Prince* determined not
to part with Duke of *Argyle*. *Prince* wrotc to
the *King*.

The *Princeſs* ſays the *Prince* rèſolves to ſeem *July 3.*
to part with *Argyle*. Lord *Townſhend* and *Sun-*
derland with the *Prince* : cry, make Profeſſions ;
ſay thcy know thcmſclvcs undone. The *King*
anſwers thc *Prince* : copy thc Lcttcr.¹ *Princeſs*
thinks the Stylc M. *Robethon's*. Shc may buy
Robethon, if it 's donc artfully. At Night at Lady
W. Powlett's. Madame *Robethon* there. How it
ſtands between thc *Prince* and *Robethon* as to thc
Pcnſion promiſcd. Clears him as to this Affair.
All Lies. Remember what he ſaid to me and
my Lord about thc Regency.

Go to thc *Princeſs* beforc Ten. *Prince* not up. *July 4.*
Princeſs ſays he is reſolvcd to ſend for Baron *Bern-*
ſtorff, and tell him that hc is rcſolved to ſacrifice
Everything· to pleaſe and livc well with the *King*,
ſo will part with the Duke of *Argyle*. Deſigns
to ſend alſo for Monſicur *Robethon,* to givc him
a Penſion. Duchcſs of *St. Albans* huffcd the
Princeſs about her not being always with hcr.

M. *Robethon* ſays thc *King* will come back *July 5.*

---

⁹ *William Cadogan*, Eſq., afterwards Lord (1716) and Earl *Cadogan* (1718), was more than once Ambaſſador to *Hol-*
land, and fought under *Marlborough* at *Ramiliɩs*, and under *William III.* at the *Boyne*. He was Commander-in-Chief in 1722, and one of the Lords Juſtices during the *King's* Abſence on the *Con-*
tinent in 1723. He died in 1726, and is buried in *Weſtminſter Abbey*. Some noble Lines in his Honour were written by *Tickell*.

¹ *Vide* Appendix D.

1716. again, which he did not intend to have done if thefe Things had not been arranged. The Fo‑reigners take their Leave of the *Princefs*. The Duke of *Devonfhire* made Prefident, and the Duke of *Kent* Steward. The *King* will not ftay above fix Months. Baron *Bernfiorff* came to take his Leave. Go to take mine of the foreign Ladies; the *King* to take his Leave of the *Princefs*. Go to the Drawing-room. The King in mighty good Humour. When I wifhed him a good Journey and a quick Return, he looked as if the laft Part of my Speech was needlefs, and that he did not think of it. At Night Lord *Lovat*[2] brings a Man called *Barnes* to the Council, who depofed upon Oath that two *Sulivants*, Coufins to *Sulivant*,[3] whofe Head is upon *Temple Bar*, told him that *Sulivant's* Brother, who is a Partizan, was to kill the *King* in a Wood between *Utrecht* and *Loo*, and that he was to command a 'Party Blue,' which is a cant Phrafe for fifty Men. The Men were feized. This Lord *Lovat* was profecuted for the Rape of one of the Duke of *Athol's* Sifters, and durft not appear in the World till by his good Services in *Scotland* he had merited his Pardon. Madame *Buckenburgh* would not let the Doc-

[1] *Simon Frafer*, Lord *Lovat*, born in 1667, after many Acts of Violence, fled to *France* and gained the Confidence of the old *Pretender*, which he made ufe of, on his Return to *Scotland*, to ruin his perfonal Enemies. He was rewarded by the Government of *George I.* with the Title of *Lovat* and a Penfion. He en‑gaged in the Rebellion of 1745, and after having difplayed his ufual Craft and Audacity, he was executed in 1747, at the Age of eighty. The whole Plan for the Rebellion of 1745 is fuppofed to have originated with him.

[2] *Jofeph Sulivant*, alias *Silver*, was executed at *Tyburn* for High Treafon, *October* 28, 1715.

tor's and one of the Councillors' Wives fit down in the Dreffing-room where we were all fitting, and the *Princefs* in the next Room.

The *King* went in the Morning, and the *Prince* in the Coach with him. Almoft all the great Officers followed, except the *Chancellor*, who was obliged to fit in the Caufe Room that Morning. The Duke of *Argyle* and my Lord *Iflay* went to kifs the *King's* Hands, and affure him that their future Behaviour fhould fhow that they had been falfely reprefented to *His Majefty*.

In the Morning at *Court.* The *Princefs* bids my Lord *Cowper* come to the *Prince*, for he has Confidence in Nobody elfe. She fays M. *Robethon* is entirely gained with a Penfion of 300*l.* a Year (but I doubt that, for M. *Robethon* is a cunning Fox). *Stanhope*[4] fwears he will write all that paffes (I doubt that alfo). She fays that the *King*, in his Vifit laft Night, faid he had feen above fifty People that Day, and Everybody had afked him Something but my Lord *Cowper*. She faid to him, ' Sir, you look ill To-day. Are you well ?' He laughed, and faid, ' I may well look ill, for I have had a world of Blood drawn from me.'

The *Princefs* complains that Monfieur de *Torcy*[5] opens all her Letters.

---

[4] *James* Earl *Stanhope*, celebrated as a General and Statefman, was named Secretary of State in 1714, and became Prime Minifter in 1717. Died fuddenly in 1720.

[5] *J. B. Colbert*, Marquis de *Torcy*, Nephew of 'Le Grand *Colbert*,' was a diftinguifhed Diplomatift, and a Member of the Council of Regency during the Minority of *Louis XV*.

1716.   Lady *St. John*[6] here. She talks of her dead

July 8.   Son, cries, and tells of the Ingratitude of the Duke of *Marlborough* to him. That *George* had been twice at *Antwerp* to wait upon him, to the hazard of his Place. That the *Duke* made such a Rout with him, that he went to the Inn and fetched him to his House in his Chariot, and treated him with all the Expreffions of Kindnefs in the World; and when he took his Leave, faid, ' Mr. *St. John*, you are going to *England.* I have a Favour to beg of you. Pray give my humble Service to my Lord *Oxford* and my Lord *Bolingbroke.* I always had a Refpect for the one and an Affection for the other.' ' My Lord!' fays Mr. *St. John*, ' Lord *Oxford* and my Brother?' ' Yes, Mr. *St. John*,' fays the *Duke*; ' I never was againft them in my Life.'

Lady *St. John* faid my Lord *Marlborough's* Behaviour to her Son had broke his Heart; and that Half-an-hour before he died he faid to his Servant, ' Tell my Father I die a Whig, and always was one.'

She fays that the Duchefs of *Munfter* had told her that fhe was againft turning out *Argyle* at this Juncture, and that fhe believed it was the Minifters had put the *King* upon it. In the Afternoon at *Court.* My Lord *Radnor* replaced at the Council. I met the *Archbifhop*, who told

---

me that my Lord *Cowper* and he had agreed to 1716.
ftand and fall by one another. My Lord *Cowper*
with the *Prince* almoft two Hours. He promifes
to hear him in Everything. My Lord perfuades
him to live well with all thofe he thought had
not done their Duty, becaufe it was for the Good
of the Whole. He promifes him to do fo. He
tells my Lord *Cowper* he fhould not have known
what to have done without me, who had been
very neceffary to him and had done purely.

The Death-warrant came down for twenty-
four, all to be reprieved but Juftice *Hall*[7] and
Parfon *Paul*. The Duchefs of *Shrewfbury* in
Waiting. She pleads hard for a Pardon for all
the twenty-four. Go to Mrs. *Clayton's*. The
Duke of *Marlborough* very ill; he goes this Week
to the Lodge, and fo to the Bath.[8] Mrs. *Clayton*
faid he knew Nothing of what was doing in public Affairs; but they did Everything without acquainting him. I could have afked her what was
then the Meaning of my Lord *Cadogan's* going
down twice in one Day to *St. Albans,* as he did
that Day the Reftrictions were accepted; but I
won't enter into any of their Broils if I can help
it. Everybody believes that the Duchefs of *Munfter* had 5,000*l.* for making Lord *St. John* a Lord.

With the *Princefs* foon after Ten. She thinks *July* 10.

[7] *July* 13, 1716. *John Hall,* Efq.,
formerly a Juftice of the Peace in the
County of *Northumberland,* and Mr. *William Paul,* a Clergyman of the Church
of *England,* were drawn upon a Sledge
from *Newgate* to *Tyburn,* and there
executed according to their Sentence, as
in Cafes of High Treafon.
[8] See Letter of Duchefs of *Marlborough*
in Appendix F.

I

1716.   Lord *Townfhend* is the fneeringeft, fawningeft
Knave that ever was,[9] and adds this Reflection,
that Knavery is of very little Ufe when it puts One
fo out of Countenance. She faid Lord *Sunder-*
land owned to her he had been againft the *Prince*,
yet he was more natural than Lord *Townfhend*,
who ever ftrove to put on a Mafk, which is no
better than an Afs's Face, and that of the Two
fhe liked Lord *Sunderland* the beft. He owned
to her he had been for the Reftrictions, and faid
I fhall be the fame whenever I fee the like Occafion. He owned he was for difplacing the Duke
of *Argyle*, but not in the Manner they did, and
faid, 'I wifh Anyone durft tell me to my Face that
it is otherwife.' I told the *Princefs* I thought M.
Robethon had given the moft natural Account of
the turning out the Duke of *Argyle*. He faid
that Lord *Townfhend* and the other Secretary of
State had hoped to have governed the *Prince*
through the Duke of *Argyle*, which made them
talk of throwing up if he was turned out; but
when they faw the *King* refolved, and that they
were in real Danger of lofing their own Places,
then they fell in with the Cry againft the *Duke*,
and were the moft violent in hunting him out.

> [9] This is not the Character generally given of him. Lord *Hervey* fays: 'He was rafh in his Undertakings, violent in his Proceedings, haughty in his Carriage, brutal in his Expreffions, and cruel in his Difpofition, impatient of the leaft Con-tradiction, and as flow to pardon as he was quick to refent.' Lord *Chefterfield* fays: 'Lord *Townfhend*, by very long Experience and unwearied Application, was certainly an able Man of Bufinefs, which was his only Paffion. His Man-ners were coarfe, ruftic, and feemingly brutal; but his Nature was by no means fo, for he was a kind Hufband, a moft indulgent Father to all his Children, and a benevolent Mafter to his Servants.'

I told the *Princeſs* it was prudent not to truſt Mr. *Molineux*,[1] for Madame *Robethon* told me he had been with her and Monſieur *Robethon*, and had cried and begged to be forgiven, and had excuſed himſelf upon doing Nothing but obey his Maſter.

The *Princeſs* told me that the *King* had told her he had heard that the *Prince* had as ill an Opinion of my Lord *Cowper* as of the Reſt; but he added, 'He may truſt him, for he's a very honeſt, diſintereſted Man. He and the Duke of *Devonſhire* are the only two Men I have found ſo in this Kingdom.' The *Princeſs* is prevailed upon to live civilly with the Miniſtry, but, I am apt to believe, will hardly forgive what is paſt.

In the Morning at *Court*. The *Princeſs* gives me a Book to read to her; 't was Madame *Deſhoulière's*[2] Works. We came upon a Paſſage relating to *Brutus*, which, as much a Whig as I am, I cannot come up to; for I think *Brutus* ſhould either have been faithful to *Cæsar*, or he ſhould have refuſed his Favours; the Baſeneſs of his Ingratitude blackening, in my Opinion, all that could be ſaid for his Zeal for his Country. This occaſioned a great Diſpute among us.

I am trying to get Something for Lady *Willoughby*.[3]

---

[1] Probably the Agent ſent by the Duke of *Marlborough* to *Hanover*, in 1714, to watch the Proceedings of Mr. *Harley*, who had been ſent there by his Brother, Lord *Oxford*.

[2] Called by her Contemporaries the *Tenth Muſe*, the *French Calliope*, &c.,

a Poeteſs of the Time of *Louis XIV*.; was the Friend of *Corneille*, *Fléchier*, and *Peliſſon*. Her Tragedies are very inferior to her Paſtorals.

[3] *Heſter*, Daughter of *Henry Davenport*, of *Darcy Leven*, in *Lancaſhire*.

With the *Princefs* by Eleven. The Duke and Duchefs of *Roxburgh* have been with her to make Profeffions that they were againft putting the Duke of *Argyle* out, but would have advifed her not to fee him again. She anfwered coldly, ' Why fo ? The *King* has given him Leave to come to *Court*, and I fhould think the *Prince* did an un-grateful Thing not to countenance him, when he has fuffered fo much on his Account.'

Lord *Sunderland* did affure her that though he was¯for putting out the Duke of *Argyle*, yet he was againft the Manner of doing it. This was a Lie ; for after the *King* had agreed to Everything, and the Speech was made, and that Article in-ferted which related to the Guardianfhip, Lord *Sunderland* faid, with a great deal of Warmth and Paffion, ' But I'll go and take t' other Pull at it.' Upon which the Duke of *Argyle* was put out, though it was not fo much as talked of be-fore. For my Share, I thought it of fo abfolute a Neceffity to the public Good to keep all Things quiet, that I did heartily and fuccefsfully endea-vour to conceal this and Everything that could poffibly tend to Difunion, little thinking at that Time it could ever be called a Crime to endea-vour to keep Things quiet. It was very plain that the Foreign Miniftry had no Mind that the *Prince* fhould have the Guardianfhip. Monfieur *Robethon* owned to me that he wifhed the Re-ftrictions⁷ might be fo made that the *Prince*

---

⁷ The *Prince*, in fpite of his very limited Power, gained much Popularity.

might not accept, and when I faid, if it was fo,
I was afraid that Nobody would dare to act in
the *King's* Abfence, he faid I did not know the
Prince—that he only wanted Power to difplace
Everybody the *King* liked, and diffolve the *Parliament*. This was a ftrange Rant, and I thought
only proceeded from a Difappointment in a
Penfion of three hundred Pounds a Year the
Prince had promifed Monfieur *Robethon*, which
was a Secret I was then let into with a great
deal of Refentment, it never having been paid.
The next Morning, being with the *Princefs*, I
told her I had heard of a Promife not having
been fulfilled; that I believed it made great Uneafinefs; but I did not fay one Word of what
I had heard concerning the *Prince* nor the Reftrictions.   Within two Days the *Prince* fent for
M. *Robethon*, gave him an Order for three hundred Pounds, and promifed the Continuation of
this whilft he was his Friend.

The *King* was no fooner gone, than the *Prince*[8]
took a Turn of being civil and kind to Everybody, and applied himfelf to be well with the
King's Minifters, and to underftand the State of
the Nation.   The Duke of *Roxburgh* expected to
govern either by his Wife or Coufin; but the
Firft had been a good While out of Favour, and
his Coufin was fo far from helping him, that fhe

---

[8] On the firft Abfence of the *King*
from *England*, the Prince of *Wales* was
appointed Regent, but was never en-
trufted with that high Office a fecond
Time. It is probable that he difplayed
too much Fondnefs for acting the King.
The Father and Son hated each other
ever after.

1716. fhowed the *Prince* a Letter he wrote her to in-
fluence the *Prince* in the Affair of the Duke of
Argyle, and which fhocked the *Prince* to that
Degree, that he never fhowed the Duke of *Rox-
burgh* any Favour from that Time. The good
Archbifhop and *Chancellor* ftood upon their own
Integrity, and Defire of having Things go as well
as they could during the *King's* Abfence, which
could not be unlefs all Difputes were made up.
Stanhope was gone with the *King*, who took no
Englifh but him and *Bofcawen*,[9] and the Dean of
Exeter[1] for a Chaplain.

A new Scheme was let out by the Duke of
Marlborough's Friends for the State of the Nation
in the next Seffions of *Parliament*. By that it was
refolved, firft, that my Lord *Townfhend* fhould
be turned out (the Duchefs of *Munfter* had given
me a Hint that that was refolved upon before
fhe left *London*), and Mr. *Methuen* continued in
his Place (which alfo proved true), Mr. *Methuen*
having had the Seals given him during the Abfence of Mr. *Stanhope* ; that *Walpole* was to be
laid afide, and my Lord *Carnarvon*[2] put in his
Room (he fays they offered it to him, and he
refufed it, becaufe he was fure they would not
change Hands if they did not want fome dirty

---

[9] *Hugh Bofcawen*, created Vifcount *Falmouth* in 1720, was at this Time Comptroller of *H. M.'s* Houfehold.

[1] *Lancelot Blackburn*, Dean of *Exeter*, is faid to have been a Pirate in his Youth. Was made Bifhop of *Exeter* in 1716, and Archbifhop of *York* in 1724. Was a great Friend of Sir *Robert Walpole*. *Horace Walpole* calls him 'the jolly old

Archbifhop, who had the Manners of a Man of Quality, though he had been a Buccaneer and was a Clergyman.'

[2] *James Brydges*, ninth Baron *Chandos*, was, on the Acceffion of *George I.*, made Earl of *Carnarvon*, and, in 1719, Duke of *Chandos*. He had been Paymafter-General of the Forces.

Work done, and he added, 'I'm too rich to do any fuch Thing for them ') ; that the *Chancellor* was to be difplaced becaufe he was not tractable (that is, would not give in to their Villanies), and fome faid Mr. *Vernon* was to be in his Room ; but after Confideration, they pitched upon Mr. *Lechmere* as the only proper Perfon to govern *Weftminfter Hall.* He had Warmth enough for *Sunderland,* and they hoped he might be fo managed that they might perfectly govern him. They knew he was capable of being mightily frightened, for when the *Aylefbury* Election [3] was before the *Houfe of Commons,* he was Counfel in behalf of *Afhby* and *White,* and that being a Tory *Houfe of Commons,* had ordered Mr. *Lechmere* to be taken into Cuftody. When the Meffenger went to perform his Office to his Chambers, up two Pair of Stairs in the *Temple,* he was fo terrified that he tied the Sheets of his Bed, and by that Means flipped out of his Window into the Court, and fo efcaped. He was the moft mortal Enemy the *Chancellor* had, who had got him turned out for an Encomium made (at the Trial of one of the Rebels) upon the good

---

[3] This was the great conftitutional Cafe of *Afhby* v. *White* and the *Aylefbury* Men, which originated in an Action by *Matthew Afhby* againft *William White,* Mayor of *Aylefbury,* and others, for refufing to receive his Vote at an Election for that Borough. The *Houfe of Commons* refolved that a Queftion as to the Qualification of an Elector was only cognifable by themfelves, and the *Houfe of Lords* fupported, againft them, the Rights of the Subject, upon which the Commons, by an Abufe of parliamentary Privilege, in the Opinion of the beft Authorities, were endeavouring to encroach. In the courfe of the Conflict, which only clofed with the Diffolution of *Parliament,* the *Commons* went fo far as to commit to Prifon the Counfel and Solicitors concerned for the Burgeffes of *Aylefbury,* and it is to this Stage of the Proceedings that the Incident mentioned in the *Diary* refers.

1716. Behaviour of the Univerfity of *Oxford* during the
Rebellion (and that only to contradict Sir *Jofeph
Jekyll*,⁵ who had fpoke before him, and had found
fault with them for their ill Conduct). But to
return to the new Scheme. The Duke of *Marlborough* had had fo great a Stroke of the Palfy,
that it was feared he would never come to the
Ufe of his Reafon again, that being in a Manner gone, as well as his Speech; fo *Cadogan* was
the Man pitched upon to fill his Place. He had
been made a Lord for his Succefs in *Scotland*,
and this Matter was to be managed with fome
Dexterity; for though he was a very brave Man,
there were a great many that were by Right between him and the Command of the Army. The
Duke of *Argyle* was the moft formidable of his
Competitors, and I'm apt to believe it was the
true Secret of his Removal, though other Pre-
tences were made ufe of with the *King* to perfuade
him to agree to it.

There were a great many Removes more; as
the Duke of *Kingfton*⁶ to be Privy Seal, the Duke
of *Roxburgh* Secretary for *Scotland*, and the Duke
of *Montrofe*⁷ to be in his former Place, and many
more, which have efcaped my Memory. The
Scheme I have mentioned was given out with

* Mafter of the Rolls :—
⁵ A Joke on *Jekyll* or fome odd old Whig,
Who never changed his *Politicks* or Wig.'
  Pope's Epilogue to the Satires.
⁶ *Evelyn Pierrepoint*, firft Duke of
Kingfton, was named four Times a Lord-
Juftice during the *King's* Vifits to *Hanover*;

was the Father of Lady *Mary Wortley
Montague.*
⁷ *James* firft Duke of *Montrofe*, a
zealous Hanoverian, appointed one of
the Lords of Regency by the *Elector.*
He proclaimed *George I.* at *Edinburgh.*

fuch Affurance that it put the whole Town in a
Ferment, efpecially when it was known that my
Lord *Sunderland* was to go to *Hanover*, which he
did foon after the *Prince* went to *Hampton Court*,
where he refided with great Splendour the whole
Summer. My Lord *Townfhend* and his Family
were there conftantly, *Methuen* twice a Week,
the *Chancellor* once a Week. Count *Bothmar*
was there the whole Time; he was left by the
King to keep all Things in order, and to give
an Account of Everything that was doing. The
Prince behaved fo well, efpecially in regard to the
King's Perfon and Authority, that if Things were
truly reprefented, it could not fail to be for his
Advantage.

My Lord *Sunderland's* going to *Hanover* gave
frefh Life to the Schemers. They pretended they
were fure to carry their Point, and People in general were very apprehenfive that this Divifion of
the Whigs muft infallibly let in the Tories, and
that the Diffolution of this Parliament muft follow. What made People ftill more uneafy was,
that almoft all thofe who were named to fucceed
the Minifters who were to be difplaced were Men
altogether incapable of carrying on the public
Bufinefs, and who, of neceffity, muft embarrafs
Affairs to a Degree to make it of abfolute Neceffity to go to the Tories, fince it would be altogether unfit to take thofe in again who had been
fo heartily difobliged; and the Duke of *Marlborough's* good Intentions towards his old Friends,

the Tories, made People conclude he had further
Views than he let his Whig Friends into, and
that he put them upon choofing People he knew
could not go on with public Bufinefs, on purpofe
to play Everything into the Hands of the Tories.
This Sufpicion was not a little confirmed by the
Meetings and Conferences held among the Tories
at my Lord *Carnarvon's* Houfe, where it was con-
fidently reported the Duke of *Marlborough* had
been prefent feveral Times.

But Nothing was fo great a Check to the
Schemers as the Duke of *Marlborough's* Illnefs,
who was now fo ill again of the Palfy that his
Life was in great Danger. However, he recovered, though his Underftanding and Speech were
much impaired, for which he went to the Bath,[8]
where he paffed the whole Summer. The Schemers flocked thither; for though the *Duke* could
not advife, he could lend his Name and Purfe,
both which the *Duchefs* governed (a Pleafure to
her, who loved Power even more than the *Duke*).
Lord *Sunderland* came for his Inftructions twice
or thrice before he went away, and Nothing was
talked of at the Bath [9] but the great Things that
were to be done when the *King* came over.

[8] Where, as Dr. *King* fays, 'when
he was in the laft Stage of Life, and
very infirm, he would walk from the
public Rooms in *Bath* to his Lodgings,
in a cold dark Night, to fave Sixpence
in Coach-hire.'

[9] Verfes on the Miniftry about this
Time :—

'*Bothmar* is Father *Petre* in Difguife,
And *Sunderland* his Father's Place
fupplies :

Irifh and Scotch both Counfellors are
grown,
And faithful *Churchill* guards the facred
Throne.
Remember, *George*, when this Set led
the Dance,
They fent a greater *King* than you to
France.'

The *Court* meanwhile was lulled afleep by the Report of the Duke of *Marlborough's* Illnefs. People did not fo much as remember the Tafte the *Duchefs* had for Government, and that having the *Duke's* Purfe at command, fhe could do that which the *Duke's* Love of Money would never permit him to do; and 'tis no Wonder *Sunderland* was fo devoted to her, fince he was fo well paid for it; for fince this Illnefs fhe got the *Duke* to alter his Will, and take Everything from my Lady *Godolphin* he could hinder her of, and leave the Bulk of his Eftate to *Sunderland* and his Children.

But to return to *Hampton Court.* Lord *Townf-hend* being always there, found Means to infinuate himfelf mightily into the Favour of the *Prince,* but left the *Princefs* quite out, even to the fhowing her all the Contempt in the World. He made his Court to Mrs. *Howard* and Mrs. *Ballandine,* fo that, when I came to *Hampton Court,* I was never fo furprifed in my Life as to fee that fo little Refpect was fhown to the *Princefs.* She had too much Quicknefs not to feel this as much as was poffible. I faw it with the utmoft Uneafi-nefs, and got Mr. *Woodford* to reprefent to Lord *Townfhend* how wrong this Ufage of the *Princefs* was, and how much it was for their Intereft and Advantage to get her on their Side. Soon after my Lord *Cowper* made him the fame Reprefentation fo ftrongly, that from that Time he quite altered his Conduct to the *Princefs,* to the great Pleafure of thofe who had been concerned in the

Thing. This brought the *Princefs* into perfect Tranquillity.

Lord *Townfhend* was no fooner fet right in this Particular, than he began his Tricks againft my Lord *Cowper*. It was very plain he had infinuated many Things to the *Prince*, though without Effect. He violently pufhed on the Intereft of *Parker*, whom he had ftole from my Lord *Cowper*, who had made him Chief Juftice. Lord *Townf-hend* had not treated the *Archbifhop* better than my Lord *Cowper*; but, by the good Offices of the *Prince* and *Princefs*, Matters were made up, and Everything was kept quiet and right at *Hampton Court*.

About the Middle of *Auguft*, Lord *Sunderland* began his Journey. He had been at *Hampton Court* to take Leave ; and in the Gallery the *Princefs* and he had fo loud a Converfation, that the *Princefs* defired him to fpeak lower, for the People in the Garden would hear, to which he anfwered, ' Let them hear !' The *Princefs* added, ' Well, if you have a Mind, let 'em ; but you fhall walk next the Windows, for in the Humour we both are, one of us muft certainly jump out at the Window, and I 'm refolved it fhan't be me.' One may eafily guefs by this Sample what the Reft of the Converfation was.

Lord *Sunderland* took Leave of Lord *Townfhend* with a thoufand Proteftations that he would do Nothing to hurt any of them, and that his main Intention in going was to perfuade the *King* to come foon back. How this Promife was fulfilled will be known in the Sequel.

The *Prince* and *Princefs* dined in public every Day in the *Princefs's* Apartment. The Lady in Waiting ferved at Table. My ill Health prevented my doing that Service at all, except one Day that the *Princefs* went to *Windfor*. In the Afternoon the *Princefs* faw Company, or read or writ till the Evening, and then walked in the Garden, fometimes two or three Hours together, and then went into the Pavilion, at the End of the Bowling Green, and played there. This fhe did very frequently, till, one rainy and dark Night, the Countefs of *Buckenburgh* [1] fell, and put her Foot out of Joint; and I think, after that Accident, the *Princefs* went there no more, but ufed to play in the Green Gallery from Nine to about half-an-hour paft Ten. The Duchefs of *Monmouth* ufed to be often there : the *Princefs* loved her mightily, and certainly no Woman of her Years ever deferved it fo well. She had all the Life and Fire of Youth, and it was marvellous to fee that the many Afflictions [2] fhe had fuffered had not touched her Wit and good Nature, but at upwards of Threefcore fhe had both in their full Perfection.

Sometimes the *Princefs* ufed to afk Company to fup with her in the Countefs of *Buckenburgh's*

[1] Madame de *Buckenburgh* was very fat ; her Corpulence is frequently alluded to in the Squibs of the Day.

[2] ' For fhe had known Adverfity,
    Though born in fuch a high Degree ;

In Pride of Power, in Beauty's Bloom,
Had wept o'er *Monmouth's* bloody Tomb.'

Lay of the Laft Minftrel.

1716.   Chamber, and I can't but fet down that once
at Table there was the *Princefs*, the Countefs
of *Buckenburgh*, myfelf, Lady *Townfhend*, the
Duchefs of *Shrewfbury*, and the Duchefs of *St.
Albans*, and that all their Fortunes together did
not make eleven thoufand Pounds.

    The 28th *October* the *Court* left *Hampton Court*.
The Ladies came with the *Prince* and *Princefs* by
Water in a Barge.   The Day was wonderfully
fine, and Nothing in the World could be plea-
fanter than the Paffage, nor give One a better
Idea of the Riches and Happinefs of this Kingdom.   The *Sunday* fe'nnight following, being the
4th of *November*, the *Princefs* fell into Labour,
upon which the Council was called.   There was
a German Midwife (whofe Countenance prognof-
ticated ill, fhe being the very Picture of the French
Refident), and Sir *David Hamilton* waited as Phyfician.   The Englifh Ladies all preffed to have
the *Princefs* laid by Sir *David Hamilton*, but
fhe would not hear of it.   The Council, as well
as the Family, fat up all Night, but there were no
Signs of Delivery.   On *Tuefday* the *Princefs* had a
fhivering Fit, which held her a good While, and
violently.   Everybody but the *Princefs* and the
Germans were now in a great Fright, which
caufed the Council to fend down for the Countefs
of *Buckenburgh*, to defire her to let the *Prince*
know that they were there to befeech him to have
the *Princefs* laid by Sir *D. Hamilton*; which he
was angry at, and when I came on *Wednefday*

Morning I was in Amaze to fee the Hurly-burly   1716.
there was about this Affair. The Midwife had
refufed to touch the *Princefs* unlefs fhe and the
Prince would ftand by her againft the Englifh
'Frows,' who, fhe faid, were high Dames, and had
threatened to hang her if the *Princefs* mifcarried.
This put the *Prince* into fuch a Paffion, that he
fwore he would fling out of Window whoever had
faid fo, or pretended to meddle. The Ducheffes of
St. Albans and *Bolton* happened to come into the
Room, and were faluted with thefe Expreffions.
Everybody's Tone was now changed, and Nothing
was talked of but the *Princefs's* good Labour and
Safety. Nay, Lord *Townfhend*, to fhow his Readi-
nefs to comply, met the Midwife in the outward
Room, and ran and fhook and fqueezed her by
the Hand, and made kind Faces at her: for fhe
underftood no Language but German. This I
think the Tip-top of all Policy and making One's
Court.

The poor *Princefs* continued in a languifhing
Condition till *Friday* Night, when fhe was delivered of a dead Prince.

1720.

April 9.　THE *Princefs* fays that *Walpole* came to her with Offers of Reconciliation, and fhe bid him go to Lord *Cowper* and acquaint him. He did, and Lord *Cowper* was not come to Town; and the Servants faid, as reported, that he would not come till *Monday* (though he came that Night); but *Walpole* was glad to put off the Meffage as long as he could.

April 10.　*Walpole* came to Lord *Cowper* in the *Houfe of Lords*, and told him he had Overtures of the *King* from *Craggs*, that no Terms were to be infifted on on either Side, but the *Princefs* was to have her Children again, and that the *Prince* was to write to the *King*, and that he fhould return to live again at *St. James's*; that Lord *Sunderland* had promifed to come into all Meafures of the *Court*, and in particular that of raifing 600,000*l.* to pay the Debts of the Civil Lift, and that this was the only Opportunity for the *Prince* to make an advantageous Bargain for himfelf, for the Tories had promifed to come up to any perfonal Thing againft

him. About three o'Clock I had a Letter from
the *Princefs* to defire Lord *Cowper* to come to
her immediately, which he did. The *Prince* and
Princefs in great Anguifh of Mind. Lord *Cowper*
advifes the *Princefs* to infift upon the reftoring her
Children. The *Princefs* perfuaded by *Walpole* to
truft him in Everything, and, inftead of taking
Lord *Cowper's* Advice to infift, defires *Walpole* to
get them if he can, and that in a very faint Manner. The *Prince* won't go to live at *St. James's.*
Lord *Cowper* perfuades him, and fays it will not
appear to the World to be real without it. A
Letter agreed upon to be writ to the *King.*

I go to the *Princefs* alone, and beg of her to
infift upon her Children for her own Credit, and
not let them be in the Hands they are; for if
the *Princefs* gives up, fhe will never have a faithful
Friend again, nor be thought a good Mother, but
her Enemies will always fay that fhe had hitherto
only acted the Part fhe thought moft hurtful to
the *King.* The *Princefs*, in great Anguifh, fays
the *Prince* will not be prevailed upon to return
to *St. James's.* Says that the *King* looks upon
this as a Triumph to the *Prince* and *Princefs*,
fince they bring back with them all the People
the *King* hates; that all the Friends of the *Prince*
are to be replaced; that the *Speaker* [3] faid the
Servants of the *Prince* could not decently vote

[3] The Honourable *Spencer Compton*   He was created Baron *Wilmington* 1728,
(M. P. for *Suffex*) was Speaker of the   Vifcount *Pevenfey* and Earl of *Wilming-*
Houfe of Commons from 1714 to 1727.   *ton* 1730, and died unmarried 1743.

K

1720.   againſt the Civil Liſt; that the *Prince* is to be
at the Head of the Regency (a Thing unheard
of for a Prince of *Wales*) if the Reconciliation
goes on; that *Bernſtorff* knows Nothing of all
this Affair. The *Princeſs* deſires me to take my
Week, 'for,' ſays ſhe, 'I would have you with
me when I firſt go to *St. James's*.' Lord *Cowper*
goes to the *Archbiſhop*, and tells him in ſecret of
the Affair in hand. Lord *Townſhend* tells Lord
Cowper in the *Houſe of Lords* that he had inſiſted
to the Biſhop of *Norwich* [4] upon Lady *Portland's* [5]
Diſmiſſion, but it could not be granted (as if it
was likely that the Miniſtry would inſiſt upon
this after what has paſſed), but that *Walpole* and
Townſhend have undertaken that the *Prince* and
Princeſs ſhall be content with Everything they
agree to.

April 13.   With the *Princeſs*. She weeps, and tells me
ſhe was betrayed; that they had bribed the *Prince*
with conſenting he ſhould ſtay where he was;
that the Miniſtry had gained the *Speaker*, who was
to have come into the Council with Lord *Cadogan, Haverſham*, [6] and *Trevor*, if this Reconciliation
had not taken place; that the Biſhop of *Norwich* had fallen down upon his Knees to *Townſ-
bend* and *Walpole*, and ſwore that the *Princeſs*

[4] *Charles Trimnell* was Biſhop of *Norwich* 1707 to 1721, when he was
tranſlated to *Wincheſter*. He died 1723.

[5] *Jane*, Siſter of the firſt Viſcount
Palmerſton and Widow of the Earl of
Portland, was appointed, in *April* 1718,
Governeſs to the three Princeſſes.

[6] *Maurice Thompſon*, ſecond and laſt

Lord *Haverſham*, ſerved in the French
War, was dangerouſly wounded at the
Siege of *Namur*, and was a Member of the
Houſe of Commons, before his Acceſſion
to the Title, on the Death of his Father,
in 1709. He himſelf died in 1745, when
the Barony of *Haverſham* became ex-
tinct.

fhould have her Children ; that they (*Sunderland* 1720.
and *P.*) fhould, in two or three Days after the
Reconciliation, come and receive her Orders from
the *Princefs* ; that many would be turned out.
Aiflaby[7] and *Bofcawen*[8] both to be made Lords.
Newcaftle[9] and *A.* would be dropped ; that Lady
Portland would be put out ; that the *Prince* and
Princefs might come as often as they pleafed to
Court ; that *Walpole* had promifed the *Princefs*
to keep *Clayton* in ; that *Walop*[1] would be out ;
that *Sunderland* faid he had never found the *King*
cool to him till he mentioned a Reconciliation ;
that the Bifhop of *Norwich* offered to fwear upon
his Knees to the *Prince* and *Princefs* that all Terms
fhould be made good and fatisfactory to them ;
that all the *Princefs's* Friends were to be reftored.
The *Princefs* cried and faid, ' I fee how all thefe
Things go ; I muft be the Sufferer at laft, and
have no Power to help myfelf. I can fay, fince
the Hour I was born, I have not lived a Day without Suffering ;' and added, that the *Prince* had ordered the Letter to be brought to Lord *Cowper,*
who underftood the Laws, for he would write
Nothing that fhould tie his Hands ; that the *King*
would not hear of parting with Lady *Portland,*

[7] *John Aiflabie,* a Lord of the Admiralty, 1710 to *April* 1714 ; Treafurer of
the Navy from 1714 to 1718 ; Chancellor of the Exchequer from *March*
1718 to 1721 ; was expelled the *Houfe
of Commons* and fent to the *Tower* for
the Share which he took in the Working
of the *South Sea* Scheme.

[8] *Hugh* firft Lord *Bofcawen,* Comptroller of the Houfehold, 1714 ; created
Peer as Lord *Bofcawen* and Vifcount *Falmouth* in 1720.

[9] Yet *Newcaftle* continued to be Lord
Chamberlain till 1724, and *A.* (*Argyle*)
Lord Steward of the Houfehold till 1725.

[1] *John Wallop,* a Lord of the Treafury.
from 1710 till 1720. He was afterwards
Vifcount *Lymington* and Earl of *Portfmouth.*

but *Walpole* promifed upon his Faith and Honour
it fhould be done in a few Days, and argued fhe
ought to truft her Friends, who muft play this
Part to ferve them, without which they could do
Nothing, for that the *King* was inexorable if ruffled, and that there was no Way but to feem thus
to fubmit, and let them work underhand for
them, and that he (*Walpole*) would give them his
Head if Everything was not to their Minds in a
very fhort Time. The *Princefs* faid to him : ' Mr.
Walpole, this will be no jefting Matter to me ;
you will hear of me and my Complaints every
Day and Hour, and in every Place, if I have not
my Children again.' Archbifhop of *Canterbury*
at Night with the *Princefs*. She fays Nothing of
this Thing to him.

Lord *Cowper* ftayed but little with the *Prince*,
who fends *Walpole* Home with him. *Walpole*
tells Lord *Cowper* that he would not wait upon
Duchefs of *Kendal* till Things were far advanced ; that now he intended it, and that her
Intereft did Everything ; that fhe was, in effect
as much Queen of *England* as ever any was ;
that he did Everything by her.

He faid abundance of Things to perfuade Lord
C. that all this was right, but Lord *C.* told him
that notwithftanding he faid he took care not
to be duped, for all the World would laugh at
them, they certainly would be laughed at, for
they would certainly be duped ; that the very
Thing they engaged in was betraying the Li-

berties of the People, for what Ufe was having a 　
Civil Lift if they could run in Debt and have it
paid as oft as they would? *Walpole* ftammered,
and faid, 'Truly, it is not quite right.' 'No,'
fays Lord *C.,* 'for 't is quite wrong; but you of
the *Houfe of Commons* are to look to that, not
the *Houfe of Lords,* who have no Blame to fhare
with you upon that Score.'

It alfo appeared to Lord *C.,* from *Walpole's*
Difcourfe, that this Thing was agreed upon before the Duke of *Devonfhire* went out of Town;
that Lord *C.* had not been made privy to it, and
the *Princefs* had refufed to hear Anything before
Lord *C.* was acquainted with it. The *Prince*
faid to Lord *C.,* 'If I and my Friends are not well
received at *St. James's,* I won't go not above
once in a Month, and let them ftay by themfelves.' (Is not that the Thing moft wifhed at
St. James's?) That *Argyle* knows Nothing of his
being to be out. That the *Prince* and *Princefs*
have been half frighted, half perfuaded to this,
by making them believe the following Things:
that the Minifters were fure of the Tories; that
Atterbury faid he would come up to Anything
perfonal againft the *Prince*; that the *Speaker* was
with the Tories, and was to come in with them
into the *Court* Meafures; that he betrayed the
Prince and *Princefs,* and made all their Servants
betray them; that it was better to have the
Minifters make up with their Friends than their
Enemies; that all would be well if they played

this Part; that *Prince* and *Princefs* might come to *Court* as oft as thcy will.

Walpole told Lord C. that he got the better of *Bernftorff* by proving to thc *King* that *Bernftorff* had bought up vaft Sums owing to the foreign Troops at fifty per Cent., which the Public had paid, and that Principals had hardly got any of, the remaining fifty had been fo difpofed of. ' Yet,' fays my Lord, ' I can prove he has done much more of that kind than ever *Bernftorff* did.' *Walpole* faid the *Princefs* was to fend a Meflage of Excufe to Duchefs of *Kendal*, as thc *Prince* did to the *King*. *Walpole* faid, two or three Times, ' I faid fo and fo to the *Princefs*, but durft not tell the *Prince* fo yet.'

Walpole has engroffed and monopolifed the *Princefs* to a Degree of making her deaf to Everything that did not come from him. He ftirred up the *Prince's* Zeal againft *South Sea* Stock, which he was well enough pleafed with till *Walpole* had a Mind to fignalife himfelf upon that Head, and then the *Prince* and all Friends cried out againft it.

Walpole and *Townfhend* would never come into any vigorous Meafures againft *Sunderland*, though many fair Opportunities were offered.

Walpole let the *Prince* intrigue with his Wife,[2] which both he and the *Princefs* knew.

Walpole was every Day this Winter once, if not twice, at *Leicefter Houfe*. *Townfhend* pre-

---

[2] *Catherine*, Daughter of *John Shorter*, Efq.

tended to be angry and sullen, no doubt a Pretence to make up with *Norwich*. Lord *Cowper* not told of this Cabal which the Rest were for. There were several Meetings at Duke of *Devonshire's* about it, a Week before he went out of Town. The *Prince* and *Princess* get Nothing in reality by this Agreement, but Leave to come sometimes to *Court*; and for that they give up their Children, suffer their Friends to betray and quit them, and take Service where, in a little Time, they will hear it is a Fault to be civil to those they have betrayed: and no doubt the *King* likes that the *Prince* and *Princess* should not come back, and only seems to be reconciled to get this Debt paid, for here's Nothing to satisfy the People that this is new. No Return to live together, no Children restored, no Guards, Nothing that is great or princely; and all this to procure *Walpole* and *Townshend* the Benefit of selling themselves and their Services at a very dear Rate to the *King*, whose Affairs have suffered more from those two than from any since he came here.—Their Insolence having disobliged Everybody at first, and at last been the Cause of all the Broil at the *King's* first coming back, and which was the Cause of all the ill Blood between the *King* and *Prince*, and which ended at last in an open Rupture, and which, though it seemed by Appearance to be upon another Account, was nevertheless owing to that secret Spring. The *King* directly stipulated that those two Perfons fhould be removed from his Acquaintance; and that not without Reafon, for I fear, as now it is too plain, they only made the *Prince* their Cat's-foot to compafs their own Ends, fince he is thus betrayed into this moft infamous Way of making Peace, without any real Benefit for himfelf and the Kingdom.

Query. Whether *Walpole* and *Townfhend* have not thrown cold Water upon the Attempt of the *Prince's* beft Friends for his Service, with a View to this Bargain? If they have not all along made a Merit to the *Court* of keeping the *Prince* bound Hand and Foot as they pleafed, and letting his Friends fignify Nothing, and if they have not all along acted like Men that had a Defign to get into Place again, the firft advantageous Opportunity to themfelves of doing it?

The *Princefs* has been made to fufpect me all this Winter fince the Meffage for correfponding and wifhing well to the *King* and *Bernftorff*, and that to a Degree to fhow it very much, and the *Prince* has hardly looked at me, nor any of my Friends, for the fame good Reafon without doubt. The *Prince* has been fo rough with little Lord *Stanhope*[3] about voting in the *South Sea* Affair, that he has talked of refigning for a good While.

April 15.   Lord *Cowper* had a Letter from the *Archbifhop*. He fays he had been with the *Princefs*, who had faid Nothing of the Affair to him, nor he to her.

---

[3] The celebrated Earl of *Chefterfield,* and a Lord of the Bedchamber to the then Lord *Stanhope,* M.P. for *Loftwithiel,*   Prince of *Wales.*

Amazing! How has *Walpole* got fo far Power over them that they don't fee and know their beft Friends but through the Perfpective he holds to their Eyes? About One, *Walpole* brought Lord *C.* the Copy of a Letter to the *King* from the *Prince.* He told him that he was to carry the Meffage from the *King* to the *Prince* that Night, who was to meet him and *Townfhend* at ——.

Sunderland fays the *King* is fo out of Humour with him about this Thing, that if the *Pretender* were in *England* he could cut them all down. The *King* faid to him, ' Did you not always pro-mife to bring me the *Prince* bound Hand and Foot, and don't you bring him back without my having Power to put any one Servant in or out about his Perfon?—and what 's become of all the Money you promifed me?' *Sunderland* fays he is quite grown cold with them fince they men-tioned it to him, but the *Princefs* fays fhe heard the Duchefs of *Kendal* fay, fome Time ago, they ruled fo tyranically that the *King* was weary of them; which agrees with a Story told by very good Hands of *Mohamed* [4] the Turk. The *King* won't hear yet of turning out Lady *Portland*, but *Walpole* and *Townfhend* fwear to the *Princefs* it fhall be done, and their Arguments are moft from the Neceffity of the Thing; that the *King* has run out 600,000*l.*, and when once thefe Debts

[4] *Mahomet* and *Muftapha* were taken Prifoners when *George I.* was ferving with the Imperial Army, and were ad-mitted into his Service. When he arrived in *England*, they were named Pages of the Backftairs, and were fuppofed to have much Influence with their Mafter.

are paid they muſt fall into all Methods of good
Huſbandry, one of which will be to retrench
20,000*l*. a Year, and that they will force Lady
Portland to quit, by telling her ſhe ſhall have
neither Penſion nor Money paid her if ſhe don't.
The *Princeſs* ſays they will ſend them the
Guards again, and they promiſe in a little Time
to ſend the Children again ; but 't is only a Promiſe.   The Duchefs of *Kendal* ſaid ſhe heard the
King ſay that Lord *Cowper* was the only Man in
England who had treated him with good Manners whilſt in his Service.   *Princeſs* ſaid Nothing
of her Submiſſion to Duchefs of *Kendal*.

Duke of *Kingſton* deſigned to be out.   *A.*
moſt zealous and eager for Reconciliation, though
he was truſted with it only at ſecond Hand.   He
ſwore he would go to *Devonſhire Houſe*, and do it
with the Duke of *Devonſhire* in a Minute.   Before this he had agreed to retire, and have his
Retirement made eaſy and honourable, though I
can't hear upon what Terms.

Biſhop of *Norwich* is ſick, but yet takes bodily
Pains in hopes to be Biſhop of *Durham*, who,
though much older, is yet in a better State of
Health than himſelf.

I don't hear that any Terms are made, or that
we are to have any Aſſurances of not being as ill
treated as ever, as ſoon as the Miniſters have com-
paſſed their Ends.   I aſk the *Princeſs* if the Removes were reſolved upon.   She ſaid, 'Yes, but not
who is to come in ;' ſo 't is as in the Triumvirate,

only the Executions are agreed upon. *Walpole* is
very tenacious, and won't hear of taking Service
under *Sunderland*.

The *Princess* fays we are to trust to them—'t is
their Interest, *Walpole* fays, to keep their Words
with the *Prince* and *Princess*—but methinks 't is
a good old English Saying, that the lefs you
believe, the lefs you'll be cheated. One must
needs own *Sunderland* has the Afcendant of thefe
People, and has outjockeyed *Walpole*, though he's
a *Newmarket* Man.

I verily believe *Townshend* and *Walpole* have
agreed for themfelves only, exclufively of all the
World. Lord *C.* has been fo fick of the whole
Affair, he goes out of Town To-morrow, to hear
no more of it, and 't is more than Odds, if he is
not pleafed with his Treatment, that he will take
me away.

Communion. *Eafter Day.* Both *Prince* and
Princess received in their own Chapel. A full
Court afterwards.

I came into Waiting, not very well. *Princess*
tells me all goes on well; that the Letter had
been feen by the Minifters. Some Words dif-
agreed to, but that the *Prince* infifted it should
remain as it was. *Bernstorff* knows Nothing of
this, nor do any of the Germans. The *King* in
an intolerable Humour Yefterday. They did not
dare fpeak to him.

In the Morning fent for very early, for Princefs
Ann was ill. I went, and found the *Princefs*

1720.

a dreffing. She had fent *Perche* to the *King* to afk Leave to fee her Daughter, fhe being allowed to fee her Children but every *Sunday* Night. *P——* brought Word he had fpoken to *Mahomed*, who faid the *King's* Anfwer was, the *Princefs* might go, but fhe muft carry neither Doctor nor Phyfic, for he had appointed *Schezeldart*, and *Sloane*,[6] if any more was wanted. The poor *Princefs* went, and found the Small-pox come out. The little *Princeffes* were removed into the Prince of *Wales'* Apartments at *St. James's*, and no Communication between the two Families. We waited all the Day at *St. James's*, and the poor *Princefs* left her Daughter at paft eleven o'Clock. The *Princefs* very preffing to *Walpole* to have her Children again (but I fuppofe the Bargain is made, and they muft ftand to what *Walpole* thinks is for his own Intereft). The *Prince* in great Anxiety.

April 20.

The *Princefs* twice at *St. James's*, as every Day, from Eleven to Three, and from Six to Eleven. The Service of the Week very hard, being dreffed every Day but this. No Opportunity to hear Anything. Princefs *Ann* in a very hopeful Way. The *Princefs* fent us away from *St. James's*, and we came at her appointed Hour to wait upon her back to *Leicefter Fields*.

April 21.

The *Princefs* had a Letter from the *Archbifhop* Yefterday, to enquire how Princefs *Ann* did, and

---

[6] Sir *Hans Sloane* was Phyfician to *George I.*, by whom he was created a Baronet.

to offer to wait upon her. The Servant brought *1720.* one by miftake from the *Archbifhop* to Lord *Sunderland*, which the *Princefs* opened, read, and gave me to read. The Contents were, that Princefs *Ann* being ill, and he not knowing how foon he might be fent for to do his Duty to the afflicted Mother in her comfortlefs State, he defired Leave to go as often as he was fent for without troubling him again. The *Princefs* faid Nothing but 'Voyez quel Homme!' and bid me give the Letter to the Servant (and fay fhe opened it by miftake), and at the fame Time the Anfwer to his Letter, which fhe fent.

Lord *Cowper* goes to *Walpole*, and then to the *April 22.* Prince. *Walpole* gives him a Copy of the Letter, altered from its firft Original, and the Paragraph interlined is of the Minifters' putting in. It is to go To-morrow. *Walpole* has agreed to Everything beforehand, and it muft be as he fays. My Lord *Dorfet*[7] takes my Lord afide at *Leicefter Fields*, and enquires into the Succefs of the Negotiation, and tells him as much as he knows of it.

I begin to find that my Lord is taking a Refolution to come no more into Bufinefs.

Princefs *Ann* in a very hopeful Way, and not very full.

St. George's Day, Patron of *England.* At *Saturday, April 23.* Twelve Lord *Lumley*[8] waited upon the *King* with

---

[7] *Lionel* feventh Earl and firft Duke of *Dorfet*, K.G.
[8] The eldeft Son of the firft Earl of *Scarborough*; was a Lord of the Bedchamber and Mafter of the Horfe to the Prince of *Wales*.

the Prince of *Wales*' Letter, and Mr. *Craggs* [9] went back with him to the *Prince* with a Meffage from the *King*. The *Prince* took his Chair and went to *St. James's*, where he faw the *King* in his Clofet. The *Prince* made him a fhort Compliment, faying it had been a great Grief to him to have been in his Difpleafure fo long; that he was infinitely obliged to *H. M.* for this Permiffion of waiting upon him, and that he hoped the Reft of his Life would be fuch as the *King* would never have Caufe to complain of. The *King* was much difmayed, pale, and could not fpeak to be heard but by broken Sentences, and faid feveral Times, 'Votre Conduite, votre Conduite;' but the *Prince* faid he could not hear diftinctly Anything but thofe Words. The *Prince* went after he had ftayed about five Minutes in the Clofet, and from thence went to fee the two youngeft *Princeffes*, and after, Princefs *Ann*, who was told of the Reconciliation by my Lady *Portland* before the *Prince* came into her.

The *Princefs* was gone Home from *St. James's* Time enough to meet the *Prince* going there. She found my Lord *Pembroke* [1] in her Apartment, and went into the Clofet with him, and ftayed till the *Prince* came back, with the Beefeaters round his Chair, and Hallooing and all Marks of Joy which could be fhown by the Multitude.

He looked grave, and his Eyes were red and fwelled, as One has feen him upon other Occafions when he is mightily ruffled. He immediately difmiffed all the Company, and I was ordered to be there at Five in the Afternoon.

At Five I went, and found the Guards before the Door, and Square full of Coaches; the Rooms full of Company; Everything gay and laughing; Nothing but Kiffing and wifhing of Joy; and, in fhort, fo different a Face of Things, Nobody could conceive that fo much Joy fhould be after fo many Refolutions never to come to this, as I have heard.

I was called by the *Princefs* into the Clofet to feal a Letter to the *Archbifhop*, who was entirely kept out of this. I wifhed the *Prince* Joy and Comfort of what had been doing. He embraced and kiffed me five or fix Times, and with his ufual Heartinefs when he means fincerely. He faid he knew the Part I took in all his good or ill Fortune, and he knew my good Heart fo well, he was fure I was pleafed with this. The *Princefs* burft out into a loud Laugh, and faid, ' So ! I think you Two always kifs upon great Occafions.'

All the Town, feignedly or unfeignedly, tranfported. I kiffed Lord *Cowper* at coming Home ; faid to him, ' Well, I thank *God* your Head is your own, and that 's more than One could be fure of two Months ago.'

A Meeting at *Devonfhire Houfe* to fettle the

Ceremonial of going the next Day to *Court*. The *King* could not be brought to fee the *Princefs* that Night, and faid, when he was preffed to it feveral Times, ' L'Occafion fe trouvera.'

This Thing was carried on at *Horace's*[2] Lodging, who lives in a By-place, and keeps but one Servant, which was always fent out of the Way upon thefe Occafions.

The *Speaker* was in another Scheme with *Carlton*,[3] *Harcourt, Atterbury*,[4] *Trevor*, and all the Tories.

A third little Scheme was a carrying on at this Time by *Bernftorff* with *Chandos* and the moderate Tories.

A fourth little Scheme was laid down between *Lechmere, Bolton, Cadogan*, and *Roxburgh*.

In fhort, there was not a Rogue in Town that was not engaged in fome Scheme and Project to undo his Country.

The Debts of the Civil Lift were to be paid by the Bubbles. *Walpole* had not got fo much as he wifhed in the *South Sea*, and fo he was refolved to make up his Mouth now, and the two Infurances were the Things he pitched upon. They were to give 600,000*l.* for the Difcharge of thofe Debts. Infurance was fo low that *Walpole* and *Craggs* bought in vaft Sums at four-and-a-half.

---

[2] *Horace Walpole,* Brother of Sir *Robert,* afterwards Ambaffador at *Paris.*

[3] *Henry Boyle,* Lord *Carlton,* once Se-

cretary of State.

[4] *Atterbury,* Bifhop of *Rochefter.*

Bernſtorff, nor *Bothmar,* nor none of the Germans, knew of this except the Duchefs of *Kendal,* whom Englifh Money and an Englifh Title had made true to the Englifh Miniſters.

Stanhope came up to the two German Miniſters in the outward Room, and faid in French to them, in his fhrill Scream, ' Eh bien ! Meſſieurs, la Paix eſt faite . . . . la Paix eſt faite.'

B.—' Les Lettres sont-elles arrivées ? '

S.—' Non, non, c'eſt la Paix ici. Nous allons revoir notre Prince.'

B.—' Notre Prince ? '

S.—' Oui, notre Prince, notre Prince ; nous l'attendons pour être réconcilié avec le *Roy.*'

B.—' Monfieur, vous avez été bien fecret dans vos Affaires.'

S.—' Oui, oui, nous l'avons été, . . . le Secret eſt toujours néceſſaire pour faire les bonnes Chofes.'

Bothmar could not bear the Infult, nor the being given up by his old Maſter, and burſt into Tears, which was very faithfully reported to the *Prince* and *Princefs.*

The *King* very hardly brought to fee the *Prince* when propofed to him. He faid, ' Can't the Whigs come back without him ? '

The *Prince* and *Princefs* not to live in the Houfe with the *King*—the true Reafon becaufe the *King* won't bear it—fo 't is artfully made a Merit to the *Prince* to be fuffered to ſtay where he is. The *King* told that the Whigs don't

L

defire any Places, only to be Friends again.   He
faid, ' What did they go away for ?   It was their
own Faults.'
Every one of the *Prince's* Friends at *Court*, to
wifh Joy.

Lord *Cowper* came to my Bedfide, and faid,
' My dear Girl, I am come to let you the firft
into my Secrets.   I have, with you, thought to
take Service again, and by that fhow them,
though I was not originally in this Thing, yet
I think a Reconciliation fo right and fo neceffary, that I will help to making Everything in its
own Condition again.   And I did think to accept
of that Offer made me of my Friend *Kingfton's* 5
Place, who has behaved himfelf fo fhamefully ill
to me, that it was a Piece of Juftice upon him ;
but upon further Confiderations, all the Reafons of my Quitting fubfift ftill, except the unfortunate Breach in the Royal Family.   I am
old and infirm, and rich enough, and I have refolved not to enflave myfelf to any Power upon
Earth.   At Five-and-fifty 't is Time to think
of making Life eafy ; my Infirmities will not let
me ftruggle with Knaves and Fools.   My Tranquillity will content me more than all they can
give me under their Power and Influence.'   I
faid all I could to diffuade him, and told him
that the World would fay he was in a Pet at
his not having the Doing of the Reconciliation.

⁵ *Evelyn Pierrepoint,* Duke of *King-*   was Lord Privy Seal.
fton, Father of Lady *M. W. Montague,*

Lord *Cowper* replied he had Thoughts of that too, and found any Reproach better than the Lofs of his Tranquillity; that he told this as his pofitive Refolution, not to afk Advice, and that he defigned to fhow that he was not out of Humour by afking for the Key for me which had been promifed me, and would take a Place in the Cabinet if they would fummon him, but neither Office nor Penfion, for he was refolved to live a Freeman and an Englifhman, and let them have no Hold of him in any Occafion.

The Whigs of the late Cabinet all met at *Devonfhire Houfe* to wait upon the *King*, as had been agreed the Night before at a Meeting to fettle the Ceremonial. The Duke of *Devonfhire* made the *King* a fhort Speech in the Name of the Reft (which had been made for him the Night before; *God* having made him a very honeft Man, but no Speechmaker). The *King's* Reply was fo low, few of them heard it; thofe who did, faid the Main of it was to fay he was glad to fee them all united. After which they came out of the Clofet, and then waited on the *King* to Chapel. The *King* went to Church a Quarter of an Hour fooner than ufual; the *Prince* was by that coming upftairs when the *King* went in. He followed, but they fpoke not to one another, nor looked at one another all the Time, which caufed many Speculations.

When the *King* came out, the *Prince* ftood by him. The *King* fpoke to moft People except

1720.　the *Prince*: they two only looked grave and out of Humour.

The *Princeſs*, as uſual, with Princeſs *Ann*, who is almoſt out of Danger. *Walpole* told her the Secretary had been with him, to ſay the *King* would ſee the *Princeſs* in the little *Prin-ceſſes'* Apartment; ſo I was ordered to come by Five, the *King* not having appointed his Hour, which accordingly I did, and found the *Princeſs* dreſſing the *Prince* in the Room, who ſtayed all the Time till the *Princeſs* went to *St. James's.*

The *Prince, Princeſs,* and myſelf alone. The *Prince* ſays he told *Argyle* he might ſee he (the *Prince*) was no Scoundrel; for he now made up for himſelf and all his Friends whom he brought in with him. 'And now,' ſaid he, 'I have the Comfort of having done well; for if in this Time I had given up my Friends, by G——! it had broke my Heart, and before this Time I had died; but now I can bring my Friends in with Honour. We have drove them to this Peace, —— in the *Commons,* and Lord *Cowper* in the *Lords,* for Nobody elſe has ſtirred, and the firſt and greateſt Blow was in the Affair of *C.,* which Lord *Cowper* did againſt the Con-ſent of all my Friends, who were Cowards on the Bout; but now is the Time to reward them, and I hope ſoon to ſee Lord *Cowper* have the Seals again.' I made a Curtſey, and ſaid, all the Praiſe was charming, more ſo than the Re-ward; that Lord *Cowper* had found the Seals ſo burthenfome, I believed, he would never think of it.' Says the *Prince*, ' He muft. All my Friends muft be reftored, for I won't come in among my Enemies ; and I fhall want him and his Affiftance more than Anybody's.' I faid, ' I don't know, Sir, what your pofitive Commands may do, but I 'm fure Nothing elfe will.'

Lord *Cowper* more confirmed in his Refolution. The *King* came into the little *Princeffes'* Apartment about Six. The *Princefs* was in the front Room to receive him, and my Lord *Grantham*[6] and I as Attendants ; and he brought the two Turks with him. The *King* and *Princefs* went into a little Clofet, where they ftayed an Hour and ten Minutes, during which Time the Turks ftayed with us. *Mahomed* entertained us with the Praife of the late Queen of *Pruffia*, Sifter to the *King*, who died at *Hanover* of two Days' Sicknefs, fufpected of having been poifoned, before fhe left *Berlin*, with Diamond Powder, for when fhe was opened her Stomach was fo worn, that you could thruft your Fingers through at any Place, as did *Mahomed*. The *King*, he faid, was in fuch Sorrow, that he was five Days without eating or drinking, or fleeping, but kept walking and wailing all the Time, and by hitting his Toes againft the Wainfcot (which he ever does when he walks), he had worn out his Shoes till his

---

[6] *Henry de Naffau Auverquerque*, fecond Earl of *Grantham*, Lord Chamberlain to the *Princefs*. His Daughter and Heirefs married *William* fecond Earl *Cowper* in 1732.

1720. Toes came out two Inches at the Foot. He
refufed to fee Anyone till *Mahomed* found the
Duke of *York* in the outward Room, and carried
him in without afking Leave. As foon as he
faw the Duke of *York*, he flung his Arms' about
his Neck, and faid, ' Quelle Perte venons-nous
de faire, mon Frère ! . . . eft-il poffible que cette
charmante Femme nous puiffe quitter en fi peu
de Temps ? ' When his Paffion was a little over,
they got him to Bed, and fo, by degrees, brought
him to Bufinefs again.

The *Princefs* came out tranfported at the
King's mighty kind Reception, and told the Doctors and Everybody how mighty kind he had been
to her.

Walpole told my Lord that the *King* was very
rough with the *Princefs*—chid her very feverely
in a cruel Way. He told her fhe might fay
what fhe pleafed to excufe herfelf ; that fhe could
have made the *Prince* better if fhe would, and
that he expected from henceforward fhe would
ufe all her Power to make him behave well.

Monday,
April 25.   The *Princefs* faw the Ladies in the Morning.
Lord *Grantham* in Waiting. All the Cabinet
to wait upon the *Prince,* and, I think, all the
World befide. We were ordered to go at Night
into the Drawing-room.

A Reconciliation Dinner at my Lord *Sunder-*
land's ; fix old Minifters, fix New. Lord *Cowper*
one of them.

Duke of *Kent* with the *Princefs* above two

Hours. The Archbifhop of *Canterbury* ftayed to fee the *Princefs*, but could not. He left his Ex-cufe with me, and faid he had received a Letter on *Saturday* from the *Princefs* (which was the One I fealed), to tell him of the Reconciliation; and that fhe would have told him fooner, but that fhe did not know it till the Night before.

Mrs. *Wake*[7] afterwards told me the Contents of the Letter, which was that fhe did not know a Word of this till the Day it happened. And yet, although fhe had heard it talked of, fhe had no more Reafon to fuppofe it would come to Any-thing than all the Reports of Reconciliation ever fince the Quarrel. That the Morning fhe met the *Prince* in the *Pellmell*, and was fo frighted, thinking he had heard ill News of the Princefs *Ann*, that fhe ftopped to tell him how fhe had left her, and afked him where he was going. He anfwered, 'To *St. James's*.' She faid, 'I hope you have no ill News of *Ann*, whom I have juft now left?' He faid, 'No; I am going to wait upon my Father.' That this ftruck her, not knowing Anything of it, and that fhe was more fo when fhe faw him return with his Guards, of which fhe fent to give the *Archbifhop* Notice, being fure of the Part he would take in this good News.

At Night in the Drawing-room, though my Face was fwelled : it could not be put off. The *King* fpoke not to the *Prince* nor none of his

---

[7] Wife of the *Archbifhop*.

Friends but the Duchefs of *Shrewfbury*, who fpoke once in vain; but the fecond Time fhe faid, whingeing, 'Je fuis venue, Sire, pour faire ma Cour, et je la veux faire.' It happened Lady *Effex Robartes* was in the Circle when our Folks came in, fo they all kept at the Bottom of the Room, for fear of her, which made the whole Thing look like two Armies drawn up in Battle Array; for the *King's* Court was all at the Top of the Room, behind the *King*, and the *Prince's* Court behind him. The *Prince* looked down, and behaved prodigious well. The *King* caft an angry Look that Way every now and then; and One could not help thinking 't was like a little Dog and a Cat—whenever the Dog ftirs a Foot, the Cat fets up her Back, and is ready to fly at him. Such a Crowd was never feen, for not only Curiofity but Intereft had brought it together. It had been ufed to keep the Drawing-rooms fo empty for fome Time, there was hardly fix Women at once, to fhow the Neceffity of a Reconciliation, and that the People were difgufted.

Walpole made the *Prince* fend a Meffage by him to ——. The *Prince* refufed, and would not. *W——* faid, 'If you won't, I will make fuch a One as is fit for you to fend, and carry it in your Name. I am fure when I have done you will thank me.' He did as he faid, and the *Prince* thanked him when it was over.

Walpole has undertaken to make the *Prince* do Everything the *King* pleafes. The *Prince* knows

Nothing of this, but thinks he governs Every- thing.

Walpole to make up his Mouth by a Bubble, becauſe he did not get enough in *South Sea.*

The *Prince* and *Princeſs*, eſpecially the *Princeſs*, in Tranſports of Joy. *Bernſtorff* here. He carefully avoids talking of any News, and neither ſays he did nor did not know of this Thing.

Great Crowd of Ladies above Stairs at *Court.* Great Crowd of Men below.

At Night at the French Play with Ducheſs of *Shrewſbury.* Everybody took Notice of the Scene of the Drawing-room.

Madame *Kielmanſegg* ill, and could not go to the *Princeſs* when ſhe ſaw Company. She had applied before, but the *Princeſs* ſent her Word, ' que toutes Choſes ſe faiſoient par Ancienneté, et que par conſéquent il falloit que la Ducheſſe de *Kendal* vînt la première.'

Kielmanſegg had been left quite out of this Secret. She had been out of the Miniſtry's Favour.

At *St. James's* with Madame de *Montandre.*[3] The *Chancellor* there. The *Princeſs* laughed, and ſaid, ' I dare ſay, Lady *Cowper*, you are glad to ſee the Purſe in that Hand ? ' ' Yes, truly, I am right glad to ſee it in that Hand, and I wiſh that Hand may hold it till it is as weary of it as ours was.' The Chiefs had been there the Day before, and becauſe the *Chancellor* was not to *ſ'encanailler,*

---

[3] Wife of the Marquis de *Montandre,*   was made a Field Marſhal in 1739. one of King *William's* old Officers, who

1720. he came alone, and a very little While after, the Mob of the Cabinet, with little *Kent* at their Head, who looked of all Sort of Colours, except that of Health. They put me in Mind of the Ballad :--

> For my Lord Privy Seal, and my Lord Prefident,
> The one Duke of *Kingſton*, the other of *Kent* ;
> *Newcaſtle*, *Roxburgh*—theſe are ſuch Things
> That *Pinky* 9 would ſtarve if he ſhowed them for Kings.
>   Which Nobody can deny.

There was *Kent, Newcaſtle, Bolton, Kingſton, Roxburgh*, and *Craggs.* The Duke of *Bolton's* Tongue was out, as when we left the *Court*, and I can't but remark that the only Things I found as we left them was his Tongue lolling out of his Mouth, and Lady *E. R. [Eſſex Robartes]* ſtanding in the very Place of the Circle in the Drawing-room where I left her.

Lord *Cowper* continues in his Refolution, and ſays he intends to ſpeak to *Walpole.* He defigns to go out of Town.

This Affair has been two Months in Hand. It was by Concert with *Sunderland* that the *Prince* was received ſo very coldly.

At Night, *Radamiſtus*, a fine Opera of *Handel's* Making. The *King* there with his Ladies. The *Prince* in the Stage-box. Great Crowd.

Thurſday, April 28. Lord *Cowper* goes out of Town.

The *Princeſs* much importuned by *King* to take

---

* Probably one of the *Penkethmans*,   at *Bartholomew* Fair, &c. who were ſucceſſively Owners of a Booth

Duchefs of *St. Albans* again. It is alfo faid the Salary is to be but 800*l.*, and many other Things of that Kind, faid for me to hear, that it may not be afked. ' Put not thy Faith in Princes, nor in any Son of Man,' fays the *Pfalmift.*

Bernftorff mightily out of Countenance. He had been quite left out of the Thing; and though he had no Mind to appear quite difgraced, yet he did enough to fhow the great Anguifh and Anxiety of Mind he was under. He hinted that the Reconciliation would not go fo far as was defigned by both Parties. He faid he had been with the *Princefs*, who had received him kindly; that fhe faid, 'You always agreed with your old Friend, Lord *Cowper.*' 'Yes,' fays he, 'in Everything but two : he left us much againft my Will, and he went to the *Court* when I would have had him neuter.'

Prince at Chapel. Time enough before the *King* went. Obferved the *King* did not fpeak to him. The *Princefs* not there. If fhe don't go to the Drawing-room To-morrow, I fear People won't believe the *King* received her kindly.

Princefs not willing to give the Key to me. Pretends Lady *D.*[1] will be difobliged and quit. When the *Princefs* promifed it to me, fhe offered it herfelf, and faid that the *King* had afked it for —— ; but fhe anfwered, that 'after the Obligations I have to my Lady *C.*, None but fhe can ever have the Key.' To which he replied, ' In-

---

[1] Probably Lady *Deloraine.*

1720. deed, Madam, 'tis true when One reflects upon it; it is her Due, and I afk Pardon. I am in the Wrong.'

How comes Lady *D.* to be difobliged now, when it was refufed her thus? Does flying about at *Richmond* with the *Prince* make this neceffary?

The *Princefs* knew of this Affair long ago—long before the *Prince* did—as *Walpole* fays, who durft not tell him till about the Time firft mentioned in the Paper.

They raife a new Clamour for the Duchefs of *St. Albans,* and the *King* is to fend a Meffage of it.

I am quite fick of this Ufage.

Monday, May 2. Lord *Cowper* comes Home. Goes to the *Princefs.* Waits an Hour. Don't fee her. *Sunderland* there. She writes an Excufe at Night, and bids Lord *C.* go next Day.

The Drawing-room full, as ufual. The *King* don't fpeak to the *Prince,* and looks ill at all the People.

Tuefday, May 3. Lord *C.* at the *Houfe of Lords.* Confideration of the *Calico Bill* [2] to be put off for fix Weeks.

[2] There are fome Particulars about the *Calico Bill* in the *Political State of Great Britain* for *May* 1720. The Bill was entitled, 'for the preferving and encouraging the Woollen and Silk Manufacturers of the Kingdom, and for the more effectual employing the Poor, by prohibiting the Ufe and Wearing of printed, ftained, or dyed Calicoes and Linens, except fuch as are of the Growth and Manufacture of *Great Britain* and *Ireland.*' On the 28th and 29th of *April,* the *Lords* had heard Counfel for and againft the Bill, but on *May* 3rd they wifhed to put off the further Confideration of the Bill for fix Weeks. At the fame Time, to allay the Murmurings of the Silk Weavers, they ordered that an Addrefs be prefented to His *Majefty,* to order the Commiffioners of Trade to prepare a Scheme to carry out the Intents of the Bill, and to be laid before

The Weavers very difcontented; People affaulted by them in the Streets that are dreffed in Calico. Lord *C.* invited to a Miniftry Dinner at *New-caftle.* Does not intend to go. It is not con-fiftent with his Health.

In the Afternoon Lord *C.* goes to the *Princefs.* She very angry with *Sunderland* for propofing an Eftablifhment for the little *Princeffes,* and *Prince* and *Princefs* to pay for it. He fays the *King* will give Lady *Portland* a thoufand Pounds a Year Penfion here to do Nothing; or if fhe will go to *H.* [*Hanover*], fifteen hundred Pounds a Year there. The *Princefs* faid fhe was rich enough to pay all thofe that ferved her faithfully. She difliked the Impetuofity and Infolence of *Sunderland,* whom fhe faid was worfe than ever.

Lord *C.* would have taken an Occafion to afk the Key for me, but fhe did not give him the leaft Handle, but avoided giving the leaft Opportunity to fpeak of any fuch Thing. The *Prince* not to be fole Regent. She fays he won't accept otherwife. We fhall fee how it will be when *Walpole* fets himfelf to perfuade her.

'T is fure now this Reconciliation has been hatching thefe three Months, though *Prince* nor *King* knew Nothing of it, nor does the *King* know any Particular of the Agreement yet.

Parliament in the following Seffion. To this His *Majefty* affented on the follow-ing Day, which was the more expedient as that fame Morning 3,000 Silk Weavers, &c., came in a riotous Manner to *Weft-minfter,* and it was neceffary to call out fome Detachments of the Life Guards and the Train Bands of the *Tower* Ham-*lets.* The Mutineers, however, commit-ted no further Difturbance than tearing off a few calico Dreffes from fome of the Women who fell in their Way.

The *Princefs* was let into it by *W.* from the Beginning, and it was from that that when Anybody that loved her this Winter faid Anything for her Service, fhe would laugh in their Faces, and fay fhe feared Nothing and wanted Nothing, and bid them learn Courage from her.

A world of Difcontents among People that have been zealous on both Sides, and that are dropped.

Great Hugging and Kiffing between the two old and two new Minifters. They walk all four, with their Arms round one another, to fhow that they are all one.

My Lady O. [*fic*] all Day conftantly to play and laugh with the *Prince*, and bring Intelligence. One of *W.'s* [*Walpole's*] great Arts to pleafe the *Princefs* has been by making her a Stockjobber in the *South Sea.* They bought in for her that very Morning before the great Debate, and it was ufed to the M. of P. [Members of *Parliament*] as Arguments they (the *Prince* and *Princefs*) were both for the Project.

Since they fubfcribed at a hundred and fifty— he twenty thoufand, fhe ten—many Members of Parliament were ftruck out for this; and they were told they muft fubmit, for *Prince* and *Princefs* had fo much they could not help it; and at length many People had this faid to them, and confequently were made Enemies—they lofing fo much certain Profit to enrich thofe whom they thought did not want it.

To-day a Meffage to the *Houfe of Commons*

from the *King*, to fay *Onflow's* and *Chetwynd's*
Bubbles³ had been fo well recommended by great
Numbers of Merchants and other fubftantial
People, and appeared fo beneficial to Trade, that
he defired they might be incorporated; and that
the Civil Lift being in Debt, they had offered fix
hundred thoufand Pounds, which he defired might
be applied to the Payment of thofe Debts.

Thefe Bubbles *Walpole* and *Craggs* had engaged
in. They would hear no other Propofals, though
others offered double which thefe did; and *W.*,
at a Meeting of *Commons* the Night before, had
openly faid to *Poult.* [*Poultney*] : ' By *G*——! Sir,
I tell you we will hear no Propofals, for thefe
will do.'

Prince fays, fince he has helped to do this, he
expects the fame to be done for him when he is
King. Whether he wants it or not, to what
Purpofe will be the fixing the Civil Lift after
this Example?

*Wharton*⁴ at *Newmarket* has loft a great Sum
of Money: fome fay 13,000*l.*

³ Thefe ' Bubbles,' as they are termed
here, were two Infurance Companies, one
of which was headed by Lord *Onflow*,
and the other by Lord *Chetwynd*, and
they were doubtlefs the fame as the ' Infurances' mentioned already on P. 144.
The Lords *Onflow* and *Chetwynd* had
been negotiating with the Miniftry for
Charters for the Eftablifhment of their
refpective Companies, and had offered
600,000*l.*, 300,000*l.* for each Company, in
the event of the Charters being obtained.
The *King*, as above ftated, fent his Meffage of Affent to the *Houfe of Commons* on
the 4th of *May*, and a Bill was ordered
to be brought in to enable him to grant
Letters of Incorporation. See the Particulars in the *Political State of Great
Britain* for *May* 1720. The two Infurance Companies were both incorporated on the 24th *June*, 1720, the
Statute in favour of them having received
the Royal Affent fourteen Days before.
(*Anderfon, Origin of Commerce*, vol. iii.
P. 101.)

⁴ ' *Wharton*, the Scorn and Wonder of
our Days,' was created Duke of *Wharton*
in 1718. Soon after he had received

1720.
Thurfday,
May 5.

The Bubbles fall, notwithftanding the . . . .
of the *Prince.* A Meeting in order to raife it.
Sir *John J.* and my Uncle *Allanfon* voted Yefterday againft the *Court.*

*Shippen*⁵ upbraided *Walpole* terribly in the Debate with having chid the Committee of Supply
for fear of fuch an indifcreet Method as this to
raife Money, and now with moving and helping
the *Court* to it in this Manner. He fpoke long,
and very well—the better for being in the Right.

The Miniftry, to all Appearance, will certainly
quarrel with the *Prince,* and ufe him and the
Princefs ill after they have got the Money, if they
don't do Everything they would have them.

Friday.

Saw the *Princefs.* Very angry with *Bernftorff* ;
fays he made the wretchedeft Figure when with
her. He was more in countenance with the
Prince. Infinuated they fhould not forget who
turned *Townfhend* and *Walpole* out ; that he hoped
they would make up with *C.*

Craggs had been with the *Princefs,* and makes
many Profeffions and tells many Lies. He fays he
was not for taking the Children from the *Princefs.* He faid the Quarrel had been made by
Under-fervants, who had reported abundance of
Things, which they faid were true ; that for the

---

his Dukedom, he went over to the *Pretender,* and became a Roman Catholic,
retiring at laft into a Spanifh Monaftery,
and dying there in 1731.

⁵ ' Downright *Shippen,*' as he was
called, one of the Leaders of the Jacobites in the *Houfe of Commons,* made

feveral fuch Speeches about this Time,
one of which did 'much gravel Mr.
Secretary *Craggs,*' and feveral of them are
quoted in *Tindal's Continuation of Rapin* ;
but the one above mentioned, of *May*
5, is not among them.

Minifters, he would anfwer they had never done any fuch Things; that their Complaint againft the *Prince* was, that he fpoiled and oppofed the *King's* Affairs; and they ufed to fay to the *King* that the *Prince's* Friends were like a Battalion that broke through all their Meafures : ' And perhaps,' fays he, ' I myfelf have been one of the Foremoft to fay it, it being true.' She faid, ' I was told you had condefcended fo low as to call me a B——h ; ' at which he began a Volley of Oaths and Curfes of the Falfenefs of the Affertion, for fo long a Time, and with fo much Vehemence, that fhe faid to him : ' Fie! Mr. *Craggs* ; you renounce *God* like a Woman that 's caught in the Faƈt.' He talked of fending the *C.* Home, but was not clear in the Manner, nor Anything.

M. [*Memorandum.*] His Intrigue with Madame *Platen.* The *Prince* at the Drawing-room. The *Princefs* told me the *King* received her very kindly, and faid, ' Vous êtes la bien-venue, Madame. Je fuis ravi de vous voir ici. On y voit dès à préfent que vous êtes dans le Drawing-room.' After talking a great While to her, he afked her to play. She faid, ' Is it your Majefty's Commands I fhould ? ' He faid, ' Yes ; not only now, but I would have you always play, as you were ufed to do.'

The *Princefs* prefented *Alvarez* to the *King*, who talked a great deal to him. She made him tell the *King* a Turkifh Story.

This Day *Walpole* moved an Addrefs of the

M

Houſe of Commons to the *King*, to thank him for his Care of the Inſurances, and for taking their Money (in effect)—a Flattery only fit for the Reign of *Tiberius*.

Saturday.   *Alvarez* dines here. At Night at Madame G. A new Perſecution, ariſing from the Princeſs of *Wales* taking *C.* without aſking Leave of the *King*, which Lord *Sunderland* ſays ſhe promiſed, and would never take Anybody without firſt having his Leave.

Baron *Bernſtorff* here. Covers his Ignorance of what's a .doing by ſaying he would not know. Says that moſt of the Articles promiſed will not be kept, for they dare not tell the *King* what they have promiſed. That they would have him help to keep the *King* here, but he won't meddle. He was a little more in countenance, and more eaſy and cheerful, but One might plainly ſee what paſſed in his Heart. Vain Condition of a wiſe Man, whoſe Wiſdom can't put him above the undeſerved Frown of an old Maſter he had long and faithfully ſerved, and who now deſerted him for the moſt worthleſs and profligate Men the World had ever produced.

Mem. He ſaid *Walpole* ' avoit fait à merveille,' for he had moved the Addreſs in the *Houſe of* ・ *Commons*.

Sunday.   Lord *Cowper* went to Chapel. The *King*, the Prince of *Wales*, and the Princeſs of *Wales* there. Dumb Show between the *King* and *Prince*. The *King* does not ſpeak to Lord *Cowper* : looked ftrangely out of Humour and confounded. The 1720. Prince of *Wales* followed him into his Room— not fpoke to at all.

Lechmere[6] out, Lord *Cowper* tells me, who apprehended he had gone out of the Window again ; but it feems it was out of his Place.

Duchefs of *St. Albans* comes to afk Advice about the Key. Says the Princefs of *Wales* would never take it from her, and that fhe has it locked up in her Cabinet, and advifes if fhe fhall afk to wear it, or ftay till fhe is bid. Marvellous! What could provoke the Princefs of *Wales* to offer it to me, who did not afk for it, if fhe had it not in her Power to give it. To what Purpofe fuch Diffimulation as this, which, when once known, muft give fo low an Idea, both of One's Sincerity and Underftanding ?—for this, of all others, is the most foolifh Step ever was taken in fuch a Cafe, to offer what One could never give, unafked. Sure, fhe thought me a tame Fool, who minded not her Intereft at all, and who, confequently, was to be eafily impofed upon ; and that Lord *Cowper* was modeft, and would never pufh it forward if he found any Difficulty in obtaining it for me. The Germans used to fay the Princefs of *Wales* was 'gran-diffime Comédienne.' I fay No. If Actors ever played their Parts in fuch a Manner, they would be hiffed off the Stage, and muft ftarve. This Diffimulation fhows how fimple fuch Arts are,

<hr>

‘ See *ante*, Page 119.

M 2

for, inſtead of having its Effect, it has diſobliged the two very beſt Friends the *Princeſs* ever had ; and who, if they had had any Diſſimulation them-ſelves, muſt have found the *Princeſs* out before. No Talk of Places. The great Thing is obtained in the Money on one Side, and on the other the Advantage of going to the Drawing-room, and of being uſed as ill as Lord *Sunderland* pleaſes, which Laſt has undoubtedly taken Care to betray his Maſter for at leaſt thirty Pieces of Silver. 'T were well would he follow the whole Example, and hang himſelf.

The *Prince* does not ſee he is betrayed, but is guided by the *Princeſs* as ſhe is by *Walpole.*

The *Princeſs* in Tranſports of Joy at the ima-ginary Succeſs of her Court Arts—much below the Underſtanding and Capacity *God* has given her. But I have often obſerved, One may live ſo long among ſimple People, that One lets down One's Underſtanding ſo low, not to frighten them, that at laſt One quite loſes it. The old wiſe Man ſaid, ' Tell me thy Company, and I will tell thee what thou art.' If ſo, One can eaſily judge what *D. P., G., B.,* and *H. H. R.* will produce, added to *G.'s* Sincerity *pour tourner les Choſes.*

Lady *Powlett* aſks me if I know when the Ducheſs of *St. Albans* is to wait. I anſwered, ' I don't know if ſhe is in.' ' Yes,' ſays ſhe ; ' a Relation of hers told me To-day ſhe was never out.' And yet the *Princeſs* never would take the Key from her, which fhe has now locked up in her Cabinet.

In the *Houfe of Lords* Lord *Stanhope* wifhed Lord *C.* Joy of *Lechmere's* being out.   He re-plied, ' My Lord, 't is you that muft be wifhed Joy upon this Occafion.   I have Nothing to do with him, fo his being in or out is a Matter of Indifference to me.   But your Lordfhip has to do with him, and I 'm fure Everybody that has muft be glad to be rid of him.'

Craggs told the *Princefs* that he was the Man propofed taking the Children away, and fo he fhould be put out for that Thing.   To how many Ufes does the turning out of this Man ferve to !

Archbifhop *Wake* with the *Princefs.*   He ftayed *Wednefday,* but a little, for fhe was going to the Opera; but 10. repeated fome Parts of the Converfation he had. He faid to her, ' Madam, we muft now wifh ourfelves and the World Joy.   Firft, of this happy Reconciliation ; and next of the Honour and Integrity, the Difintereftednefs of the Minif-ters, as well as their profound Wifdom and Vir-tue.   They would be matchlefs for *King* and *Prince,* if they were not equalled by the two great Governors of this *Court, W.* and *T.* [*Wal-pole* and *Townfhend*].   What glorious Things muft we not expect from the Conduct of the Firft in the Miniftry, and the two Laft here !   What Happinefs for the People to be under fuch Di-rectors ! and how glorious a Figure we muft makc, all the World over, when we are influenced by fuch Counfels!' She looked out of Counte-nance at this, and faid, ' No, furc, my Lord ; *T.* and *W.* are not our only Advifers.   Pray, what do you make of your Friend Lord *Cowper* ? ' ' If you go to that, Madam,' faid hc, ' pray what do you make of him ?   Come, come ! in truth he is not at all fit for an Advifer, or to be put upon the Level of thofe great Men.   He may make One to affent to what thcy have firft agreed on among themfelves, and then let him into.'   Somebody fcratched at the Door, and fhe faid, ' It's the Duchefs of *St. Albans*, coming to torment me about the Key.'   ' And will fhe have it ? ' fays hc. ' No, never,' fays fhe.   ' You would have more Charity than I take you to have,' faid he, ' if fhe fhould have it.'

Thurfday,
11.

Go to fee *F. G.*   She enquires after what they are doing, and believes them fincere.   She will have fome Caufe to be fure of the Contrary, or I am deceived.

The Duchefs of *Shrewfbury* made me wait for her this Afternoon.

Sunday,
14.

Lord *Cowper* at Chapel.   *King* don't fpeak to him, more than to the *Prince.*

Monday.

Lord *Cowper* with *Bernftorff.*   Finds him in his Garden.   A good deal of free Talk.

Wednefday.

In the Morning Lord *Cowper* with the *Prince.* Tells him his Defign to go into the Country and take Nothing.   *Prince* faid feveral he heard were of the fame Mind, the Duke of *Devon-*

ſhire, and ——, Men of the ſame Opinion. He
dropped to a Piece of Advice that Lord *C.* gave
him, that he would confult his Friends about it,
and ſpeak to Mr. *Walpole* of it the firſt Time he
ſaw him.   Same Morning Lord *C.* went with
me to Duchefs of *Kendal*, who received him very
civilly.

Bernſtorff to Lord *C.*, in pretty good Humour
and Countenance.   Seems upon better Terms
than ordinary, but accufed Lord *C.* of running
away without giving him Notice.   I told him I
did not go fo foon ; fo he promifed to come to
me the following *Sunday*, which he did.

Lord *Cowper* into the Country for good. Leaves
me to make ready.   *Alvarez* dined with me, and
brought *Remond* with him.

Bufy packing all Day.

In the Evening I went to the *Princeſs.* I had
not been in a Minute before —— came in with
a Phyſic Book, and whifpered the *Princeſs* that
Mr. *Walpole* wanted to fpeak with her.   She gave
me the Book to write out three Pages of a large
Octavo, when I had got a violent Headache, and
had complained to her of it. I took it, and went to
write, till I grew fo fick I could bear it no longer,
and was forced to give over, and excufe it to the
Princeſs, and ——, who only wanted to employ
me whilft ſhe ſaw Mr. *Walpole.*   The *Princeſs*
afks Lord *Cowper* what was the Meaning of his
going into the Country.   Lady *Cowper* ſaid, ' To
avoid Importunity, and be quiet.' ' And,' added

1720. the *Princefs* to me, 'what makes you go fo foon ?'
'Becaufe he commands, Madam ; and I have Nothing to do but obey.' The *Princefs* was going
to Lord *L.*, and bid me follow, who was forced
to go Home, and then meet the *Princefs*, to go to
the Drawing-room with her Family. I did not
ftay it out, but went to fup with *R.* at *M. G.*'s.
Nothing was more evident than the Tranfports
of Joy in which the *Princefs* was with this new
Acceffion of Flatterers, and Mr. *Walpole* had fo
poffeffed her Mind, there was no Room for the
leaft Truth.

Saturday,   They went to *Richmond.* I would have gone
21.   to *Lambeth.* The Water was fo rough, I durft
not.

Sunday,   I had a Vifit from Baron *Bernflorff.* He was
22.   with the *King.* Said he thought Lord *Cowper* in
the Right not to take Office in fuch Company,
but hoped, if it was changed, he would lend his
Affiftance to the *King.* I faid, ' Not among thefe
People ; and there was little Hopes they would
be changed.' Baron *Bernflorff* faid, ' Not fo ; for
they go on fo madly ; and from Abroad as well
as from Home, there are fuch univerfal Complaints, it is impoffible to go on ; and the *King*
begins to be fenfible how he is ufed.' I faid,
' Whenever that happens, and if the *King* trufts
Baron *Bernflorff* again as he did, I dare anfwer
Lord *Cowper* will take Anything Baron *Bernflorff*
fhall command him ; but fure they are now too
ftrong.' He faid, ' That's a Miftake ; and the next

Change we muſt reform the Error we have been in to let the *Secretary of State* be Maſter inſtead of Servant.' 'This will remind you,' ſaid I, 'that it was Lord *Cowper's* ſincere Opinion that it was more the *King's* Intereſt to have a Treaſurer than the Treaſury in Commiſſion ; and now you ſee it. All the vile Things that will happen from this Projeƈt of the *South Sea* had not happened if there had been a Treaſurer; for no one Man durſt have taken that Load upon himſelf which this Treaſury in Commiſſion has divided : and if the *King* will ever be happy and proſperous, he muſt make a Treaſurer ; but he muſt have both Diſintereſt- edneſs and Sincerity, and make Mr. *Clayton* Chan- cellor of the Exchequer, and I 'll pawn my Head all will go right.' He liſtened, and then ſaid, ' But your Treaſurer has ſuch unlimited Power here in *England*, that One can't think of it as endurable.' I ſaid, ' What do you think of the Power of the Earl of *Sunderland*? I have ſeen ſe- veral Treaſurers, but None with the Authority and unlimited Power of the Earl of *Sunderland*. The Earl of *Oxford* never had the Quarter of the Power, nor the Inſolence, that Lord *Sunderland* has.' Baron *Bernſtorff* pauſed, and ſaid he had, and would, with Pains and Inſinuation, make the *King* Maſter of the very ill Conſequences that this Projeƈt of the *South Sea* brought, and ſpoke in a Manner I have never heard him ſince *Feb- ruary* ($17\frac{16}{17}$), which plainly ſhowed he thought himſelf in a very good Situation. He ſaid a world

1720.   of kind Things of me, and told me he would fee
me at my Return.

Monday,
23.   Go into Country.   Nothing material there.
Friday,
27.   I return to *London*, to go to the Birthday and
wait the Week following.   I went to pay my
Duty to the *Princefs*, and waited with Dr. *Clark*
till the *Mafter of the Rolls* was gone from her.

Saturday,
May 28.   The Birthday of our moft gracious *King*.   In
the Morning we waited on the *Princefs* to *Court*,
where was one of the greateft Crowds I ever faw,
it being greatly increafed by our new Lords and
Mafters of the *South Sea*, who had much more
Court made to them than the Minifters themfelves.
At Night we all went in the fame Train.
The Duke of *Newcaftle*[7] had got drunk for our
Sins; fo the *Princefs's* Ladies had no Places, but
ftood in the Heat and Crowd all the Night.
The Duchefs of *Shrewfbury* downright fcolded
aloud about it, and he told her, for Conclu-
fion, that Places were provided for the *Princefs's*
Family, which they did not keep, but that Ladies of the Town came and took them.   'T was
not his Fault; and he could not turn out the
Ladies of the Town for us.   There was fo great
a Crowd, and we were fo ill ufed, that four of us
went away, and left only Lady *Dorfet*[8] in Waiting.   It was plain we were to be ufed thus; and
I am almoft tempted to think it was alfo one of
the doughty Articles of Reconciliation.

[7] The Duke of *Newcaftle* was at this
Time Lord Chamberlain.   [8] *Elizabeth Collier*, Countefs of *Dorfet*,
a Lady of the Bedchamber.

Kendal and *Kielmanſegg* very civil to me. *Newcaſtle* ſtood before me both Morning and Night. If I had not ſeen his Face, I ſhould have known it had been him, it being his Peculiar ever to turn his Back upon thoſe he has any Obligations to.

Dined with Aunt *Allanſon.* Go to the *Maſter of the Rolls.* The Servants got ſo drunk, I was forced to ſend one of them Home.

Begin my Waiting. Great Crowds at our Court this Morning. The Waiting much longer; we are not releaſed till half-an-hour after Three. The *Princeſs* in high Delight with the Folks, and they as much with her. No Opportunity to ſpeak of Anything. I am ordered againſt Eight at Night to go to the young *Princeſſes* before the Drawing-room. At Night the *Princeſs* went as ſhe deſigned, and had a great Mind to be out of Humour with me, and put on a Frown. When the *King* ſpoke to the *Princeſs,* he turned his Back to me who was playing. But a ſudden Curioſity took him, and he turned his Face round, and had his Eyes fixed upon me, and looked all Night ſo intently, and was not angry, that it was talked of.

The *Princeſs* ſaid to me that —— had been with her that Morning, and ſaid that the *King* could not help liking me as well as ever ; and that ſhe ſaw plainly by the *King's* Manner laſt Night that I could do what I pleaſed, and that it was my Fault if I did not rule them all. I an-

fwered, for the Thing itfelf, I did not believe it at
all; and, fuppofing it were true, Power was too
dear bought when One was to do fuch difhonourable Work for it.

In the Morning I waited. A good deal of
Company. The Talk is that l'Abbé *du Bois*, Archbifhop of *Cambray*, made fome Reprefentations to
the *King* againft Laws which he did not like, and
that the Reprimand he had got went fo far as two
or three good Kicks. It proved a Lie; but had
it been true, how would the *King* have helped
himfelf if the new-made Archbifhop had excom-
municated him? — for in that Church the Prieft
pretends to that Power. In the Afternoon the
Prince and *Princefs* went to the French Play. A
moft difmal Performance. No Wonder People
are Slaves who can entertain themfelves with
fuch Stuff.

Baron *Bernftorff* with me by Appointment.
He complains grievoufly of the Miniftry, and is in
better Heart than before the Reconciliation. He
hopes for a new Miniftry. I faid, by Order of Lord
Cowper, to him, when Baron *Bernftorff* preffed
Lord *Cowper* to take Service, that he had no Objection to it, provided it were a Whig Miniftry,
but if he quitted thefe, and came into any new
Scheme, it muft be a Tory Miniftry. In fhort,
to be plain, if Earl *Cadogan* and Duke *Chandos* were to propofe the Scheme, it muft be
Tory, and he would not take Service with Lord
Harcourt and Lord *Trevor*, and all that Set of

People; that fuch a Scheme muft end in Baron *Bernftorff's,* and the *King's,* and the Kingdom's Ruin, and that, like a good Friend, he gave him this Notice; but if the Miniftry continued to be Whig, and the *King* reftored to Baron *Bernftorff* his Friendfhip and Power, he had no Objection to take Service.   I faid, 'You fee now your Error.   When the *King* is to be happy, it muft be from returning to the Place from whence you came out of your Way.   Let the *King* make an honeft Treafurer, and make Mr. *Clayton* Chancellor of the Exchequer, and all will be well.' Baron *Bernftorff* replied, 'The Thought is not bad; and one Reafon Everything has been fo wrong is, that the *Secretary of State* is Mafter inftead of Servant.'   I afked if Mr. *Walpole* was to be Lord of the Treafury.   He faid, ' No; fure the Earl of *Sunderland* won't give up that: but Everything goes fo madly, both at Home and Abroad, I can anfwer for Nothing.'   He faid that Princefs *Ann,* Princefs *Amaly,* and Princefs *Caroline* would remain with Lady *Portland*; and, as the Judges had declared the Right the *King* had to their Education, they might perhaps be with the *Princefs* in Summer, but when the *King* returned he would expect them again.

At the French Play.   News came Princefs *Amaly* was ill.   The *Princefs* went from thence to *St. James's,* and found her pretty well.   At Night I fupped with Madame *Kielmanfegg,* with *R., M.,* and Madame *M.,* Mrs. *Clayton,* Mr.

1720. *Hilten*, and Mr. *Plaifance*. One buys thefe Ho-
nours very dear, by the late Hours One has to
keep.

Wednefday. Waiting in Morning.

Thurfday. Morning in Waiting.
Evening the *Princefs* went to Princefs *Amaly*,
who is very well again. Sup at Madame G.'s
with *R*.

Friday. Morning in Waiting.
I dine with Mrs. *Clayton*. Am left by Chair-
men and Servants—all drunk. I can hardly get
to the *Princefs*.
In the Afternoon Lord *Lovat* came to me.
Says that the Miniftry is very low. Baron *Bern-
ftorff* will never ceafe till he has got the Better.
He extols the *Baron's* Love and Efteem for Lord
Cowper and myfelf.
Afternoon the *Princefs* went firft to Princefs
Amaly, and then to the Drawing-room, which
was very long, and not over full. The good
King faid not a Word to the *Prince*, nor any
Soul belonging to him, but his *Princefs*. He
looks as if he would take the very firft Oppor-
tunity of leaving them all.

Saturday. Waiting in the Morning. At Night None, fo
had the Afternoon to myfelf. Made Vifits. Sup
at Duchefs —— with Madame *K.*, *R.*, *Plaifance*, and Le Comte de *Laval*, *Remond* having
begged a Play of the *Princefs*.

Sunday,
July 5. The *Princefs* at Church twice this Morning.
After Chapel fhe went into the Drawing-room,

and fo Home, which concluded my Waiting, never having had any Opportunity to fay one Word to the *Princeſs* alone without the Door being open.

When Mrs. *Wake* came to take her Leave, be- fore the *Archbiſhop* went his Viſitation, ſhe ſaid to Mrs. *Wake*, ' Our Children we ſhall have, and the Regency they promiſe us, but the Laſt I don't believe ; and I tell you naturally, my dear Mrs. *Wake*, I will venture my Noſe we ſhan't have it.' I was pulling on her Gloves, and ſaid, ' Yes, Madam ; if your Highneſs had thirty Noſes you might venture them all without the leaſt Danger to them.'

APPENDICES.

APPENDIX A.

Duchefs of Marlborough to Duchefs of St. Albans.

I beg your Pardon, dear Madam, that I could not write fooner, being at Dinner with Company. In all the Courts that I have feen, the *Groom of the Stole* has the firft Place, and next to her the Lady in Waiting, whatever Quality fhe may be of, and after them two all the Ladies are placed according to their own Titles.

I am, &c.,

S. MARLBOROUGH.

APPENDIX B.

Lord Bolingbroke to his Father.

Thurſday.

Yours of *Tueſday* came to my Hands laſt Night. Be pleaſed to depend on what I told you in *London,* and to have no Concern on that Head. I not only never figned or writ fuch a Letter as is fuppofed, but I never directly or indirectly [*had Dealings*] with that Perfon, or with any Man living or dead, in his Behalf. I had not an Opportunity of making my Court to the *King* before his Acceſſion, but I was always as true a Friend to his Succeſſion as any of thoſe who clamoured the loudeſt, and a better than ſome of them. It is hard to anſwer in this perfidious diſſembling World for what any Man has done or may do, but I am confident my Lord *Harcourt* is as innocent as I know myſelf to be. We have often converſed in the utmoſt Confidence together during the *Queen's* Time, concerning what was likely to happen after her Deceaſe. He was, in his Opinion, the moſt concerned I ever ſaw a Man that our Whole depended on the inviolate Preſervation of our legal Settlement, and I re-member particularly that he uſed to lament, juſt before Her late *Majeſty's* Death, that we ſhould be branded as Jacobites if ſhe died ſoon, without having the leaſt Share of that Guilt.

A thouſand Thanks for your ſpeaking to *Lord Trea-*

ſurer, and for all other Inſtances of your Care and Tenderneſs.

I have Letters from *Wotton,*[1] and Accounts by the Servants I ſent thither, neither of which pleaſe me at all. I ſhall write more fully to you in a Day or two, on this and other Subjects.

---

[1] *Lydiard,* his Country Seat, was near *Wotton Baſſet.*

APPENDIX C.

Letter from Lord Cowper to the King on the breaking out of the Rebellion in 1715.

Sire, — I would not trouble your *Majefty* in this Manner but on fome very great Crifis, as I take the prefent to be, when I fhould defire not to be in the leaft miftaken by a fudden Interpretation.

On your *Majefty's* receiving certain Advice from *Scotland* of an open Rebellion, not only begun but declared there, and even Hoftilities commenced.

I own my Concern to find Nothing moved to be confidered but whether Circular Letters fhould not go to the *Lord Lieutenant*, &c., to feize Papifts and Nonjurors in the North of *England.* Your *Majefty's* Attorney and Solicitor were both of opinion with me that the Law doth not warrant the Import of fuch Letters. The *Chief Juftice* did not give an Opinion either Way.

Two or three Precedents were found in the Council Books of fuch Letters, which were indeed Strains of the Law, in hopes of fome good Effect, which always failed.

However, the moft of your *Majefty's* Council were for making the Experiment once more, and to that I refer myfelf to have it feen what Fruits it will produce when the Returns come to be made, if any.

It was agreed that the Method I preferred, of learning the Names of all the great Papifts and Nonjurors in the *North*, and taking them up and fecuring them by

Warrant of fix Privy Councillors, or a Secretary of State, in virtue of a plain Law made on purpofe this Seffion, fhould be likewife practifed. And left the ufing the firft infufficient Remedy fhould, as is ufual, flacken the making Ufe of the true, I humbly beg your *Majefty* to remind your Servants that this be done forthwith, and effectually done, fince the former Method will take up only the inconfiderable People, if any, and be longer in doing alfo.

But what feems to me to be the more important and natural Confideration on this News from *Scotland* is, whether the Forces now in *Scotland*, or going thither, are probably fufficient to ftop the March of the Rebels, and if not, whether the Confequences of that are not bad enough to require fome Augmentation wherever it can be had, without expofing too much this Part of the Kingdom.

As to the firft, I think your General or the *Secretary-at-War* fhould ftate plainly before your *Majefty* in the Cabinet, what Number of effective Men are now or will be in a fhort Time of your Forces in the Field ; and then, by comparing that Number with what the Rebels will probably march, or your *Majefty*, by the next Advices, may hear they have got together, a Judgment may be formed on that Point.

If your *Majefty's* Forces are found infufficient to ftop the Rebels, I humbly think your Troops there fhould be immediately augmented, by all Means confiftent with the not leaving this Part of the Kingdom fo unguarded as to invite an Infurrection or Invafion to be made here.

For it feems certain that if any Difgrace befall your *Majefty's* Troops in *Scotland*, Infurrections will immediately follow in *England* in many Places, and probably the *Pretender* will be encouraged to land here too.

On the other Hand, if the Rebels get no Advantage in *Scotland*, my Conjecture is, there will be no confiderable Rifing in *England*, and I take it to be much eafier to prevent Commotions in *England*, by fecuring the Rebels fhall make no Progrefs in *Scotland*, than it will be when any Succefs of the Rebels in *Scotland* fhall have made many Infurrections to break out in *England*, to find Means to fupprefs them.

The Scotch magnify their Danger fomething, and perhaps prefs for more Affiftance than can be reafonably fpared from hence. But I beg Leave to affure you I cannot but obferve the prevailing Inclination here is to fupply the Forces there but too fparingly, and as on the one Hand it would be extremely wrong to draw the Bulk of your *Majefty's* Forces to that End of the Kingdom, fo on the other the not making the Duke of *Argyle* ftrong enough to fecure himfelf againft a Defeat, or a Neceffity of retreating, or of letting them go by him towards the *South*, will thoroughly involve *England* in a Civil War, of which None can anfwer for the Confequences, and therefore I humbly advife that this great Point fhould be thoroughly ftated and confidered by all fuch as have the Honour at any Time to advife your *Majefty*.

Extract of a Letter from Baron Bernftorff to Lady Cowper.

London: Sept. 28, 1715.

Le *Prétendant* fe tient encore ferme à *Bar*. Il ne veut pas venir ici avant qu'on lui faffe voir un ' Party ' qui fe puiffe maintenir. Pour affembler ce Party, *Ormona* et *Bolingbroke* devoient venir dans le *Weſt*, mais les Priſes que l'on a faites, et qui découvrent tout le Complot, ſemblent les déconcerter extrêmement, ſurtout puiſque la Rébellion en *Écoſſe* va d'une Manière à ne pas leur promettre de grands Succès.

Extract of a Letter from the Duchefs of Marlborough to Lady Cowper.

London: Oct. 1, 1715.

I hope this will find my dear Lady *Cowper* much the better for the country Air, and the Happineſs of being ſo long in the Company you like in Quiet. The Laſt is what can't be had in this Place, and I fear it will yet be worſe before it is better; for my Lord *Stair* ſays, in his laſt Account, that the Duke of *Ormond* is gone with a few Servants poſt from *Paris*. The Duke of *Berwick* was ſeen the Day before, which is all that is ſaid of him in Lord *Stair's* Letter; but another Perſon has given an Account that he had lately pawned his Jewels and Plate. My Lord *Stair* had no Notice of the *Pretender* being gone from *Bar* when he writ, but the Duke of *Ormond* may have better Intelligence of his Motions, and if he is not yet removed, that would agree with other Intelligence that he will not come to us till his Friends are in ſome Order here to receive him. I don't find that the News from *Scotland* is ſo bad as ſome reported, and I am apt to believe the Duke of *Argyle* aggravated that Matter a good deal; for at the very ſame Time that a very terrible Account came from His *Grace*, I ſaw a Letter from the Poſtmaſter of *Scotland*, which ſaid our Enemies there were not above 2,600, and there is no Certainty of any Numbers that have joined them fince ; but from fo many Men having efcaped being fecured, and the Duke of *Ormond* having left *Paris*, I fear we fhall foon hear of fome Rifing. They fay the Duke of *Somerfet* is at *Petworth*; but before he went he did what Service he could to our Enemies. When I fee my Lord *Townfhend*, I fhall have a great Mind to defire him to compute what Good and what Mifchief the Duke of *Somerfet* has done fince our Friends fhook Hands with him. I have fent this Morning *Hodges* to get Mr. *Wymondefold* to advife what is to be done with the Bonds; for that of the *South Sea*, which is for 2,100*l.*, is not worth fo much by 2 or 300*l.* at this Time, and upon the Duke of *Ormond's* Landing, or any Diforder, all Stocks will fall very much, and, though I am not fo much frighted as to part with my own, I think I fhould not run the Hazard of other People's for 5 per Cent. Intereft, which I agreed with Mr. *Wymondefold* to take upon the firft Money he paid me at 6, though I did not change the Security.

(Signed)   S. MARLBOROUGH.

Mr. *G.*, the Jeweller, was with me juft now, and told me there was 28 Men fent to *Newgate* laft Night out of *Convent Garden* Parifh.

One may write Anything by the Poft very fafe, as long as Mr. *Craggs*¹ is in the Office.

---

¹ This was the elder *Craggs*, Poftmafter-General.

Letter from John Johnson, Esq., to Henry Liddell, Esq.

Newcastle-upon-Tyne: Oct. 9, 1715.

Honoured Sir,—A great many Gentlemen and Others, to the Number of 300, or thereabout (moſt whereof are Papiſts), are now in Arms, and laſt Night lay at *Warkworth.* We are informed they are for ſeizing the Militia at *Killingworth Moor* on *Tueſday* next, and take from them their Horſes and Arms ; for my Lord *Scarborough* giving ſo long Notice as 14 Days for the Militia and Train-bands to riſe, they took this Opportunity of riſing firſt.

They are believed to have proclaimed the *Pretender* at a Place called *Rothbury* laſt *Thurſday.* Mr. *Robert Liſle,* who was with them, came to Town laſt Night very privately, and Alderman *White* and I being at *Pandon Gate* (the Reſt of the Gates in Town being all barricaded), immediately ordered him to be ſeized and carried before the Main Guard, and he is now in *Newgate.* Ten Keel-boats (two whereof are mine) are ordered for *North Shields Fort,* to bring up the Cannon, to prevent their being ſeized by the Rebels, who deſigned to batter the Walls of this Town with them. *Tinmouth Caſtle* is very well fortified againſt them. I don't queſtion but we ſhall keep them out here till ſuch Times as we get further Aſſiſtance, moſt People in Town being better inclined than thought of. Mr. *William Coteſworth* and I, with much Ado, this Day ſe'nnight got the Train-bands up here, otherwiſe I am apt to believe they would not have been up till the 11th Inſtant, according to Lord *Scarborough's* Orders, in which Time the Town was deſigned to be furprifed. Alderman *White* joins with Mr. *Cotefworth* and me, and is very zealous and hearty. Sir *Charles Hotham's* Regiment is expected here, upon their Rout for *Berwick* (but hope, through the Infinuations of Lord *Scarborough*, to keep them here till further Orders from the Government), three Companies whereof are expected on *Tuefday*. I am this Day raifing the *Poffe Comitatus*, to prevent the Rebels further ftrolling into this Country, and am in Expectation thereby entirely to fecure this Town, which they fo much aim at, expecting a great many Friends at their Entrance. I am very credibly informed from *Rothbury* that the following Perfons are amongft the Rebels, viz., *Thomas Forfter*; Earl of *Derwentwater*, and his Brother; *Philip Hodfhon*; the Chief of *Beaufront*; *Clavering* of *Callalee*; *Clavering* of *Berrington*; *John Talbot*; Chief *Collingwood* of *E——*; Mr. *George Morrifon*; *Ephraim Selby* of *Bittlefton*, and his Steward, *D——*; *Philip Walker*; *William Shaftoe* of *B——*, and three more *Shaftoes*; *Thornton* of *Netherwitton*; *Charleton* of the *Bour*, and his Son; *Widdrington* of *Cold Park*. *Lifle* informs me that my Lord *Widdrington* joined them Yefterday at *Warkworth* with about 20 Men.

(Signed)   JOHN JOHNSON.

Extract of a Letter from William Cotefworth, Efq., to Henry Liddell, Efq.

Gatefhead: Oct. 11, 1715.

We got the Town of *Newcaftle* put into a State of holding out againft 2,000 Men, if they come without a

Train. On *Monday* Sir *C. Hotham's* Regiment came in. Yeſterday Colonel *Liddell* muſtered above 1,200 Horſe and Foot out of the Eaſt and Weſt Diviſions of *Cheſter Ward* on *Gateſhead Fell.* The County Horſe and part of our Poſſe Horſe marched this Morning into the *Shield* Field. The Militia Horſe for *Durham* are to march to *Gateſhead* To-night. Sir *William Williamſon* has called upon me to talk about their continuing here. I was this Morning with my Lord *Scarborough*, and have propoſed that the Militia Horſe of both Counties, as ſoon as my Lord *Cobham's* Dragoons come up, ſhall join with them, and as many other armed Horſe as we can get, and go out and drive the Rebels into the Sea, for they lie down by the Sea-ſide. I have promiſed my Lord, that if but 20 Gentlemen in our County will go upon this Expedition, I will make one. This, I am ſure, is the Way to ſtrike Terror into all the Enemies of our happy Conſtitution and Government.

What theſe Rebels hoped for was that the High Church would have joined them, and no doubt there was but too good a Diſpoſition in ſome People to it. They talk now of a great Number of Horſe and Foot they expeƈt will join them from the South of *Scotland*; but our Communication is in a great Meaſure cut off, ſo that the Miniſtry is the beſt Judge of the Strength of the Duke of *Argyle* and *Mar.* The Recorder of *Newcaſtle*, the lately-made Serjeant, was keeping the Earl of *Der-wentwater's* Courts when the Lord of them was in open Rebellion againſt his Prince. I find it is always a Work of Time for me to perſuade my Friends I can diſcern men. I ſhould tell you that Dr. *Sacheverell's* Brother is a Preventing-Officer between *Shields* and *Sunderland*, which is a dangerous Thing, in my Opinion. I have taken a good deal of Pains to have Sir *W.*

Blackett fecured from going over to the Enemy. *T. Wilkinfon* is now with him at *Wallington.* I do not think it advifable that he be feized till we are in a more quiet or fecure State.

Extraƈ of a Letter from John Johnfon, Efq., to Henry Liddell, Efq.

Newcaftle: Oƈ. 16, 1715.

The Enemy have entered *Morpeth*, and from thence marched to Lord *Derwentwater's* and *Hexham*, where they ftill continue. We daily expeƈt *Cobham's* Dragoons, but are afraid the Rebels will march into *Lancafhire* and quit this Country before we can give them Battle. They plunder None as yet, but feize Horfes and Arms. Lord *Derwentwater* and *Tom Forfter*, our fcandalous Member, give out that my Under-Sheriff fhall hang me, and one of my Bailiffs my Under-Sheriff; but fuch Menaces I value not. I know my Caufe is good, and will venture my Life and Fortune and lay down my all for His Majefty King *George.* A Spy of mine met with a Scotchman fourteen Miles beyond *Carlifle*, who had feen my Lord *Kenmure* with about 200 Horfe on *Friday* laft, going to join the Rebels in this Country. Upon the three Meffengers coming down for Lord *Derwentwater*, I ordered four of my truftieft Bailiffs to attend them. They traced my Lord into his Houfe about 7 o'Clock at Night, and fearched next Morning by 6, but could not find him. This occafions me many Threats from the Papifts, who are mightily affronted that I fhould order my Bailiffs to affift the *King's* Officers in apprehending fo great a Perfon and Rebel.

Letter from John Johnfon, Efq., to Henry Liddell, Efq.

Newcaftle: Oct. 23, 1715.

I am informed that the Rebels who were at *Wooler* croffed the *Tweed* at *Coldftream*, and joined the Rebels that came over the *Firth*, and continue there in full Rendezvous, taking all the Horfes, Saddles, and Arms they can meet with. They defign to prefs the Duke of *Argyle's* Camp on this Side, whilft Lord *Mar* does the Like on the other. It's thought advifable by General *Carpenter* that Sir *Charles Hotham's* Regiment of Foot and two Regiments of Dragoons fhall march for *Scotland* To-morrow, in order to ftrengthen *Argyle's* Camp, and the Regiments that are upon march are to follow ; but he has ordered a Regiment of Foot, who are like- wife upon march, to ftay here till further Orders, fo that at the prefent we fhall have the Guard of the Town to ourfelves. The Soldiers were very uneafy for their Clothes. Major *Green* came to my Houfe on hearing that the two Ships that brought their Clothes and Bayonets were arrived at *Tynemouth*, and defired my fpeedy Affiftance. On this I fent two Keel- boats, double-manned, to *Shields*, who brought up the Clothes this Morning ; but the Ship that brings the Bay- onets, &c., is not yet arrived, fo that they'll be obliged to march without them. The Rebels are, I am forry to

acquaint you, as ſtrong as 1,500.   Another Regiment
of Dragoons is expeƈted here on *Tueſday.*   We hear
Nothing certain, as yet, of the Dutch Forces, but hope
by this they are arrived in *Scotland.*   I hear Lady *Crew*
is dead, but could have wiſhed it had been his *Lord-
ſhip,* for as long as we have ſuch Biſhops we can't expeƈt
good Clergy, a great Part of this Trouble being occaſioned by them.

APPENDIX D.

Letter from George I. to the Prince.

La première Lettre que je reçois de votre Part, mon Fils, eft fur des Sujets auffi peu dignes de vous que de moy. A l'égard du Duc d'*Argyle*, j'ay eu de bonnes Raifons pour faire ce que j'ay fait fur fon Sujet, mais je ne fçay ce qui vous eft moins défavantageux, d'avoir été induit par luy ou d'autres à faire le Pas que vous venez de faire, ou bien, de l'avoir fait par votre propre Mouvement. Vous aurez de la Peine à redreffer cette Démarche dans le Public. Quand on en fait de pareilles l'on n'eft pas en droit d'accufer mes Miniftres de me faire des Rapports défavantageux, et c'eft le Monde renverfé quand le Fils veut préfcrire au Père quel Pouvoir il doit luy donner ; ce n'eft pas non plus un Motif de mettre le Deftin de mes Miniftres et autres Serviteurs à la Merci de votre Modération. Il ne paraît pas auffi, à la Conduite que vous avez tenue pendant les Séances du Parlement, que vous avez fi peu de Friandife, comme vous le dites, pour le Gouvernement, vous mêlant de Chofes qui ne vous regardoient pas, et ne vous empêchoient pas de pouvoir être tranquille. Je voudrois fçavoir quel Droit vous aviez de faire des Meffages à la Chambre contre mon Intention. Eft-ce à vous de faire des Claufes aux Dons que je fais au Public ? Vous dites à cette Occafion que vous avez voulu foutenir l'Autorité

royale, mais qui vous en a donné le Soin ? Vous con-
viendrez que quand on n'eſt pas reſponſable ni chargé
d'une Choſe on ne doit pas ſ'en mêler. Il ſ'agit pré-
ſentement du Duc d'*Argyle*, lequel, malgré ce que j'ay
été obligé de faire à ſon Sujet, vous voulez ſoutenir et
garder à votre Service, en montrant par là à tout le
Monde que vous vous oppoſez à mes Sentimens. En
même Temps vous aſſujettiſſez à votre Caprice le Re-
tardement du Voyage que j'ai le deſſein de faire. Je
demande que vous mettiez Fin à tout cela, et que
vous ſatisfaſſiez aux Propoſitions que M. de *Bernſtorff*
vous a faites de ma Part. Vous empêcherez de cette
Manière les Démarches que je ſeray indiſpenſablement
et contre ma Volonté néceſſité de faire pour ſoutenir
mon Autorité. Voilà ce que j'ay à vous dire en Réponſe
à votre Lettre. Je ſouhaite que vous en profitiez, et que
vous vous mettiez en État de mériter mon Amitié.

GEORGE R.

APPENDIX E.

Letter from J. Clavering, Esq., to Lady Cowper.

Hanover: July 7, 1716.

I cannot exprefs the Surprife we are in here at Mademoifelle *Schulenberg* being naturalifed and made an Englifh Duchefs. The Countefs de *Platen* is mightily mortified, for you muft know we have two Parties here more violent than Whig and Tory in *England* (which are the *Schulenberg* and *Platen* Factions). Madame *Kielmanfegg* writes here that fhe's very unwilling to give Place to the new Duchefs; therefore fhe will petition *Parliament* to be naturalifed, that fhe may have a Title equal to the Other.

His Czarian *Majefty* [1] did us the Honour to pafs by *Hanover* twice, and ftayed two or three Days at *Herrenhaufen*, a Country Houfe of the *King's*, about an Englifh Mile, fo I had the Honour to eat at his Table feveral Times, which I was not very ambitious of, for he never ufes Knife nor Fork, but always eats with his Fingers, never ufes a Handkerchief, but blows his Nofe with his Fingers; therefore you may guefs how agreeable it is to be in His *Majefty's* Company. He has a Scotch Gentleman with him, Coufin of the late Lord *Mar*, who is both Chamberlain and Phyfician (but a rank Jacobite), who

---

[1] What follows is of a piece with the Experiences of *Evelyn* and of the Auftrian Secretary of Legation, recently tranflated by Count *Macdonnell.*

O

told me that Lord *Wharton* had promifed the *Czar* to go with him as Volunteer when he makes the Defcent in *Schonen*. His Lordfhip has received a great many Prefents from the *Landgrave*—a gold Snuff-box, with his Picture; 7 fine brown Horfes for a Coach; two others to ride upon. He lives very magnificently at *Caffel*; has 6 Footmen, a running Footman, a Valet de Chambre, a Secretary (for he will not allow People to call him his Governor), two Sets of Coach-horfes, &c. All this is to be done out of 1,000*l.* a Year, which is his Allowance. I am certain if he lives two Years he will fpend every Farthing he has in the World.

Extract of a Letter from J. Clavering, Efq., to Lady Cowper.

Hanover: Sept. 4, 1716.

I fupped with the Duchefs of *Munfter* laft Night, when we drank my Lord's and your Health. I go there very often, and muft own I have not been fo civilly treated by Anybody here as by her and her Family. Since the *King's* Arrival from *Pyrmont* we have a Drawing-room every Night at *Herrenhaufen*, in the Green-houfe, which, with walking in the Garden, is very plea-fant. His *Majefty* was very much indifpofed for the three or four firft Days after he came, having loft his Stomach, and not fleeping, but now, thank *God*, is very well. Lord *Peterborough*[1] has been here five Days. He

---

[1] The famous *Charles Mordaunt*, Earl of *Peterborough*. See *Swift's* Verfes :—
' *Mordanto* fills the Trump of Fame.'
He was noted for the Rapidity with which he travelled.

came from *Venice* here in nine Days, only to fee the *King*, and will return there in the fame Time he was coming. He told us the *King* lived fo happily here, that he believed he had forgot the Accident that happened to him and his Family the 1ft of *Auguſt*, 1714. Madame *Kielmanſegg* tells Everybody ſhe deſigns to return to *England*. Mademoiſelle *Schulenberg* is gone to drink the Waters of *Emps* (*ſic*). We Engliſh here live very fociably, dining with Mr. *Stanhope* very often, whom we put at the Head of us.

Extraɛt of a Letter from J. Clavering, Eſq., to Lady Cowper.

Dec. 15, 1716.

Mr. *Wortley Montague* and his Lady[1] are here. They were fo very impatient to fee His *Majeſty* that they travelled Night and Day from *Vienna* here. Her *Ladyſhip* is mighty gay and airy, and occaſions a great deal of Difcourſe. Since her Arrival the *King* has took but little Notice of any other Lady, not even of Madame *Kielmanſegg*, which the Ladies of *Hanover* don't reliſh very well; for my Part, I can't help rejoicing to fee His *Majeſty* prefer us to the Germans.

---

[1] Lady *Mary W. Montague*, Daughter of *Evelyn*, Duke of *Kingſton*, was born in 1690. Married to *Edward Wortley* *Montague* in 1712, and died in 1762. She was admired by both *George I.* and his Son.

Extract of a Letter from the Duchefs of Marlborough to Lady Cowper.

Bath: Sept. 3, 1716.

The Duke of *Marlborough* is, I thank *God*, better than he was when we left *St. Albans*, but I think he wants a good deal yet of being well. However, one is told every Day of fo many People that have been much worfe than he ever was, and have recovered, either by Time or thefe Waters, that it gives One great Reafon to hope. My Lady *Grandifon* is one great Inftance. She told me the other Day that fhe underftood or fpoke but very little for a great While, and one of her Hands was dead and withered, which is now filled out like the other, and Nobody would think fhe ever had had the Palfy.

I am very glad of a Victory fo much to the Honour and Advantage of Prince *Eugène*,[1] whofe Friendfhip to the Duke of *Marlborough* alone is enough to make me wifh him well. I am very forry for the Account which you give of your Health, which I have always feared would not be mended by being at *Court*. I don't wonder that you find it melancholy to be away from your Lord and Children; for though the *Princefs* is very eafy and obliging, I think Anyone that has common Senfe or Honefty muft needs be very weary of Everything One meets with in Courts. I have feen a good many, and lived in them many Years, but I proteft I was never pleafed but when I was a Child, and after I had been a Maid of Honour fome Time, at Fourteen I wifhed my-felf out of the *Court* as much as I had defired to come

---

[1] *Peterwardin* and *Temefvar*, two great Victories over the Turks, were gained by him in 1716.

into it before I knew what it was. Her Grace of *Shrewf-bury* is here, and of a much happier Temper. She plays at Ombre upon the Walks, that fhe may be fure to have Company enough, and is as well pleafed in a great Crowd of Strangers as the common People are with a Bull-baiting or a Mountebank. I have been upon the Walks but twice, and I never faw any Place Abroad that had more Stinks and Dirt in it than *Bath*; with this Difference only, that we are not ftarved, for here is great Plenty of Meat, and very good, and as to the Noife, that keeps One almoft always awake. I can bear it with Patience, and all other Misfortunes, as long as I think the Waters do the Duke of *Marlborough* any Good.

INDEX.

Index.

www.ingramcontent.com/pod-product-compliance
Lightning Source LLC
Chambersburg PA
CBHW030123030726
47498CB00007B/2524